WINGS OF FIRE

WINTER TURNING

by

TUI T. SUTHERLAND

SCHOLASTIC INC.

Text copyright © 2015 by Tui T. Sutherland
Map and border design © 2015 by Mike Schley
Dragon illustrations © 2015 by Joy Ang

This book was originally published in hardcover by Scholastic Press in 2015.

ISBN 978-93-5275-091-7

First printing 2016
Book design by Phil Falco

This edition : August 2021
Printed in India

To Catherine and Ella, because you
are awesome and could definitely save the world
(from dragons or for dragons, either way)!

Queen Glacier's Palace

Ice Kingdom

Sky Kingdom

Queen Thorn's Stronghold

Kingdom of Sand

Scorpion Den

Claws of the Clouds Mountains

Jade Mountain

Queen Ruby's Palace

Ruins of the Summer Palace

Diamond Spray River

Kingdom of the Sea

Diamond Spray Delta

Bay of a Thousand Scales

Mud Kingdom

Scavenger Den

Queen Moorhen's Palace

Scavenger Den

Rainforest Kingdom

W E

Ice Kingdom

Kingdom

A GUIDE TO THE
DRAGONS

Sand

Scorpion Den

Jade Mountain

Queen Ruby's Palace

Ruins of the Summer Palace

W

Scales

OF PYRRHIA

UPDATED AND EDITED BY
STARFLIGHT OF THE NIGHTWINGS

Scavenger Den

Queen Moorhen's Palace

Scavenger De

Rainforest Kingdom

WELCOME TO
THE JADE MOUNTAIN
ACADEMY!

At this school, you will be learning side by side with dragons from all the other tribes, so we wanted to give you some basic information that may be useful as you get to know one another.

You have been assigned to a winglet with six other dragons; the winglet groups are listed on the following page.

Thank you for being a part of this school. You are the hope of Pyrrhia's future. You are the dragons who can bring lasting peace to this world.

WE WISH YOU ALL THE POWER OF WINGS OF FIRE!

JADE WINGLET

IceWing: Winter
MudWing: Umber
NightWing: Moonwatcher
RainWing: Kinkajou
SandWing: Qibli
SeaWing: Turtle
SkyWing: Carnelian

GOLD WINGLET

IceWing: Icicle
MudWing: Sora
NightWing: Bigtail
RainWing: Tamarin
SandWing: Onyx
SeaWing: Pike
SkyWing: Flame

SILVER WINGLET

IceWing: Changbai
MudWing: Sepia
NightWing: Fearless
RainWing: Boto
SandWing: Ostrich
SeaWing: Anemone
SkyWing: Thrush

COPPER WINGLET

IceWing: Alba
MudWing: Marsh
NightWing: Mindreader
RainWing: Coconut
SandWing: Pronghorn
SeaWing: Snail
SkyWing: Peregrine

QUARTZ WINGLET

IceWing: Ermine
MudWing: Newt
NightWing: Mightyclaws
RainWing: Siamang
SandWing: Arid
SeaWing: Barracuda
SkyWing: Garnet

SANDWINGS

Description: pale gold or white scales the color of desert sand; poisonous barbed tail; forked black tongues

Abilities: can survive a long time without water, poison enemies with the tips of their tails like scorpions, bury themselves for camouflage in the desert sand, breathe fire

Queen: since the end of the War of SandWing Succession, Queen Thorn

Students at Jade Mountain: Arid, Onyx, Ostrich, Pronghorn, Qibli

MUDWINGS

Description: thick, armored brown scales, sometimes with amber and gold underscales; large, flat heads with nostrils on top of the snout

Abilities: can breathe fire (if warm enough), hold their breath for up to an hour, blend into large mud puddles; usually very strong

Queen: Queen Moorhen

Students at Jade Mountain: Marsh, Newt, Sepia, Sora, Umber

SKYWINGS

Description: red-gold or orange scales; enormous wings

Abilities: powerful fighters and fliers, can breathe fire

Queen: Queen Ruby (although some dragons still support Queen Scarlet, who may be alive and in hiding)

Students at Jade Mountain: Carnelian, Flame, Garnet, Peregrine, Thrush

SEAWINGS

Description: blue or green or aquamarine scales; webs between their claws; gills on their necks; glow-in-the-dark stripes on their tails/snouts/underbellies

Abilities: can breathe underwater, see in the dark, create huge waves with one splash of their powerful tails; excellent swimmers

Queen: Queen Coral

Students at Jade Mountain: Anemone, Barracuda, Pike, Snail, Turtle

ICEWINGS

Description: silvery scales like the moon or pale blue like ice; ridged claws to grip the ice; forked blue tongues; tails narrow to a whip-thin end

Abilities: can withstand subzero temperatures and bright light, exhale a deadly frostbreath

Queen: Queen Glacier

Students at Jade Mountain: Alba, Changbai, Ermine, Icicle, Winter

RAINWINGS

Description: scales constantly shift colors, usually bright like birds of paradise; prehensile tails

Abilities: can camouflage their scales to blend into their surroundings; shoot a deadly venom from their fangs

Queen: Queen Glory

Students at Jade Mountain: Boto, Coconut, Kinkajou, Siamang, Tamarin

— NIGHTWINGS —

Description: purplish-black scales and scattered silver scales on the underside of their wings, like a night sky full of stars; forked black tongues

Abilities: can breathe fire, disappear into dark shadows; once known for reading minds and foretelling the future, but no longer

Queen: Queen Glory (see recent scrolls on the NightWing Exodus and the RainWing Royal Challenge)

Students at Jade Mountain: Bigtail, Fearless, Mightyclaws, Mindreader, Moonwatcher

THE
JADE MOUNTAIN
PROPHECY

Beware the darkness of dragons,
Beware the stalker of dreams,
Beware the talons of power and fire,
Beware one who is not what she seems.

Something is coming to shake the earth,
Something is coming to scorch the ground.
Jade Mountain will fall beneath thunder and ice
Unless the lost city of night can be found.

PROLOGUE

It was one of those days so blue and sunny that you *had* to be flying. The sky reached in your window first thing in the morning and dragged you out, flinging you up and up and up into the beautiful wing-catching wind. You had to soar and spin and dive because a day this perfect might never come again.

And sometimes you had to take your little brother with you, and sometimes you had to hurl his cautious tail into wonderful danger, because the wind was roaring and the sky was glorious and the sunlight promised that nothing bad could possibly happen.

Hailstorm did a flip in the air, laughing. "The currents are mine to command!" he shouted. "Can you catch me? No, you cannot! No one can! I'm the commander of the sky!"

"I think the SkyWings would disagree," Winter called. He twisted to scan the cloudless blue emptiness around them.

"Stop worrying!" Hailstorm said, spinning into a dive. There weren't any dragons within flight-sight. It was a perfect day for Winter's first expedition into SkyWing territory, especially if he really wanted to find a scavenger.

"This doesn't feel safe," Winter observed as they landed. His talons sank into a pile of leaves and he jumped back, eyeing them with suspicion. "Yikes! What are all these flappy things on the ground?"

"They come from the trees," Hailstorm said, laughing. "No need to panic, little brother. We're here for *your* weird little obsession. So get excited!" He took a deep breath, inhaling the smells of the forest, and sneezed loudly.

"SHHHHHH," Winter protested. "This is the Sky Kingdom! There could be enemy soldiers everywhere!"

"Lounging around in the woods near a scavenger den?" Hailstorm said skeptically. "Doubtful." He flicked his brother's wing with his tail. Winter was only three, but he was very amusing — a lot more fun to tease than their sister. He also tried so hard, and still had so much trouble with the rankings. Poor dragon. Hailstorm wished he could relax a little bit. Not everyone could be the best at everything, although it most likely didn't help that his big brother actually was.

Despite his worry, Winter couldn't hide the excitement spilling over his face. "Is there really a scavenger den here?" He blinked at the trees, as if hoping a scavenger would suddenly fall out of one of them.

"That's what the patrol reported," Hailstorm said with a shrug. "They said they saw at least five scavengers, and that many usually means a den nearby."

Now that they were surrounded by trees, though, he had no idea how they were going to find one of the little creatures for Winter. Hailstorm had never actually seen one himself. There were hundreds of furry smells in the forest, but he couldn't even figure out which ones were scavengers and which ones were squirrels. The only thing he was sure of was that none of them were polar bears.

"What are you going to do if we *do* catch one?" Hailstorm asked, turning over a fallen log and checking underneath. Nope. No scavengers there. "You know they can't survive in the Ice Kingdom. You won't be able to keep it."

"I just want to look at it," Winter said. "Have you ever seen a scavenger up close? I read that they wear other animals' skins on top of their own skin. Isn't that bizarre? Why would they do that?"

"Same reason Mother has that necklace of SkyWing teeth," Hailstorm said authoritatively. "To make themselves seem more dangerous and scare off any possible predators. Obviously."

Winter glanced at the sky. "Speaking of SkyWings . . ."

"We're FINE," Hailstorm insisted, tempted to jab Winter's worrying snout with one of his claws. "We're several mountains away from Queen Scarlet's palace. No one is going to find us here."

"But won't Father be furious?" Winter asked, twitching slightly.

Hailstorm ruffled his wings as though he was trying to shake the idea of their parents right off his scales.

"Who cares?" he said. "I'm going to be second-in-command of the IceWing army one day. Queen Glacier already said so. Mother and Father can't do anything to me."

"They can do plenty to *me*," Winter said.

"Not if you get high enough in the rankings," Hailstorm said with a grin. "Which you do by being brave and strong and bold."

"I thought it was by being smart and following orders," Winter said.

Hailstorm dismissed this with a wave of his tail. "Dragons in the Third Circle and below can worry about following orders. First Circle dragons have to prepare to be leaders one day. Besides, I'm the best fighter in the Ice Kingdom. Even if we do get caught, I think I can take a couple of SkyWings."

"Oh, really?" said a mocking voice behind them. "How about fourteen SkyWings?"

Hailstorm whirled around. Red and orange drag-ons were slithering between the trees, surrounding them. Their eyes glittered in the golden light and their enormous wings were tucked in close to avoid the snarling branches above.

His heart sank. This couldn't be happening. Bad luck wasn't a thing that ever wandered into Hailstorm's life, and this was the worst luck he could have imagined.

Fourteen SkyWing warriors were more than he could fight alone. Definitely more than he could fight and still keep his little brother safe.

"Second-in-command of the IceWing army?" said the one who'd spoken, a dark red female dragon with an unusually long neck and tail. Small rubies glittered from between the scales around her eyes; larger ones clicked together on spiky silver rings around her claws. "Then you are a prize, aren't you? Mother will be *so* interested to meet you."

"Let us go," Winter said fiercely. "Queen Glacier will have your heads on spikes by morning if you dare touch us."

"Oh, very attached to you, is she?" the dragon said, arching her brows. "That's absolutely our favor-ite kind of prisoner. Seize them," she ordered the other SkyWings.

"Perhaps you can take us," Hailstorm said, drawing

in a hissing breath. "But how many of you are going to die first? Do you know what happens when frost-breath touches your eyes? Do you know what it feels like to watch your leg snap like a broken icicle? Or how long it takes frozen ears to turn black and fall off?" His voice was cold, his threats slicing the air between them like a freezing wind.

Winter raised his tail and inhaled, working up a gust of frostbreath of his own.

"So a few dragons die," said the female SkyWing with a shrug. The other SkyWings exchanged uneasy looks. "You'll be our prisoners in the end, either way."

"Here's another idea," said Hailstorm. "Take me and let Winter go, and nobody has to die."

"What?" Winter cried.

"You don't need him," Hailstorm said, ignoring his brother. "He's completely useless. Queen Glacier won't trade any prisoners for him — nobody back in the Ice Kingdom would care whether they ever saw him again. And he wouldn't even be interesting in your queen's arena. He can barely fight. He'd be dead in two heartbeats."

Winter looked as though the world was crumbling beneath his talons. "Is that true?" he whispered. "Hailstorm, is that really what you think?"

"If he's so useless," the SkyWing asked, "why do you care if we let him go?"

Hailstorm lifted and settled his wings again. "Call me sentimental. He's my little brother and I quite like him, even if I wouldn't want him beside me in a battle. Besides, I know I'm worth trading, whereas he'll be bones in your arena sands before the month is up."

"Ouch," said the SkyWing, giving Winter an amused, pitying look. "I think I'd probably rather die in battle than listen to my brother talk about me that way."

"I'm not useless," Winter said furiously. "Fight me and you'll see!"

"Oh, go *home*," Hailstorm said, swatting Winter's wing. "You want to be useful? Fine. Get out of here. Go tell our parents where I am."

"I'm not leaving you," Winter protested in a half-choked voice. "I'm not going to hand you over to them without even *trying* to save you —"

"Yes, you are," Hailstorm said. "This is the real war, little brother. Go away and let the true warriors fight it. Nobody wants to watch you pathetically flail around and then die pointlessly."

"Oh, my, *I* can't even listen to this anymore," said the SkyWing. "IceWing, I'm going to be more merciful than your heartless brother and let you go. You can tell Queen Glacier that Queen Scarlet will consider a trade, if she'd like to send a messenger to open negotiations."

Trade for who? Hailstorm wondered. The IceWings didn't have any political prisoners of importance. Where would they even keep them? The Ice Palace was too cold for dragons from any other tribe to survive it for long.

He shoved Winter away, trying to ignore the anguished look in his brother's eyes. "Fly away," he growled. "Right now." He could see that the only way to make Winter leave was to be as cruel as possible. He lowered his voice and shoved in the last blade. "Don't be a mewling RainWing in front of our enemies."

Winter stepped back, tense, like a wolf about to spring. He stared into Hailstorm's eyes for one long, final moment, and then he suddenly pivoted and leaped into the air. His pale blue scales glinted orange-red as they caught the sun, and then he swooped into the wide sky, heading west.

He's safe, Hailstorm thought with relief. *Even if he hates me now, at least he's alive.* Winter wasn't useless, but it was true that his current ranking wouldn't make him worth rescuing — and it was also true that Hailstorm didn't want to see his brother die in Scarlet's notorious arena.

The SkyWing smiled as Hailstorm turned back to her. "Aren't we civilized?" she said. "Somebody club this IceWing over the head and let's drag him off to prison."

"That's not necess —" Hailstorm started to protest, but suddenly a sharp bolt of pain cleaved through his head and everything went dark.

He woke up in a bright throne room, so bright he instantly got a headache, although the brightness of the sun on ice had never bothered him. But here the sun reflected hotly in all corners of the room and every surface seemed to be plastered with gold, loud and gaudy and yellow and way, way too shiny.

"Oh, finally," said an impatient voice nearby. "You've been so horribly boring. I hope you intend to be exceptionally thrilling now to make up for it."

Hailstorm gathered his wings and stood up slowly, rubbing his head. Chains weighed down his talons and strange metal bands prevented his wings from unfurling all the way. But there were no guards around him; only one other dragon was in the room. He lifted his eyes to the throne.

Orange scales. Glittering rubies. A circlet of gold and diamonds. Yellow eyes peered down at him through veils of smoke. He'd only seen the SkyWing queen from a distance once, during a battle, but there was no doubt this was her.

"Greetings, Your Majesty," he said. "I'm sorry we have to meet this way."

She studied him for a moment, and then an unexpected smile quirked the corners of her mouth. "Instead of in combat?" she guessed.

He gave her a similarly small smile in return. "Yes. The battlefield is where I prefer to meet all my enemies. Although then the acquaintance doesn't last very long."

"Arrogant," Queen Scarlet mused. "Like all IceWings. Take a note of that," she said over her shoulder.

Hailstorm saw the shadows move behind the queen, as if something were pushing itself slowly out of the wall. He blinked, feeling a strange shiver of eerie fear, but when he looked again, an ordinary SkyWing soldier was standing beside Queen Scarlet, writing on a small scroll.

He hadn't seen her come in — but maybe all the gold had dazzled his eyes so he'd just missed her before. She was an orange color very close to the golden yellow of the room, with warm amber eyes. She looked young, and quiet. Her voice when she finally spoke was soft.

"Are you sure you want to do this, Your Majesty?" she asked.

"Yes," Queen Scarlet said with a hiss. "He's dangerous the way he is — anyone can see that. I can't use him in my arena if I want to trade him later, and I don't want to deal with any messy escape or rescue attempts."

"You understand I'm not sure what the consequences will be," said the soldier. "If we stick to your . . . unusual specifications, I mean."

"I told you I'd only use you for special cases." The queen lashed her tail. "This is one."

"Very well. Then he's gone," said the other SkyWing. "No one will ever be able to find him. Trust me."

Queen Scarlet snorted. "Not one of my favorite activities, trusting other dragons," she said. "But I'll give it a whirl just this once. He's all yours."

The dragon smiled sideways at Hailstorm, and for the first time in his life he felt cold — cold all the way through his bones and claws.

She stepped toward him, reaching for something around her neck, but he was too hypnotized by her eyes to run or fight or even scream.

Her eyes were not normal SkyWing eyes anymore. They were dark black, black as the darkest abyss in the ocean, and they were coming to swallow him whole.

PART ONE

A COLD WIND

━━ CHAPTER 1 ━━

The first time Winter disappointed his family, he was two years old.

Or at least, the first time he *knew* he'd disappointed them. Perhaps it had been happening all along, and they'd hidden it behind the stern, demanding faces they showed all the royal dragonets.

He could remember the dawn that day, the morning of his eleventh hunt — the subzero chill in the air, the paling purple of the sky, two moons still high overhead while the third slid its thin crescent sliver down below the horizon. A snowy owl was perched on one of the palace outcroppings, its talons digging into the ice. It glowered beadily at Winter as if it saw his disgrace coming.

His sister, Icicle, was in the hunting party, and his brother, Hailstorm, too, along with two of Glacier's dragonets, one of Winter's royal uncles, three attendants, and Winter's parents, Tundra and Narwhal. They gathered in the courtyard of the ice palace, stamping their feet and beating their wings as the glorious freezing air filled their lungs. The sharp crunch of snow beneath their claws broke the stillness of the morning.

Winter remembered looking up at his mother as she hissed for attention.

"This hunt is for the table of the queen herself," Tundra growled. "Whoever brings down the first polar bear will be invited to sit at her side this evening." She shot a glittering look at Icicle, coiled beside Winter.

Icicle was only two years old as well, but she already knew the future her parents had planned for her. So did Winter, although he suspected he wasn't supposed to.

He couldn't remember how he knew. Had he overheard his parents whispering when they thought he was too young to understand? Or had he figured it out from their behavior over the years?

But he did know. One day Icicle would challenge their aunt, Queen Glacier, for the throne. That was the reason she was hatched, and the destiny she was trained for: to kill Glacier and become queen herself. The only question was when.

Glacier grew older and larger and stronger each year. And Icicle had to strike before one of Glacier's own daughters seized the queenship. Daughters, sisters, or nieces could try for the throne; cousins could not. Neither could sisters-in-law, or Tundra surely would have thrown down the challenge herself.

So Winter's parents couldn't wait forever — but they also needed to be sure Icicle was ready. She'd have only one chance. Kill or die, that was how it worked.

Icicle lifted her snout and returned her mother's arch, calculating look. "It'll be me," she said, sounding almost bored. "Find a polar bear? Easy. I have a much better nose than these two." She flicked her tail dismissively at Hailstorm and Winter.

"We'll see about that!" Hailstorm said. He grinned and hopped from foot to foot, full of energy the way he always was. Winter often wished some of his brother's confidence would spill over onto him.

The five dragonets set out first, flying away from the palace in five different directions. At their age, every hunt was still a test — a chance to prove your worth and climb higher in the rankings. Not that Hailstorm needed to climb any higher; he'd been at the very top since he was not quite two years old himself. He made the top of the list the same day Icicle and Winter hatched, in fact.

Winter knew it was risky, but he decided to try flying out to sea to hunt. Sometimes polar bears could be found on the islands off the coast, or drifting on the icebergs, or swimming from one to another. He had yet to catch a polar bear after ten hunts, and as a result his place in the rankings was lower than anyone in their family had ever been. ("Hailstorm killed a polar bear the first time we took him out hunting," his mother would observe coldly during their tense family meals, sliding a bowl of dripping meat down the table. "Icicle has killed three so far. You obviously need to try harder.")

He scanned the waves for a long time, hoping to see a bobbing white head. Nothing moved except the sea itself and the shifting reflections of the rising sun.

Finally he swerved down toward one of the larger islands, not much bigger than the ice palace, but studded with caves where bears might hide.

And suddenly — there!

Standing at the edge of the water, staring south. She was *huge*, with a yellowish tinge to her dingy white fur. The wind was blowing his scent away from her, and he was gliding; she hadn't heard him or smelled him yet. In a few heartbeats he could be down there, sinking his claws into her shoulders. She'd put up a fight, but he would win.

He'd bring home a polar bear at last, and if he hurried, it might even be *him* sitting next to the queen at dinner tonight, while Queen Glacier ate *his* polar bear.

He wheeled upward, ready to dive . . . and then a movement caught at the corner of his eye, and he tilted his head toward the caves.

A pair of tiny cubs was wobbling out onto the snow. One of them tripped and sprawled out, paws flopping every which way, and the other growled with delight and tackled him. They rolled, wrestling playfully, and their mother swung her head around to grunt at them.

Winter hesitated. *Don't be a fool,* he told himself. *Just kill them, too; that's the way to impress Mother and Father.*

But there was something else watching the bears. It was well hidden, higher up among the rocks above the cave, but Winter's sharp IceWing eyes spotted it when it moved.

A scavenger! A scavenger here, this far north?

The creature was wrapped in so many furs, at first Winter almost thought it was another polar bear cub. But there was no mistaking those clever, thin brown paws for the great clumsy paws of bears. The scavenger was carrying a kind of rough spear and its eyes were fixed on the polar bears, so it hadn't noticed the dragon overhead yet either.

Winter scanned the island and spotted a wooden canoe that had been hauled onto the pebbly beach. How far had this scavenger traveled through the rough arctic waters? Was it hunting the bears for prey, just like Winter was?

If so, why wasn't it moving? Why had it lowered its spear as if it was already giving up?

Winter stared intently, tracking the scavenger's gaze. The way it was watching the cubs . . . was it hesitating, the way he had? Did it feel sorry for them, too?

Surely that was ridiculous. Scavengers couldn't feel pity. A hungry scavenger wouldn't spare the life of a bear just to protect her cubs. Would it?

He wished he could scoop up the scavenger and study it more closely.

"What is wrong with you?" Tundra's voice suddenly shrieked across the sky. Winter nearly leaped out of his scales. "Are you hunting or sightseeing? Are you an IceWing or a RainWing? *Kill that bear!*"

Winter twisted around and saw, to his horror, that his mother, father, and uncle were all winging toward him with disgusted expressions. Right behind them was Icicle, with a polar bear carcass dangling from her claws.

He dove frantically toward the bear, but the noise had alerted her to the danger, and she was already charging up the slope and bundling her cubs back into the cave. Winter beat his wings and lunged with his talons outstretched — but they closed on empty air as the three polar bears vanished into a narrow, stony passageway where dragons would never be able to follow.

Winter scrabbled at the cave entrance for a moment, but there was nothing he could do. The bears were gone.

He carefully forced himself not to look up at the scavenger. If his parents knew it was there, they'd make him kill it for the dinner feast, and for some reason he didn't want to. He couldn't imagine anyone eating those little paws, or the scavenger's head with its wide dark eyes. A shiver went through his wings.

"How could you let it get away?" Narwhal roared, landing beside him. Winter's father slammed one talon into the side of the cliff and a small avalanche of snow crashed over Winter's head. "It was right there! No kill could be easier!"

"Maybe he was worried about the little baby bears," Icicle offered, coming down with a thump and a splattering of bear blood. "Maybe he didn't want to leave them all alone with no mummy to take care of them, poor wittle furballs." Her voice was sneering and triumphant.

"No!" Winter cried. "That wasn't it! I was — I was just watching for a minute. I would have gotten it if —"

"If you hadn't been wasting time mooning around," Narwhal hissed. "We have to report this, you know. Your uncle saw the whole thing."

Winter stared miserably at his talons. He knew his parents would have reported it anyway, even with no other witnesses. They believed in the strict IceWing codes of behavior. They agreed that the only way to make him strong was to expose all his weaknesses. Shame and fear were powerful weapons for teaching young dragonets. If everyone was disappointed in him, surely he would fight harder to prove himself.

I will, he thought fiercely. *I will be better. I will claw my way up the rankings. I won't make a mistake like this again.*

But he still did not tell his parents about the scavenger hiding nearby. He glanced back only once, as they were all swooping away, to make sure it was all right.

That incident sent him down into the Fifth Circle, above only one-year-old dragonets in families that barely counted as aristocrats. For months, his mother had made him memorize long sagas about dragons who'd attempted the Diamond Trial to get back into the First Circle, including about a hundred verses speculating how gruesomely they might have died. The Trial was a last resort, rarely used, but she made it clear that no dragonet of hers would reach his seventh hatching day any lower than Second Circle, even if it meant turning to an ancient, mysterious, most likely deadly ritual.

With that threat hanging over him, he had struggled to claw his way back up through the rankings, bit by bit, and he had tried as hard as he could for so long.

And then losing Hailstorm — actually, *leaving* Hailstorm, abandoning him to his fate without a fight — had wiped out all that work, and he'd had to start all over from the Sixth Circle.

Which I deserved, he thought. *It was my fault we were on that mountain; my fault he got caught. My stupid, cowardly decision to leave him there.*

But everything was different now. Now he knew Hailstorm was alive, not dead as they'd all thought. Queen Scarlet still held him prisoner, hidden somewhere secret. And Icicle had been bargaining for Hailstorm's life, before Winter had ruined her plan. She'd agreed to kill the dragonets of destiny in exchange for Hailstorm . . . but Winter had stopped her.

Which meant if Scarlet killed Hailstorm *now*, it would be even more Winter's fault.

He clenched his talons.

But maybe he could get to her before that happened. If he could find Scarlet, maybe there was still a chance to save his brother.

He swiped raindrops off his face, inhaling. The downpour was incessant and repulsive; he'd take a howling snowstorm over this dripping soggy horribleness any day. The forest floor squashed between his claws and the wet tree branches lashed his wings as they swayed in the storm.

Below him, his pet scavenger stood in the open doorway of the cage Winter had built. Bandit squinted up at the dragon and the thunderstorm.

"I'm letting you go," Winter said impatiently. "Don't just stand there. I can't carry a pet with me while I'm searching for Hailstorm, especially not one that flops around moping all the time." He rattled the cage and the scavenger flinched.

Winter had spent days and days on planning and constructing this cage, making it beautiful for his very first pet scavenger. And then Bandit hadn't appreciated it at all. He'd never used the swing or the running wheel. Mostly he'd cowered under the furs and squeaked, or he'd tried to run away.

"Isn't this what you wanted?" Winter demanded.

Bandit was the most disappointing pet of all time, but Winter couldn't help it; he still cared about him. Otherwise he could have abandoned Bandit to be someone's dinner back at Jade Mountain.

Winter still remembered the expression on that first hunter-scavenger's face, all these years later. The curiosity and the dragonlike sympathy in its eyes. He'd hoped to see something like that in Bandit one day . . . but it didn't matter now. Nothing mattered except finding Hailstorm.

"Go on, get out of here," Winter grumbled. He poked at Bandit with one claw, but the scavenger dodged and retreated farther into the cage, covering his head. Winter felt a flash of pity for the creature, and then felt furious with himself for caring, when there were more important things to worry about. "I know it's raining, but it's better than the Ice Kingdom, trust me."

If I take him with me to the Ice Kingdom, he'll either freeze to death or be eaten within the first day. Queen Glacier had granted him permission to have an exotic pet while at the academy, but where he saw an exotic pet, his parents were likely to see a delicious snack.

"Winter!" he heard a voice yell, somewhere off in the trees.

A plume of fire lit up the faces of four dragons, hurrying toward him through the forest. To his astonishment, it was the rest of his winglet from the Jade Mountain Academy: Qibli, Turtle, Kinkajou . . . and Moon.

He pushed back against the little jump that his heart made when he saw her.

Just what I need right now — a bunch of glaciers slowing me down.

"By all the snow monsters, what are you doing here?" Winter demanded. How had they even found him? And why?

"Looking for you," Moon said simply. Her eyes caught on his, shining in the bits of moonlight that fought through the storm clouds. She always looked at him as if she could see more of him than anyone else. As if she saw dazzling mountain peaks where his parents saw nothing but a lump of gray ice.

"And we found you!" Kinkajou added. "We're amazing!" She flapped her wings as Qibli sent out another burst of flame, and Winter could see that she had turned bright yellow with purple spots. *Ridiculous*, that's what RainWings were, all of them. Flamboyant and ridiculous, with their feelings splattered all over their scales like that. It was embarrassing to be around.

Winter glanced down at Bandit. He couldn't let these dragons distract him. "I'm not going back to Jade Mountain," he said firmly. No matter what they said, they wouldn't change his mind. "I'm going to look for my brother."

"I thought so," Moon said, her voice quiet but as determined as his. "We want to help you."

"We *do*?" Turtle said, stamping his feet.

"Yes!" Kinkajou said. "I didn't know we did but now I totally do!"

No way. Absolutely not. I can't be around them — not even Moon. I mean, especially Moon.

He saw Qibli staring intently at him, as though the SandWing was figuring out his next move. Qibli had done that all the time in the cave they shared on Jade Mountain, and it had been very unsettling to live with. Winter could just imagine what it would be like to have the SandWing's black eyes inspecting everything he did on the path to finding Hailstorm.

"You can't come with me," he said. "I'm going to Queen Glacier. I need to explain it all to her and get her to help me find Hailstorm." Perhaps she would give him a wing of soldiers of his own to command. Or perhaps she would send out all her warrior dragons to search for Hailstorm. Regardless, he knew he needed the power of the IceWing queen to save his brother. That was the smart thing to do. Wasn't it?

"Wouldn't it make more sense to go to the Sky Kingdom?" Kinkajou asked. "Your brother must be imprisoned there somewhere, right? We could all look for him in, like, all the mountain caves, or something."

"Or you could go after Icicle," Qibli said. "Try to find out more about what Scarlet told her."

This was exactly what he didn't want: more options. More *doubt*. Qibli was right; Icicle was the only one who knew anything about Hailstorm and Scarlet. Following Icicle *would* make sense, except . . .

"I don't know where she's gone," Winter said bitterly. Back to the Ice Kingdom, he hoped, although she had to know Queen Glacier would be furious about her breaking the Jade Mountain truce.

"I have a guess," Qibli said. Of course he did. "You won't like it, though," he added, nodding at Kinkajou. "I think she's gone to the rainforest. She knows the one Scarlet hates the most is Glory — everyone knows that, if they know the story of what Glory did to her face. So I think Icicle might think that if she kills Glory, Scarlet will forgive her for failing to kill the others."

Nobody spoke for a long moment.

Thrice-cursed moons, Winter thought. *He's right. That's exactly what she would think. Icicle is brilliant, dangerous, and prefers to hunt alone. She would find a way to solve this problem, instead of running for help.*

Thunder rumbled overhead.

"Then *I'm* going to the rainforest," Kinkajou said fiercely. "I'm not letting her kill *my* awesome queen."

Suddenly Moon let out a yell of pain and crumpled forward, her wings collapsing around her.

Winter stepped toward her, but Kinkajou was faster, catching the NightWing in her wings.

"Moon?" she cried, staggering sideways.

A flash of lightning lit up Moon's face as the black dragon lifted her snout to the sky. Something blank and weird had taken over her eyes, like frost on a lake.

And then she began to speak in a voice nothing like her own.

"Beware the darkness of dragons,
Beware the stalker of dreams,
Beware the talons of power and fire,
Beware one who is not what she seems.

Something is coming to shake the earth,
Something is coming to scorch the ground,
Jade Mountain will fall beneath thunder and ice
Unless . . . unless the lost city of night . . . can be found."

The voice lurched to a stop and Moon closed her eyes, releasing all the tension out of her wings.

Everyone stared at her. Winter's heart was hammering like the pelting raindrops. Those words — that couldn't be what it sounded like, could it?

"By all the snakes," Qibli said at last. Winter met his eyes in the next flash of lightning. Qibli looked as terrified as he felt — as shaken as he'd been the day of the explosion in their history class. "What was that?"

"That's what you've been muttering in your sleep," Kinkajou said to Moon.

"It sounded like a prophecy," Winter said slowly. But it *couldn't* be. The NightWings had sworn to everyone that their powers were gone. Tsunami, Sunny, Starflight, Clay, and Glory had confirmed it. No more mind reading. *No more prophecies.* Ever again. That was what they'd said, exactly.

So someone was lying, but who?

Moon shook her head and pressed herself upright, her wings unsteady. "Turtle," she said, "please give him one of the rocks."

The SeaWing fumbled with the armband he always wore. Winter could see that a couple of the black stones were missing from it, and as he watched, Turtle pried out another one and passed it to Winter.

The stone was small, about the size of a dragon's tooth, and had a strange sheen to it, although that might have been the effect of the rain and the lightning. It was jagged around the edges, but not sharp. It looked fairly ordinary.

"What's this?" he asked. *What does this have to do with prophecies?*

"I have a lot to explain," Moon said. She sounded nervous, as though he might stab her with his tail spikes any moment. Which he'd refrained from doing to anyone so far, so he thought that was rather unfair. "Everything, the whole truth. I'm going to tell you everything."

"That sounds ominous," Winter said.

"No more ominous than *Jade Mountain will fall beneath thunder and ice*," Qibli said. "I hope we're all planning to talk about that, because I'm extremely unsettled right now."

"She said we have to find the lost city of night," Kinkajou said. "That's all, and then everything will be fine. Right? Isn't that what everyone else heard?"

"I'm pretty sure I heard that we're all going to die," Turtle said. "Death, death, monsters everywhere, death."

"Is that it?" Qibli asked Moon. "Is that what you saw? Jade Mountain is going to fall on us all?"

"I don't know," Moon said. "I've had visions, but none of them ever came out in words like that before. I don't know what it means."

Visions? Winter didn't like the sound of that. He closed his claws around the rock, frowning at her, but Moon had gone quiet, staring into the dark as though she were hearing something else.

A few moments passed, and then she seemed to snap back into herself. "Winter," she said. "There are a few things you need to know about me."

"I'm listening," he said. "Not that I have a choice, apparently."

"It's true what you've heard about the NightWings," she said. "They really have lost their powers. There hasn't been a NightWing who could read minds or see the future in . . . well, a very long time." She took a deep breath. "Until me."

Winter's tail twitched. His heart felt like the rock in his talons, small and hard.

"Because I hatched in the rainforest," she went on, "under two full moons, I can do both."

"Both what?" he forced out past the claws that seemed to be closing around his throat.

"See visions of the future," she said, then hesitated. "And . . . read minds."

— CHAPTER 2 —

No.

Thunder rumbled through the dark clouds like boulders sliding down a mountain.

What had Moon seen in his mind? What did she know?

Did she know that he felt — that he'd been thinking about *her* — her eyes and the way she tilted her head — her claws that could gently shield his scavenger one moment and rip apart a goat the next — the way she stood up to him the first time they met . . . but looked at him as though he was worth listening to . . .

She must know that he thought about her all the time.

Stop thinking about it. Don't think it — don't let her see any more —

"But you're safe now, I promise!" she said quickly, reaching toward him as he leaped back. "The rock you're holding — it's skyfire. It can shield your thoughts from me. As long as you're holding it or wearing it close to your scales, I can't hear anything you're thinking."

"Sounds like another NightWing lie," Winter snarled. *What have you seen in my head?* he thought fiercely.

Moon wiped raindrops from her eyes and took a deep breath. "I promise you, Winter. I can't hear anything in your mind right now. And even before, it was very . . . confusing."

Behind her, Qibli let out a snort that sounded a bit too amused.

"That's how I knew about Icicle and Scarlet," Moon said. "I heard them talking in Icicle's dream. And I heard Icicle planning to kill Starflight on her way to the library. But I can only hear what dragons are thinking right at that moment — I can't reach in and rummage around in anyone's brain or anything like that."

Winter found this image not very reassuring at all.

"You've been listening to us from the moment you met us," he said. "Deceiving us. Spying on us." He hissed out a wisp of frostbreath, turning the raindrops around him into tiny chunks of ice that clattered to the ground. "I should have expected as much from a NightWing."

But not from *this* NightWing. He'd thought Moon was different. He'd begun to think she might be the only NightWing in the world he could trust.

And the whole time she'd been lying and snooping around in his thoughts.

He must be the most dim-witted dragon who'd ever lived.

I shouldn't have let my guard down. I've always been taught that NightWings are conniving, underhanded backstabbers; I know the history of what they did to us. This is just more proof of that.

"Go back to Jade Mountain, all of you," Winter said. "Leave me alone." He turned to the cage where his scavenger was still standing, staring mournfully out at the rain. "And you, GET OUT OF HERE!" he roared as loud as he could.

Bandit stumbled back with a cry of terror, then bolted out of the cage. The little creature tripped and sprawled on the wet leaves, scrambled upright again, and went galloping off into the dark forest.

Winter saw the look on Moon's face as she watched Bandit go — sympathetic, pitying, curious. No one else had ever been as interested in scavengers as he was.

He curled his talons around the skyfire rock. "I mean it. Go away. I'm going to the Ice Kingdom, and if you follow me, you'll die." He paused for a moment. "Not that I have any objection to your deaths, just to be clear. I just don't want to listen to you all breathing and flapping and saying stupid things all the way there."

"That *can't* be your plan," Qibli said. The SandWing was using his annoying "let's be sensible about this" voice. "Go home and beg for help? By the time you get there, your brother might be dead. Your best chance is to catch Icicle."

"Before she kills Queen Glory," Kinkajou said fiercely. The little RainWing was now a mango-orange color with streaks of black along her wings. She looked ready to fly into battle — but Icicle was a deadly warrior who could kill a vegetarian rainforest dragon with a snap of her tail.

"I don't need help from any of you," he growled. "Especially you." He threw a glare at Moon, who folded her wings closer around herself but didn't look away.

"You do, actually," said Qibli. "You won't get two steps into the rainforest without our help — it's full of NightWings now, and everyone knows they don't like IceWings. And if you find Scarlet, do you think she'll just tell you where your brother is? Wouldn't it be useful and much more efficient to have a mind reader with you?"

"Oh, is that what you are now?" Winter asked Moon. "A clever tool that can be used by whoever needs some quick answers?"

"I won't let anyone use me," she said with a flash of anger. "But if I can do something good with this — this gift I didn't ask for — then yes, I'll do it."

"Um," Turtle interjected. Winter shifted his glare to the SeaWing, who had been quietly pacing in circles, splashing through the puddles with his huge talons. "Excuse me. What about the creepy prophecy? Is Jade Mountain in danger? Shouldn't we . . . you know, warn someone?"

"I'm not worried," Kinkajou said. "We know where the lost city of night is. The NightWings abandoned it when the volcano erupted, but we can still get to the island from the rainforest. That's easy. So we go to the lost city and then all those awful things won't happen and Jade Mountain will be fine. Right? Nothing to panic about."

Qibli let out a plume of fire, illuminating Moon's doubtful expression.

"I don't think it's that simple," she said. "The things I saw when the words came . . . the things I see in my nightmares . . . I can't imagine that just visiting the volcanic island could stop any of that from happening."

"Well, let's try it and see," Kinkajou said enthusiastically.

"But if it doesn't work," Turtle said, fidgeting nervously with his claws, "all those dragons at Jade Mountain — my sisters —"

"Hey, I agree with you," Qibli said. "I'm completely feeling the doom right now. But do you think anyone will believe her?" He nodded at Moon. "When they've been told the NightWings have no powers now?"

"Sunny will," Kinkajou said. "Tsunami might not. She doesn't like prophecies much."

"And then what — shut down the whole school based on a maybe-prophecy?" Qibli went on. "I don't think they'll do that. Besides, Winter's problem is urgent. We have to find his brother before Scarlet kills him, so I vote we do that now and deal with the impending apocalypse afterward."

"Me too," Moon said.

What in the world made these dragons think *his* problem was *their* problem? Finding Hailstorm was urgent to Winter, but it made *no sense* for any NOT-IceWings to get involved at all.

Winter narrowed his eyes at Turtle, dripping forlornly into the puddles around his claws. It was easy to forget that the SeaWing was a royal prince as well — the son of Queen Coral. He never *acted* like royalty. Instead Turtle behaved as though he didn't want to be noticed at all — mumbly, sticking to the background, agreeing to anything.

Was he afraid of something? Or just boring?

If an IceWing acted the way Turtle does, he'd be stuck in the Seventh Circle forever.

Which meant Winter could get rid of him by applying the right pressure.

"You should go back," he said, making Turtle jump. "You don't want to tramp around Pyrrhia looking for my deadly sister, who will kill you on sight, or my brother, who might do the same because, by the way, killing SeaWings was a specialty of his. Go keep an eye on Jade Mountain instead."

Turtle's glow-in-the-dark scales flickered, illuminating his anxious face with pale greenish light. "But what if the mountain falls on me? Is it dangerous?"

"Not as dangerous as following me," Winter hissed.

"It's not going to fall on you, because we're going to stop it," Kinkajou said. "But don't you want to stay with us?"

"I can't decide what sounds worse," Turtle admitted. "Chasing killer dragons across Pyrrhia, or sitting at school waiting for some kind of thunder and ice catastrophe to drop on my head."

"It's all right," Moon said. "Turtle, you can go back to Jade Mountain. You can tell them that we're safe and where we've gone."

"That's true!" he said, perking up. "That would be useful of me, wouldn't it?"

"Probably," Qibli agreed. "Although you could be useful with us, too. But it's your choice."

Turtle shuffled backward. "I'll tell Tsunami and the others not to worry about you. And I did promise Mother to watch out for Anemone, so I should, uh, I should really do that, you know? But you go catch the bad guys and stop the prophecy, and then I'll see you all when you get back to school, okay?"

A moment later, the SeaWing had slipped away into the trees, and soon they heard muffled wet wingbeats as he flew away.

"Hmm," Kinkajou said with a frown. "That was disappointing. How can we be the second coming of the five dragonets of destiny if there's only four of us?"

"I highly doubt *we're* destined for anything special," Winter said.

"You're not getting rid of the rest of us that easily," Qibli said sharply to Winter, as though he knew exactly what Winter was trying to do.

"All right," Winter growled. "Fine, let's all go to the rain-forest together like a soppy pile of MudWing siblings. I can look for Icicle and you can go dig around in the ashes of the Night Kingdom."

"And I can save Queen Glory!" Kinkajou said, leaping into the air.

"Besides," Qibli pointed out, flicking his tail at Winter, "that'll actually bring you closer to the Ice Kingdom, since then you can use the tunnel that comes out north of Queen Thorn's stronghold."

That was true. Winter disliked it intensely when Qibli made clever observations like that, and it happened about forty times a day.

"I know," he said, looking down his nose at the SandWing. "Obviously I figured that out. That's the only reason I'm agreeing to this."

"Oh," Qibli said with a rakish grin. "I thought perhaps it was because I'm so charming and convincing."

"You are neither," Winter said. "In fact, if you don't shut up at once, I will change my mind."

Qibli pretended to wrap invisible chains around his snout and lifted his front talons innocently.

"Let's go," Moon said, spreading her wings and lifting off. Qibli and Kinkajou leaped after her.

Winter hesitated for a moment, watching the lightning flash in the sky beyond the flying dragons.

Why *was* he agreeing to this? An IceWing warrior didn't

need help from anyone else, least of all a pack of misguided dragons from *other tribes*.

Take Qibli: Everyone knew SandWings were nearly as untrustworthy as NightWings, except half as smart and twice as likely to betray you for gold and treasure.

And a RainWing! They weren't even worth mentioning in the great IceWing sagas that told the history of this world. Lazy and insignificant and weak; there was no benefit to be gained from knowing them or befriending them.

Worst of all, how could he ally himself with a NightWing — even temporarily, even if he went into it knowing not to trust her? To travel with Moon, to spend a single moment longer with her, knowing what he knew now . . .

(And yet . . . still feeling something he *should not be feeling* . . .)

I should stay as far away from her as I can.

Mother and Father would be more than disappointed in me. If they heard of this, any potential position in the palace would be gone forever. I'd land at the bottom of the Seventh Circle and have to choose between the Diamond Trial or being stationed on an arctic island outpost for the rest of my life.

He could see their faces so clearly — that look they got whenever he did something wrong. The look that said, *if only we'd lost you instead of Hailstorm. If only you met any of our expectations. If only you were everything an IceWing should be.*

"Winter!" Qibli called from above. The others were hovering up there, waiting for him. "Come on!"

This was only temporary, he reminded himself. Get to the rainforest, look for Icicle. Then he could rescue Hailstorm by himself. That's what a true IceWing prince would do.

He wasn't really working with Moon and the others. He didn't have to listen to them, and he certainly wouldn't ask them for help.

Most of all, he would never, never trust them, especially that lying NightWing.

Shaking rain off his tail with a clatter of spikes, he ascended into the storm, wheeled around in a circle, and took off toward the rainforest without a glance at the other dragons.

— CHAPTER 3 —

Winter was not surprised to discover that the rainforest was horrifying and awful.

For starters, there was something blocking Winter's view in every direction — giant trees to the left, tangles of vines to the right, a thick canopy of leaves overhead. He could barely see five feet in front of him, never mind the horizon. How could any dragon keep watch in a place like this? How could you ever know if you were being attacked or by how many dragons? It was an indefensible quagmire.

Also a literal quagmire — every time they landed, the mud was nearly enough to make him want to claw off his own scales.

Moreover, the whole place was overwhelming. Too many bright colors (what self-respecting bird would ever need to have red, yellow, blue, *and* green feathers? Black and white: those were the only feather colors for a *dignified* bird). Too many strange noises (what kind of animal howled like that? why could he hear a waterfall for what seemed like hours and yet never see it? and WHAT was that INFERNAL

NONSTOP BUZZING?). Also, far far FAR too many weird smells.

Winter couldn't decide which was the worst part: the bugs or the heat. It was painfully, oppressively hot in a sweltering, we're-being-boiled-alive-in-our-scales kind of way. He thought he'd experienced heat, traveling through the Kingdom of Sand, but this was also damp and sticky and more miserable than anything he'd ever felt before.

Then there were the insects swarming around them, finding every spot between the dragons' scales to wriggle in and suck their blood. He'd already shaken two green-striped caterpillars, a walking twig thing, and an alarmingly furry spider out of his ears. His wings kept catching on enormous spiderwebs, and creatures with millions of legs had scurried over his talons at least a dozen times. He itched unbearably from his horns to his forlornly muddy tail.

Was Icicle really here? He couldn't imagine her putting up with any of this. He couldn't imagine her with even a speck of mud on her; she had always returned from battle as pristine as when she'd left, apart from a few bleeding blue scratches here and there.

Perhaps she'd taken two steps into this rainforest and decided that murdering the RainWing queen wasn't worth it.

"You must hate this place," Moon said, appearing beside him. They'd stopped to rest near a river, and Winter was crouched on a large boulder, trying to dip his talons in the water without stepping in the oozing black mud that lined the banks.

He narrowed his eyes at her, reaching unconsciously for the small wolfskin pouch he kept tied to one of his ankles, where he'd hidden the skyfire.

She sighed. "No, I didn't get that from your head. I just figured an IceWing would probably hate it here. It must be the polar opposite of the Ice Kingdom. The anti–polar opposite," she added, then scrunched her snout, trying not to laugh at her own joke.

Is this merely idle conversation? What would be the point of that? Or is she trying to trick some information out of me?

"It is," he said finally. "And I do."

"This is where I grew up," she said, wading a few steps into the river. The water eddied around her legs with glints of reflected sunlight. "It's not so bad, actually."

"Hrrmph," Winter snorted.

"Not so bad?!" Kinkajou said indignantly from the other bank. "This is the most beautiful part of Pyrrhia! Other dragons would be lucky to live here!"

The RainWing bounded into the water with a splash that drenched Winter's nose and tail. A fat orange toad burst out of the river and made a clumsy dash for the reeds, trying to get away from the dragons. Moon tilted her head at it, then flared her wings at Qibli as he sat up from the middle of the river.

"Don't eat it," she warned him. "Seriously, one of those

gave me hiccups for days. Also some really weird dreams. I thought for a while I was having visions of a possible future where newts and anteaters took over the world."

Kinkajou giggled.

"Here, try these instead," Moon offered. She reached into one of the overhanging trees and pulled a few strange fruits from the branches. They were a curious reddish-pink on the outside, with flaps like folded-up flower petals, but as she sliced them open with her claws, Winter saw that on the inside they were white with small black flecks.

She handed one to Qibli, then glanced sideways at Winter.

"Absolutely not," he said. "Do not get that vile stickiness anywhere near me. Fruit. Yuck." His stomach growled and he tried to hide it by scraping his claws along the rock.

"You are so, so weird," Kinkajou said to him. "How can you not love it here? Don't you come from a place with no colors and no life?"

He thought of the thousand different shimmering shades of blue in the ice palace. He remembered the distant splashes of whales and seals, the way sound carried across the cool, quiet ice. He thought of how he could smell polar bears or arctic foxes from miles away and how all of his senses could detect the smallest changes in the frozen world. Here it was just *too much*.

"White is a color," he snapped at the RainWing. "Blue is a color. *That* is an eyesore." He pointed to a violently red flower as big as one of his talons.

"We also have these," Moon said. She lifted a dark green leaf on one of the trees and revealed a spiraling tendril of delicate white-blue flowers, glowing like snowflakes against the brown trunk. "Oh, and look! There's a sloth!" She pointed to a furry gray shape that was clambering slowly along a branch far overhead.

"Thank the moons," Winter said, leaping to his feet. "I knew there had to be something worth eating around here." He shot into the air, his claws reaching for the sloth's exposed white underbelly.

"Wait!" Moon cried. There was a twin shriek of dismay from Kinkajou.

The sloth peered over its shoulder and blinked enormous, confused eyes at him.

And then *WHAM* something slammed into Winter's side and smashed him against a tree. He saw a flash of red scales and sharp teeth and thought, *SkyWing!* Could it be Queen Scarlet, here? Attacking him?

He whirled and lashed out with his tail but just missed the enemy dragon as it dove under him. Winter spun again and clawed at the air where the dragon should have been, but once again it whisked out of his reach.

The red dragon swooped up to the branch, snatched the sloth in its talons, paused to glare at Winter — and then vanished.

Winter roared with surprise and fury.

"Calm down!" Qibli shouted in his ear. The SandWing ducked as Winter swiped at him. "Winter! Stop!"

"There was a SkyWing!" Winter snarled. "It attacked me and stole my prey and then disapp — oh, SEAL GUTS!"

"Not a SkyWing," Qibli pointed out, although Winter had obviously figured that out already.

"I know!" Winter roared, beating the air with his wings. "Come out and face me, you cowardly lunch-stealing RainWing!"

The dragon suddenly materialized on the branch again, her scales shifting to a furious red with splatters of black and orange. "Toe-Fur is nobody's lunch!" she shouted. "Those nasty black dragons have already eaten one of my sloths! I'm not letting it happen again!" She flexed her claws and bared her fangs at him.

"Don't make her mad," Qibli said quickly, grabbing Winter's shoulder. "I mean — don't make her *more* mad." The heat emanating from the SandWing's yellow scales was uncomfortable and Winter shook him off.

"As if a *RainWing* would ever dare fight me," Winter scoffed. "As if I couldn't claw off her face as easily as breathing."

"What is with you and faces?" Qibli said. "You should try threatening someone's elbows or ankles once in a while, just for a change of pace."

Kinkajou landed on the branch beside the angry RainWing, angling herself between the furious dragon and Winter.

"Exquisite, it's me," she said. "I'm sorry about this. I promise we were about to stop him."

"Ha!" Winter barked.

"Winter, do you *have* a part of your brain that can handle empathy?" Qibli asked. "That sloth is her pet. Just like Bandit was your pet. Can you by any chance remember about a week ago when someone tried to eat *your* pet?"

Winter hesitated. Of course he remembered that, and he remembered how Moon had saved his scavenger in her quiet but resolute way. Qibli was right. *Again*. There was nothing MORE INFURIATING IN THE ENTIRE WORLD.

"Bandit is much smarter than a flea-ridden sloth," Winter snapped, landing on one of the fat branches of a nearby tree. He flinched as a centipede as long as his foot immediately scuttled over his claws. "But FINE, I won't eat any stupid sloths. Is there anything else that's off-limits that I should know about? Beloved armadillos? Hairy giant spiders that someone is terribly attached to?"

"I think the tamarin monkeys are really cute," Moon offered, swooping up beside them. "It'd be great if you could not eat those."

Winter scowled at her. As often happened with Moon, he couldn't tell if she was joking.

"Would you really eat a hairy spider anyway?" Qibli asked with genuine curiosity.

Exquisite clutched her sloth closer, hissed at Kinkajou and Winter, and vanished again. This time Winter could see the ripple of her scales changing and the slight weirdness of the air when she moved. A moment later, the branch shook as she took off, and he saw leaves thrashing about as the camouflaged dragon flapped away.

Moon landed next to Winter and suddenly reached out to brush his wing with hers. Unlike Qibli's, Moon's scales were cool and smooth, like the icy walls of his room back in the palace.

How dare she touch me! Winter thought. But then . . . he found himself keeping as still as he could so their wings would stay connected.

What is wrong *with me?*

Moon's eyes were far away, and he wondered if she even knew she was touching him.

"Someone's coming," she whispered. "Someone with dark thoughts . . ."

Did she see darkness in my *mind?* Winter wondered. *How did she feel about the way I hate other dragons?*

"What's a dark thought?" Qibli asked with something odd in his voice. Nervousness? Was he also worried about what Moon had found inside him? What had she seen in *his* head?

"It's Obsidian. He's thinking he hates being on guard duty," Moon said thoughtfully. "Especially with the RainWing he's been assigned as a partner. He hates being told what to do by RainWings. He wishes the NightWings could overthrow

Queen Glory and rule the rainforest themselves." She paused. "All right, we're safe; they've gone by."

She realized her wing was still touching Winter's and pulled away with an apologetic expression. He tried to pretend he hadn't even noticed.

"So we're all on board with avoiding NightWings, then?" Qibli said. "Excellent. Present company excepted, of course."

"Maybe not all NightWings, but definitely him," Moon said. She sighed. "I should probably tell the queen what I can do so I can warn her about dragons like this." Her tail flicked the leaves below them. "But I worry — I mean, should dragons be punished for their thoughts? Even if they never act on them? But what if warning her means they'll never do whatever terrible thing they're thinking of? I don't know. I don't want anyone to use me as a way to spy on the private thoughts of her subjects."

"Really?" Qibli said. "But it would be useful to know if a coup or an assassination is coming. If you could prevent that, wouldn't it be worth spying on a few dragons?"

"No," Winter snapped. "Nothing justifies invading another dragon's mind."

"But that's how she stopped Icicle from killing Starflight," Qibli pointed out. "Aren't you grateful she did that?"

Winter glared down at Kinkajou, who had gone back to splashing in the river below. "I still don't like it," he said. "In the wrong talons . . . I mean, Moon could tell Queen

Glory she heard someone planning a murder, and that dragon could be punished, and who could prove her wrong?"

"I wouldn't *lie*," Moon said, looking outraged.

"How do we know that?" Winter asked. "You hid your powers from us. Why should we trust you? And even if *you* wouldn't lie, what about other NightWings? They've lied before, haven't they? They lied about having powers for years apparently. The entire tribe is full of liars, going back thousands of years to the Darkstalker and his cursed mother, Foeslayer."

Moon jumped, overbalanced, and fell off the branch with a lot of wild thrashing. Startled, Winter peered down at her as she climbed back up.

"Three moons, what was that about?" Qibli asked when she was settled again. "Are you all right?" Moon was breathing in a funny, almost panicked way.

"*Darkstalker?*" she said to Winter. "How do you know about *him*?"

"Everyone knows about him," Winter said.

"I don't," Qibli offered.

"Everyone," Winter said pointedly, "who's anyone."

"Ah, I see," Qibli said. "You mean IceWings."

"And NightWings," Moon said. "He's *our* legend. Nightmare. Ghost monster from the beyond. Whatever."

"Ours too," Winter said grimly. "Trust me."

"Why, what did he ever do to the IceWings?" Moon asked.

"Killed one of our princes," Winter said. "Stole our royal heritage. Ruined everything forever."

"Oh, my, *forever*?" Qibli asked. He gave the sunlit rainforest a mock-serious, nodding inspection. "Well, that explains it. I was wondering why everything was so very ruined all the time. Thank goodness there's one ancient dead dragon we can blame for it all."

"You wouldn't joke if you knew the whole story," Winter snapped.

Moon closed her eyes, then shook her head with an expression that looked like frustration. "I want to know the whole —" she began, and then her eyes popped open in alarm. "They're coming back. Obsidian and the RainWing guard. We should —"

"Hello!" Kinkajou called, waving her wings. "Hi! Over here!"

"— not do that," Qibli finished for Moon as she winced.

It was too late. Winter hissed softly. There was no chance of sneaking through the rain   now.

The guards were heading straight for them.

CHAPTER 4

A black dragon — the one with "ugly thoughts" — slowly stalked along the banks of the river, staring at Kinkajou. His forked black tongue flicked in and out, and his expression was calculating.

A few steps ahead of him was a RainWing, dappled green like the forest but not completely camouflaged. She splashed into the river and over to Kinkajou, frowning.

"Oh, it's you," Kinkajou said. Winter had never heard that tone of gloom from the little RainWing before. "Hi, Bromeliad. I thought you were Orchid."

"What are you doing back here?" Bromeliad demanded. "You were supposed to stay at that school the queen sent you to! I *told* her you were a terrible student and would definitely fail or run off, but would she listen? Mysteriously not! And now here you are, so I suppose I was right!"

"I'm doing something important," Kinkajou snapped. "I'm here to save the queen, if you must know!"

Winter caught the shifty expression that crossed Obsidian's

face. Maybe Moon was right. Maybe this dragon's thoughts were as dangerous as they sounded.

Then Obsidian looked up and his gaze landed on Winter. His tail began lashing furiously.

"An IceWing," he hissed. "In our rainforest. Don't just lurk in the trees, friend. Come down and say hello."

That sounded like just about the last thing Winter wanted to do, but picking a fight with a NightWing would waste time . . . time he needed to find his sister. He reluctantly spread his wings.

"Don't let him bully you," Moon whispered, catching one of Winter's talons before he could lift off. "He's afraid of you. He's planning how to be as cruel and commanding as possible because he wants to see you squirm."

"I don't squirm for anyone," Winter snarled under his breath.

"I know," Moon said. "You shouldn't. You're a much better dragon than he is. You're . . . you're a much better dragon than most anyone." She ducked her head to look down at her claws.

Winter blinked at her. Was that really what she thought? Even after looking inside him?

"Not me, though, right?" Qibli said, nudging Moon with a grin. "He's not better than *me*. I'm awesome, right? Like, the most awesome?"

The way she smiled back at the SandWing, like she couldn't help herself, made Winter's scales feel all crawly and too warm. He spun away from them and leaped down to the ground.

The NightWing guard sat back on his haunches, inspecting the dragons suspiciously as Moon and Qibli landed on the riverbank as well. Having a NightWing's gaze on him, traveling over him as though he was a half-eaten seal carcass, made Winter want to smash in some faces with his tail. He scraped his serrated claws through the damp layer of leaves on the forest floor.

"You're the peculiar dragonet," Obsidian said finally, narrowing his eyes at Moon. "Failed school already? Did they realize you can't talk and send you back? What's with the multicolored escort?" He squinted at the dragons around her. "Exactly who are *you*?"

"None of your business," Winter growled.

Obsidian's brows went up and he eyed Winter even more closely. Winter wondered if it would be a bad start if he slashed that superior expression right off the black dragon's face.

"We're here to see Queen Glory," Qibli said. Winter was interested to hear a note of hostility in Qibli's voice as well. From what he'd seen so far, the SandWing usually got along with everyone, or tried to, especially right at first. "And trust me, she'll want to see us, so don't be a camel-sniffer about it."

"I have to take you to the Night Village," Obsidian said haughtily. "That's the protocol for new dragons in the rainforest. We'll send her a message, and *if* she wants to see you, she'll come find you there."

"Um, no," Kinkajou said. "Hello, *I* am a RainWing, not a 'new dragon.' I live here! I'm practically the queen's best friend! And I'm taking my new friends to see her right now."

The NightWing shifted his wings slightly and flicked his tongue through his sharp teeth.

"Kinkajou," Moon said, touching her clawmate's shoulder. "Actually, if we go to the village, I could see my mother . . . and we could ask whether anyone's seen Icicle."

"Oh — all right," Kinkajou agreed. "But I'm going because I *want* to, not because anyone is *telling* me to." She flared the ruff behind her ears at Obsidian, turning it orange as she did.

He smiled nastily. "Well, come along, then."

"I'll go tell Queen Glory you're here," said Bromeliad, lifting off into the trees.

Winter followed Qibli and the others, staying a few steps behind so he could keep an eye on Obsidian.

He had imagined visiting the home of the NightWings many times, but in those fantasies he always arrived at the head of a battalion of IceWings. His visions generally involved swooping down in vengeful glory, blasting frostbreath across the entire city, and wiping out the whole tribe in one icy attack.

NightWings had been the sworn enemies of IceWings for hundreds of years, but there hadn't been any action between them during Winter's lifetime. The IceWings had been too busy with the War of SandWing Succession — fighting nearly every other tribe — to worry about the secretive, impossible-to-find NightWings.

But then the news had arrived about the massacre at the SkyWing palace. When the tribe heard that NightWings had descended on Scarlet's arena and slaughtered all the IceWing prisoners while they were still chained and bound . . . well, Winter wasn't the only one who'd sworn vengeance. Finding the secret NightWing home had become the ambition of every young IceWing.

And now here he was, about to walk right into it.

This wasn't *the* secret home, of course. This was their new home, the one they'd been driven to after the volcano erupted and wiped out their last home. Everyone knew about this one. Just like everyone knew the NightWings had no more powers, that they were resettling in the rainforest, and that a seven-year-old RainWing was their new queen.

They heard the village before they saw it: wingbeats, branches being ripped off trees, something that sounded like hammering. Winter could also smell meat cooking over a fire, and he wished he could order his stomach not to growl and embarrass him.

Then he saw black scales ahead and felt his talons start tingling. Two dragons were pacing across a path that had been cleared through the trees, evidently guarding it. Obsidian went on ahead to speak to them in low murmurs.

The NightWings glanced over and Winter's claws curled in. If he had to die fighting NightWings, that would be a fine way to go out. *Will they kill me like they killed Hailstorm?*

He caught himself. It was instinct to see a NightWing and think of his brother's death, but according to Queen Scarlet, Hailstorm wasn't dead.

Twelve other IceWing prisoners definitely were, though. And somewhere in this village were the dragons who killed them.

Obsidian beckoned Winter and the others forward with his tail, and the two guards stepped aside to let them pass, smirking in a horribly superior NightWing sort of way.

"What do you think those smug expressions are for?" Qibli said loudly to Winter. "Doesn't seem like NightWings have anything left to be smug about, right? I mean, they've gone from claiming to be the most powerful tribe in Pyrrhia to homeless and pathetic and bowing to RainWings."

All three guards bristled, flaring their wings.

"What's wrong with bowing to a RainWing?" Kinkajou demanded.

"Qibli, quit making things worse," Moon hissed.

"I was just *wondering*," he said calmly, with a wink at Winter.

Winter knew what he was doing, and it had worked. Qibli's words had riled up the NightWings and made Winter feel better at the same time.

All of his senses were on high alert as they walked into

the village and more and more NightWings appeared around them. His eyes darted around, assessing their activity. He expected plotting and scheming and battle training . . . but most of the NightWings seemed to be busily engaged in very ordinary things.

A group of ten were grappling with vines and bushes and stunted trees, trying to expand the open space. Three more were washing fruit in the river, near a set of cooking fires dug into the ground, where another four NightWings were roasting what looked like small pigs.

Several others were working on shoring up the ramshackle huts that dotted the cleared area. Winter saw a young dragon scramble onto a roof to add more giant palm leaves, only to have the entire structure cave in underneath her. She plummeted to the ground with a yell and a crash, and a few other NightWings began shouting at her.

"There were a few RainWings who might have helped them build all this," Kinkajou explained suddenly, glancing at Winter and Qibli. "We could have showed them how to set up their village in the treetops, like ours, but the NightWings didn't want help. Plus they thought it was too sunny up there, like, what does that even mean? How can it ever be *too* sunny?"

It was cooler down on the rainforest floor, but it was also muddier. Winter wasn't sure which option he'd prefer — but he was glad he didn't have to live here at all. He wondered if the NightWings really found it an improvement over their last home.

"Mother!" Moon cried suddenly. Her whole face lit up like the sun sparkling off a glacier. She flew across the clearing and threw her wings around a tall, thin dragon who looked a lot like Moon, without the silver teardrop scales near her eyes.

"Moon!" the NightWing gasped. Her expression went from quietly tired to startled to overjoyed, and she wrapped the dragonet in close to her with fierce affection.

Winter felt a strange twinge, watching them. *IceWings don't hug like that,* he reminded himself. *At least, royal ones don't. It would be undignified.* He couldn't imagine his mother or father wrapping their wings around him. Or looking that happy to see him, for that matter.

Was this how all NightWings were with their dragonets? He glanced around the clearing, looking for dragons younger than himself, and realized there were almost none. It took him a while to finally spot one by the river, leaning against his mother's side and helping to wash fruit. She had one wing tented protectively over him.

And there was another small dragonet over by a fallen tree, practicing her flying. A dragon who might be her father stood beside her, catching her when she fell awkwardly. There was something protective and proud about the way he was standing, too.

Winter pulled his gaze away and noticed odd looks on the other dragonets' faces. Qibli and Kinkajou — there was something faintly wistful in their expressions as they watched Moon and her mother. He caught himself starting to wonder what their family stories were.

They look like lonely cows, he thought ferociously. *I refuse to moon about like that over anything. My parents are perfect the way they are. They made me strong and dangerous — a true dragon. Stronger than anyone else here, that's for sure.*

I may not be as fearsome as Hailstorm — but still, I'm an IceWing! The greatest tribe in Pyrrhia! I must act like one, especially here, with so many NightWing eyes on me. Like Father says: Be strong, be vigilant, strike first. And trust nobody.

"What are you doing here?" Moon's mother asked, holding Moon by her shoulders.

Moon curled her wings in, her face falling. "I didn't get thrown out," she said in a soft voice. "I didn't do anything wrong, and nobody — that didn't happen, Mother."

Winter realized that Moon was responding to something her mother was thinking. He touched his skyfire pouch again and wondered if the little rock could protect him from all the NightWings here . . . or if there were other secret mind readers invading his thoughts right now.

"Shhh," said the older dragon, pulling Moon close again. She eyed Winter and Qibli warily.

"But I *did* make friends," Moon said. She wriggled out of her mother's grasp. "You should meet them." She turned toward the others and her eyes went wide.

"No, stop!" she shouted. "He's not —"

Suddenly claws encircled Winter's neck and his body was thrown to the ground with a jarring thud. Someone bigger and heavier leaped on top of him, pinning him down.

"Don't bother struggling, IceWing," said an unfamiliar voice. "You're under arrest."

CHAPTER 5

Winter roared with fury, struggling to fight back, but his attacker had him expertly immobilized.

"Stop it! Get off him!" Moon yelled. Winter couldn't see much, with his snout pressed into the ground, but he felt the weight of dragons pushing and grappling on his wings.

"He's on our side!" Kinkajou cried. "Or he *was* before you *randomly attacked him for no reason.* Now he'll never like us again!"

"I wasn't going to anyway!" Winter bellowed as best he could, seething with rage and humiliation. "I didn't like you before either! I don't like any of you! And I'm going to MURDER this NightWing!"

"I don't know, he sounds kind of murder-y, Kinkajou," said the voice. "And we heard there's an extra-dangerous IceWing on the loose right now. So I'm going to keep sitting on him until I get further instructions."

"*I'm* instructing you!" Kinkajou yelped. "He's not the dangerous one! That's his sister!"

"It's true," Qibli chimed in. "This one is honorable. He's no sneak-in-the-night assassin."

"Hey, ouch," said the dragon on top of Winter. "Nothing wrong with assassins. Who said there was anything dishonorable about assassins? They're just not allowed to kill my — my queen. It's my job to stop them and drop some violence on their heads, but I'm not *judging* them, sheesh."

"He's not here to kill Glory," Moon said. "If he were, he would tell you, and he'd challenge her in open combat."

Would I? Winter wondered. *True, I wouldn't hurt a nothing RainWing, but if I'd had a chance to kill the NightWing queen, would I have done it the honorable way, or any way possible?*

What would Mother have wanted me to do?

Any way possible, he guessed. That was how Icicle and Hailstorm had been trained.

"DEATHBRINGER!" another new voice thundered, loud enough to rattle the leaves overhead. "*What* are you *doing*?"

"Saving you, protecting the forest, defending our new home, sitting on a *very* cold IceWing," said the NightWing from his perch on Winter's back. "You know, the usual."

A murmur eddied through the village as footsteps approached. Winter tried to wriggle around to see who was coming, but Deathbringer reached out and gently pinned his head to the ground again. A grotesque greenish-brown beetle with about four thousand legs came scuttling up and began creeping curiously onto Winter's nose.

"Stop arresting my guests," said the newcomer, pausing beside Winter. "It's not romantic or heroic, it's annoying. I've told you this before."

"I *know*," Deathbringer said, sounding aggrieved. "But look, it's an *IceWing*. Sunny specifically said an IceWing tried to kill all the prophecy dragonets. This is *definitely* a pinion-before-asking-questions kind of situation."

"All right, OFF," Glory said firmly. The weight on top of Winter suddenly lifted as if she'd hauled Deathbringer off with her own talons. "I am going to replace you as my body-guard if you seriously can't tell the difference between a male IceWing traveling with my friends Kinkajou and Moonwatcher, and a lone female IceWing out to kill me. Pay a little more attention to detail, Deathbringer. Also, by the way, you're one to talk about killing prophecy dragonets."

Winter scrambled upright, flinging the beetle off his nose and baring his teeth as he spun around.

His attacker was a NightWing a few years older than him, wiry and graceful and clearly trained to fight from the way he stood and the way he was assessing Winter.

Winter lunged toward him and found his way blocked by a dark green dragon with flares of orange around her ears and along the underside of her wings. She reached out and took one of Winter's talons, pressing it between hers and lowering her head in a small bow.

"We are so honored to have Queen Glacier's nephew in our forest," she said. "I sincerely apologize for the outrageous behavior of my brain-dead bodyguard. You should have been escorted at once to my royal pavilion, not attacked in such a disrespectful manner."

She glanced around at the gawking NightWings. "Everyone back to work, right now."

To Winter's surprise, they obeyed her, although there were a few muttered grumbles and two or three dragons who moved deliberately slowly.

He hesitated. Every bone in his body wanted to fly into a rage and rip Deathbringer's wings off. He couldn't let a NightWing treat him that way, especially in front of all the other NightWings, and get away with it.

But he'd never been greeted as visiting royalty before, and there was something irresistibly compelling about the way Queen Glory beckoned him to walk beside her, as if they were equals.

"Will he be punished?" Winter demanded.

"Oh, yes," Glory said, frowning at Deathbringer. "Creatively and firmly."

"Very well," Winter said. He shook as much dirt off his wings as he could and stepped up regally beside Glory. "I don't have time to punish him myself anyway. We have urgent matters to discuss."

"Indeed," said the queen, turning to lead the way out of the village. Behind him, Winter heard Moon saying good-bye to her mother, and the others hurrying to join him. "Sunny told me some of the details, but I hope you can fill in the rest."

"I can!" Kinkajou offered, bouncing up on Glory's other side. "Winter's sister, Icicle, who is, like, wicked scary, by the way, was secretly conspiring with Queen Scarlet because it turns out Winter's *brother* is, like, actually *alive*, not dead like everyone thought, and Scarlet's totally got him locked up somewhere, so Icicle was going to kill Starflight to get him back, except then Moon and Qibli and Winter completely heroically stopped her and it was apparently amazing and I missed the whole thing! Can you believe it? And so then Icicle flew off and we figure she's coming here to kill you, so we're here to completely heroically stop her *again* and also find out what she knows so we can rescue Winter's brother ourselves. Also, hello, school is awesome, how are you?"

"You're in as much trouble as Deathbringer," Glory said sternly, looking down at the dragonet. "What were you thinking, leaving school without permission? When everyone was already in such a state? Do you know how worried Sunny and Clay have been?"

Kinkajou stopped in her tracks with an expression of deep dismay and an explosion of dark blue splotches across her scales. "Oh, no!" she cried. "I'm sorry! Didn't Turtle tell them where we went?"

"Yes, and that certainly helped," Glory said with a snort. "Good news: Four of your students have gone off to find a dragon who just tried to kill you, in order to find another dragon who has tried to kill you about ninety dozen times. Oh excellent, thanks, Turtle. Now we don't have to worry at all. I mean, we were *hoping* somebody would take care of the vengeful and deadly Queen Scarlet for us. Preferably a bunch of five-year-olds. Very reassuring indeed."

Moon ducked her head. "Sorry, Your Majesty," she said. "This felt . . . urgent."

She glanced sideways at Winter and an odd flicker of something like gratitude went off in his chest — stupid, stupid. As if he cared that she knew how important it was to find his brother.

I didn't ask for help and I don't need it.

"It *is* urgent!" Kinkajou said. "We think Icicle is coming *here* next! To kill *you*!"

"That's what *I* said," offered Deathbringer, who was trailing behind them with an expression that looked closer to amused than repentant. "Ahem. AHEM."

Glory considered Kinkajou thoughtfully. "Do you really think so?"

"Absolutely," Qibli interjected. "You're the only target she has left. It's the smart choice for her. I'd wager a month of lizards on it."

"That would be irritating," Glory said. "If Deathbringer turns out to be right, I mean. It makes him really insufferable."

"I am here to search for my sister," Winter said to Queen Glory. "I just need your assurance that no one will interfere with me while I do that." He cast a dark glance over his shoulder at Deathbringer.

"I think we can do better than that," said the queen. She stopped and tilted her snout at one of the branches overhead. "Banana?"

Winter frowned. "No, thank you."

But as he spoke, he noticed a shimmering in the air around the branch, and then all at once there was a dragon sitting there in a rather hideous shade of pink that Winter had never seen before.

"Actually, it's Heliconia, Your Majesty," said the RainWing. "But good guess."

Glory flicked her tail. "Heliconia, please tell my scout captains to meet me at the pavilion as soon as possible."

The pink dragon's scales started fading into shades of blue. "But I shouldn't leave you unguarded, Majesty."

The RainWing queen waved her talons at the surrounding trees. "I think seven guards are quite sufficient. One might call it overkill, in fact. One might even infer that *somebody* doesn't think he can do his job properly on his own. Also that he must think I'm either blind and deaf or recently hit on the head, that I wouldn't notice the addition of five more dragons following me around."

"The *whole point* of a top secret invisible guard," Deathbringer said severely, "is for them to be *invisible* and *secret*. Therefore it is *extremely unhelpful* for *certain queens* to go pointing them out and discussing them loudly with the entire rainforest."

"Go now," Glory said to Heliconia, ignoring Deathbringer. The RainWing guard bowed immediately and vanished. Winter could barely hear her wingbeats flapping away over the buzzing, dripping sounds of the rainforest.

He curled his talons and stared up at the trees. There were seven other dragons up there, watching them? He couldn't see any sign of even one.

All right, he admitted to himself, grudgingly. *That's kind of an impressive skill.* IceWings were good at hiding in the snow, of course, but here in the rainforest he stuck out like a broken wing. *Which means Icicle will, too, at least.*

"The pavilion is a short flight this way," Glory explained to Winter. "I had it built halfway between the NightWings and the RainWings for anything official." She took to the air, and Winter and the others followed her. He strained his ears to listen for the sound of seven extra pairs of wings flying alongside them, but it was impossible to separate them out from the others.

Queen Glory's royal pavilion was a vast platform in the air, built on the branches of a circle of tall, overlapping trees. Winter guessed that it was about midway between the ground and the treetops — middle ground for the NightWings and RainWings. It had a roof made of the same translucent leaves he'd seen in the library windows at Jade Mountain, constructed atop twisted wooden columns instead of walls so the pavilion was open to the air but sheltered from the rain. Purple and blue morning glory flowers hung like bells from the vines that wound around each column, and delicate white-orange-pink orchids grew from the mossy crevices of the trees.

They landed one by one, shaking out their wings and sinking their talons into the clawmarked wooden floor. Winter's gaze swept over the interior of the pavilion, which was almost empty. Two scroll racks stood on either side of a simple raised dais, only a few inches higher than the rest of the platform. *Not much of a throne,* Winter reflected as Glory climbed onto it and settled herself with her tail around her claws.

"Now," she said, "I know who you all are, but let's officially meet anyway. I'm Glory, queen of the RainWings and the NightWings. My overenthusiastic bodyguard there is Deathbringer." She lifted one talon into the air and a sleek, beautiful gray sloth clambered down from the roof beams to curl up on her shoulder. "And this is Silver."

"Royal pet, not royal lunch," Qibli said to Winter, nudging his wing. "So try not to eat it, if you can restrain yourself. I'm Qibli, Your Majesty. One of Queen Thorn's advisors."

"Welcome. And then we have Moonwatcher, Kinkajou, and of course, Prince Winter," said Glory. "My friends will be very relieved that you're all safe. Jade Mountain is a bit of a mess right now, and it didn't help to have one entire winglet disappear."

"Sorry," Kinkajou squeaked.

"Sorry," Moon agreed, looking down at her talons.

There was a pause. The queen gazed sternly down her nose at the other dragons.

"All right, I'm sorry for making them worry," Qibli said. "But Winter can't go searching for Icicle and Hailstorm all by himself."

"Yes, I can," Winter said sharply. "That's the entire plan. That's what I'm going to do." It suddenly occurred to him to wonder what would happen if someone else found Icicle before he did. Would they try to hurt her? They'd end up dead if they did; she was bigger, more ferocious, and ten times better trained than any of these little dragons.

His insides gave a weird lurch as he imagined what would happen if she found Moon unguarded. Icicle would definitely kill her — the NightWing who'd foiled her plan to kill Starflight. The NightWing who was already too close to her brother, from Icicle's point of view.

If she knew how I've been feeling about Moon — she'd be even more likely to kill her, he realized.

Not that he felt that way about Moon anymore. He *couldn't.* Moon had lied to him and invaded his mind. He could put her safely back in the category of "Despicable, Conniving NightWings I Hate."

He glanced over at her as she lifted her head and met his eyes. Something in her expression said, "I will help you whether you let me or not." Much like the first time they'd met, when she'd protected his scavenger no matter how he threatened her.

It doesn't mean anything, this twisting feeling in my chest. I can hate her and still not want Icicle to kill her. It doesn't mean that I care about her.

"Well, let's see," Glory said, sitting up alertly. "Here come my watchers."

Dragons began appearing out of the leaves, materializing like the sun coming out from behind a cloud. In alarmingly bright shades of yellow, blue, and pink, they swooped into the pavilion and landed in a row in front of Queen Glory, until there were six dragons lined up. Although a "line" was hardly the right description for the slipshod way they were standing, some of them with their wings akimbo or their tails flopping all over the place.

No discipline, Winter thought disapprovingly, remembering the rigid, perfectly coiled lines of guards that attended Queen Glacier.

He also remembered practicing for hours to get that stance just right: his wings folded exactly so, his tail in the right position, his snout up and shoulders back. It was agony to hold that pose for too long, but his mother had made him stand like that before every meal, making him wait until she approved before letting him eat. *These RainWings need someone to whip them into shape,* he thought, resettling his tail with a small rattle of spikes.

"I called you in to ask if any of you have seen any sign of an IceWing today," Queen Glory said. "For those of you who don't remember the lessons, those are the white or blue dragons with spiked tails and cold scales."

One of the RainWings leaned toward her. In a loud whisper that carried to the other side of the pavilion, he hissed, "Your Majesty, I think there's one of them *right behind me*."

The dragon next to him looked around in alarm, spotted Winter, and leaped backward, nearly knocking one of her companions off the platform.

"Oh my gosh, is *that* what they look like?" she cried. "Why's it pointy all over?"

"Look at its tail!" yelped another. "It really is all spiky!"

"And can you feel how cold it is? Whoa, that's so weird," said a fourth, reaching for Winter's wing. Winter twitched back and growled at her.

Glory exhaled slowly through her nose. "This is our guest, Prince Winter of the IceWings. Have you seen any dragons today that look like him?"

"No," they all answered, almost in unison.

"Would've noticed if I did!" one of them offered. "Look at how sparkly he is, like raindrops on a cobweb or something."

"I'll say," agreed another. "Plus brrrr, I think I'd have woken up if something that cold went by me."

"Me too!" said a third.

The queen closed her eyes eloquently.

Deathbringer cleared his throat. "Permission to check with the backup NightWing guards?" he asked.

"Yes, yes," Glory said, waving him away. "But make sure you tell them if they *do* see an IceWing, they are to follow her, not attack her, especially if they're on their own."

Deathbringer bowed and spread his wings.

"That includes you!" Glory yelled after him as he flew away. "Keep your claws to yourself!"

"Can't hear you," he called back cheerfully.

Winter glanced sideways at Moon and found her staring intently at one of the RainWing watchers.

"Um," Moon said. "Your Majesty, can I ask —"

"Yes?" Glory said, waving her talons. "Speak up."

"Just — even if they didn't see an IceWing," Moon blurted in a hurry, "anything suspicious — like something frozen or colder than usual . . ." She trailed off.

She knows that RainWing saw something, Winter guessed. *She saw it in his head.* But of course, she hadn't told Queen Glory she could read minds yet.

"Well . . . there was this weird spot near the oldest giant banyan tree," the RainWing scout mused, almost to himself. "I did notice something funny there."

"What do you mean?" Glory asked him.

"There was a spot on the ground that was all shriveled up, kind of," the RainWing answered. His scales were royal blue, dotted with little swirls of dark pink. "It looked like something had killed all the plants in a circle there, and they were kind of crusty and white-ish and the berries were as hard as rocks. Oh, and kind of cold, too. Do you think that's important?"

Winter flared his wings. "Where was this?" he demanded. "How far away?"

"I know where the banyan tree is," Glory said, already rising. She untangled Silver from her neck and deposited the sloth on a nearby branch. "We can be there in a few minutes. The rest of you, stay here."

"Can't I come, too?" Moon asked. "I can be useful. I —" She stopped, struggling for words. Winter realized that she was hoping her mind reading could help.

"Me too!" Kinkajou cried. "I want to come!"

"No," Queen Glory said firmly. "I am your queen, both of you, and I'm ordering you to stay here."

Winter wished he could insist on going by himself, but he needed someone to show him the way. And if he was perfectly honest . . . someone who could sense Icicle's mind nearby *would* probably come in handy.

"Moon can come," he said with what he hoped was an offhanded shrug. "That's fine. Not her, though; she's far too loud." He jerked his chin at Kinkajou.

"I AM NOT," Kinkajou protested. "That's so unfair!"

"Kinkajou, you wanted me to be queen, and now you have to listen to me," Glory said. "Stay here, because if you get killed by an IceWing, I'm going to be extremely mad at you." She glanced from Winter to Moon, a wrinkle of puzzlement on her forehead. "But all right, Moon, come along."

Soon the three of them were soaring through the trees. Well, trying to soar — Winter kept getting his wings tangled in unexpected vines or spiderwebs or branches or, once, snagged on the nest of a large-beaked indignant red bird.

After a few minutes of flying, Queen Glory stopped abruptly and swung around.

"That is a level of noisy that makes me think you aren't even trying to be stealthy," she said. "Come on out."

Qibli emerged sheepishly from behind a tree with huge leaves. "I *was* trying to be stealthy," he protested. "But there's too many things to crash into. I'm a wide-open-desert kind of dragon."

Winter shook off a tangle of moss and branches, disgruntled to realize he agreed with the SandWing about something.

"What did I say about staying put?" Glory asked.

"You're a great queen, I hear, but with all due respect, you're not *my* queen," Qibli said, setting his jaw. "I go where they go. Besides, Winter wants me along, he just can't admit it."

"I don't," Winter said. "You can send him back to the Kingdom of Sand for all I care."

"He adores me," Qibli said.

Glory rolled her eyes. "Fine, enough arguing. Let's go."

Qibli shot Winter a delighted grin and flapped over to fly beside Moon. She was surprisingly dexterous at moving between the trees and dodging stray branches. Even Glory still ran into things occasionally, but Moon slipped easily through the forest, like a seal diving in the waves.

Soon they were descending toward an absolutely enormous fat tree with bulging branches and knobbly roots sticking out of the undergrowth. From the air, Winter spotted the circle the RainWing had mentioned. The frozen berries had melted into mushy puddles of purple, while the leaves and undergrowth were all black and damp.

But it wasn't a neat circle — there were patches of green still left within the circumference of it. Which meant something had been blocking Icicle's frostbreath in those spots.

Something . . . or someone.

Glory and Moon circled the tree while Winter and Qibli landed and studied the rainforest floor. A sharp headache was starting to work its way through Winter's brain. He didn't want this to be true. He wanted to find Icicle, but he didn't want to find out that she'd done something else terrible.

The layers of leaves and bracken were disturbed here, as if something had been dragged away. Qibli noticed it, too; his snout wrinkled with concern. Winter followed the trail, trying to guess what he would have done in this situation.

Hidden the body. To give myself more time before I was caught. But she couldn't have dragged it far. Maybe I'm just imagining the worst. Maybe she killed a rainforest boar . . . a really big one? . . . and dragged it off to eat. Maybe . . .

Winter paced over to a wall of bushes where the ground began to slope up. The banyan's roots extended this far, some of them nearly as fat around as a dragon.

Between one of the roots and the bushes was a mound of leaves, dirt, moss, and mulch that looked too big to be natural.

His heart sinking, Winter started to clear away the debris. Moon and Qibli joined him, helping silently.

The corpse of a NightWing guard lay beneath the dirt in a hastily dug hollow, his face contorted in frozen rage, his throat slashed, and his scales ravaged by frostbreath.

Icicle was definitely here.

━━ CHAPTER 6 ━━

"Moons," Glory muttered, staring over Winter's shoulder at the corpse. Clouds of dark red were gathering along her wings and spine. "This is bad, Winter. Bad for your sister, bad for the peace of the rainforest."

"The NightWings are going to set their heads on fire," Qibli agreed. "No, wait. They're going to set the closest IceWing's head on fire. Winter, I hope your skull is as thick as it looks."

Winter didn't want to ask; he really believed that reading another dragon's mind was wrong. But if it meant stopping Icicle before she did something like this again . . . and finding her before a vengeful troop of NightWings did . . .

He gazed at Moon until she looked up and met his eyes. He tilted his chin questioningly, and she shook her head. She couldn't hear Icicle's mind nearby.

"If Icicle sees you four, she'll know you're here to stop her," Glory said. She gave Moon a worried glance. "Let's get you somewhere safe."

"And you," Moon pointed out.

The queen snorted as though she was pretty sure she could handle anything, and led the way back to the royal pavilion.

"What happened?" Kinkajou yelped as soon as she saw them. She leaped up, her scales shifting into spirals of orange and lavender. "Did you find her? Uh-oh, Winter looks mad. Well, actually, that's how he always looks. Is he mad? What happened?"

Deathbringer was there, too, stamping around making the platform shake and accidentally ripping flowers off the vines.

"By yourself?" he roared at Glory. "With three little dragonets to protect you?"

"*Excuse* me," Winter objected. "Dragons my age are seasoned warriors where *I* come from. We guard the queen all the time in the Ice Kingdom."

"Don't get your tail in a knot," Glory said to Deathbringer. Her sloth was already clambering up her tail onto her back again. "My top secret invisible guard was following us, too, and you know it."

"But *I* wasn't," he protested.

She gave him an exasperated look. "You can't always be," she said in a low, surprisingly affectionate voice that suddenly made Winter rethink everything he had assumed about the queen and her bodyguard. "So calm down and trust me to take care of myself."

"Says the dragon who got herself chained up in a lava prison," Deathbringer muttered.

"The important thing is that we know the IceWing is here," Glory said.

"She *is*?" Kinkajou squeaked. "Actually here? In the rainforest? Right this minute?"

Right this minute, Winter thought. *She's close by.* His perfect, overachieving sister was somewhere in this damp mudhole, hiding from RainWings and planning a murder.

How far would she be willing to go? If Winter tried to stop her, would she kill one brother in order to save the other?

Don't leave out the key adjectives in there. Kill one low-ranked, disappointing brother in order to save the long-lost hero with a bright future. That makes the equation a bit easier.

Glory's tail lashed back and forth as she began issuing orders. "We need to organize teams to search, starting here and spreading outward. I also need you to come look at something for me." She brushed Deathbringer's tail lightly with her own.

To identify the body, Winter guessed. *Before she tells the other NightWings what we found . . . so she can tell them who's dead.*

"As for you all," Glory said, turning to Winter and Moon and Qibli, "I think the safest place is the dragonet wingery.

It's not far, it's already well-fortified, and I'll double the guard to protect you."

"What?" Winter cried, flaring his wings. "You can't lock us up with a bunch of new-hatched dragonets! I need to look for my sister!"

Glory shook her head. "I'm sorry, Winter. But if anything happens to you, the IceWings will declare war on us, and I wouldn't blame them. Keeping you safe is the most important thing." She hesitated. "I promise to let you speak with her when we find her."

"Unless an overzealous NightWing kills her first!" Winter shouted. He lashed his tail furiously. "You can't promise me you'll keep her alive! I know how NightWings are — they'll kill her the moment they see her!"

"I am their queen," Glory said with steely ferocity, "and I will not let them do that."

"She's *my sister*!" Winter roared.

"Exactly!" Glory snapped back. "So you're in danger from her *and* from the entire tribe of NightWings, once they find out what she did! I'm *not* having any more dead dragons in my rainforest today."

Warm claws stepped down hard on Winter's back foot. He whirled around, snarling.

"Stop arguing with her," Qibli whispered through his teeth.

"She's not going to give in," Kinkajou agreed. Behind her,

Moon nodded, adding the weight of a mind reader to that opinion.

Glory was already turning back to Deathbringer and a pair of scout captains. Winter shoved Qibli away. He was not done fighting about this. There was no way he was going to sit quietly with a bunch of baby dragons while an enemy tribe chased down his sister.

"Listen," Qibli hissed, shoving him back. "If you keep arguing, she'll add even more guards. Just agree, and then we'll sneak off. It's the only way."

Kinkajou's eyes went wide and her scales turned an odd shade of yellowish-green. But Moon was nodding again.

"We'll figure it out," she agreed in a whisper. "We'll make sure you're the first one to find your sister."

Winter ground his teeth together. He'd spent a lifetime being told what to do, but that was by other IceWings. No RainWing could order him around, and he didn't have to listen to whispered advice from a SandWing either.

Mother and Father would want him to fight right now, he was sure of it. They'd wreck this pavilion and fight the entire tribe — *both* tribes — if anyone tried to stop them from hunting for Icicle.

But if he fought everyone now, Glory would see him as a threat, just like Icicle.

Whereas if he waited . . . and snuck off to search for her, as Qibli suggested . . .

It was horrible. Winter could almost *see* his ranking plummeting. Everything he'd ever worked for, vanishing as he bowed his head to obey a rainbow-bright dragonet, queen of the NightWings.

It'll be worth it if I come back with Hailstorm, he told himself fiercely. *Even if I'm the bottom-ranked IceWing for the rest of my life, saving Hailstorm would make all of this worthwhile.*

And so he agreed.

He nearly changed his mind when he saw the rainforest wingery, though.

It was even worse than he'd feared — exactly the sort of soft, cuddly, lazy, stupid setup he should have expected from a bunch of RainWings. They didn't care if their dragonets grew up to be feeble and nonthreatening, so of course they left them to roll around like mammal cubs instead of launching their training the moment they hatched.

The main play area was an enormous trampoline made of springy vines and leaves, strung between several trees high above the ground. It was surrounded on all sides by tall, soft woven mats of branches that kept the baby dragons from falling over the edge. Six full-grown dragons guarded the perimeter — three NightWings and three RainWings, all of whom looked more alert and tense than anyone else Winter had seen so far.

One of the NightWings inspected each of them carefully before allowing them inside. She poked their small skyfire bags, sniffed the rocks, studied Winter's snout with a worried expression, and spent a full minute examining Qibli's deadly tail barb.

"It's very safe," Qibli promised her. "SandWing dragonets learn early how to avoid accidentally stabbing anyone." He coiled his tail protectively inward and the guard jumped back.

"I don't like it," she said to Heliconia, the RainWing who'd escorted them to the wingery. "We're supposed to keep complete strangers *away* from the dragonets. And this one looks . . . the mildest word I can think of is *hostile*." She frowned at Winter.

"That's just his face," said Qibli. "And his personality."

"He would never harm a dragonet," Moon promised.

"I can speak for myself," Winter snapped.

Grumbling under her breath, the NightWing finally let them pass. They flew up and over the woven wall, landing lightly on the platforms around the trampoline inside. Winter scanned the space and saw that it was full of peculiar toys that didn't appear to teach anything or impart any valuable skills *whatsoever*.

Inside the wingery were nine dragonets less than a year old. At first glance, Winter thought they were all NightWings, because they all had black scales and were wrestling in a pile together. But when the newcomers landed on the platforms around them, nine tiny heads popped up, and seven of them became suddenly vibrantly pink-and-yellow.

"Pretty new dragons!" one of them cheered, and eight dragonets came rampaging over, staggering on the bouncy surface and flapping their unwieldy wings.

Winter backed up all the way until his wings hit the wall, but that didn't stop three tiny RainWings from closing in on him.

"Glittery!" yelped one.

"I can do that!" said another. "Look look look." He crouched, concentrating, and a wave of icy blue surged across his scales. A moment later he looked like a miniature version of Winter, without the extra ice dragon spikes and horns. He held out his claws and cooed admiringly at himself.

"Nice work," Kinkajou said. She squinted at Winter as though he were an ice sculpture that needed improving. "You could add a little more dark blue shading around the spine and edges of the wings."

"Sure!" The dragonet clicked his teeth together thoughtfully, and a moment later a subtle shift went through some of his scales, making the jagged ridge along his back look sharper and taller, a little more like an IceWing's.

"Try this one," called a dragonet who was circling around Qibli. The SandWing wrinkled his nose at her and she wrinkled hers right back. Her scales were already shifting to the same pale yellow as his. She spread her wings and studied the underside of them, then reached out and poked Qibli until he opened his wings for her to examine.

"Hrm," she said. A shimmer of gold and bronze appeared on her chest, and then slowly melted into a color that almost exactly matched Qibli's underscales. "Woo!" she cried. "Let's see if I can do his snout!"

Winter watched tiny brown freckles and a small dark zigzag that matched Qibli's scar appear on her scales. He tried to squash his amazement. Dragonets less than a year old could do that? Winter glanced around the wingery. Maybe they weren't completely wasting their time in here after all.

Of course, camouflage scales weren't as impressive or useful as hunting and fighting and survival skills. Hailstorm had battled a killer whale before he was one year old. Winter had been sent out to spend an entire night in a blizzard alone. Icicle was already combat training with dragons three times her size by her first birthday. These dragonets wouldn't last a minute in IceWing training; they wouldn't make a dent in the rankings at all.

His gaze fell on the one dragonet who was hanging back — a small, nervous-looking NightWing with a leaf bandage wrapped around one foreleg. The dragonet met his eyes, squeaked nervously, and tucked his head under his wings.

"Don't mind him," said the dragonet who'd turned himself the color of Winter.

"He's so useless," said the other NightWing dragonet. She was sleek and glossy, like a seal, and was studying the newcomers with more reserve than the wild curiosity of the RainWings. "He's *still* having nightmares about the volcano every night, even though that was *months* ago. Toughen up, lizard!" she barked at him.

The bandaged NightWing slowly drew his head out and folded his wings back, shivering from horns to tail. Winter could see him fighting back his terror as he squared his shoulders and faced the new dragons.

"Some NightWing he is," the female dragonet snorted. "We keep telling him what an important, dangerous tribe we are, but frankly, I'm not sure he'll ever measure up. I guess some dragons are just —"

"Hatched in the wrong tribe," Moon finished softly.

Winter tilted his head at her. Did she wish she weren't a NightWing? Or had she heard other dragons wishing they could be something different?

Not me. He couldn't imagine not being an IceWing. His whole life was about trying to be a true IceWing warrior. All he'd ever wanted was to rise to the top of the rankings and prove himself to his parents and the rest of the tribe. That was all he *should* want.

Until I met her. And now I want . . . what? To understand a NightWing? To have her care about me?

No wonder he hated himself.

"All right, scoot," Qibli said suddenly, flapping his wings at the dragonets. "Leave us alone and go play. Quietly. Over there." He herded the dragonets to the other side of the enclosure and came back, ducking his head toward Moon. "Are you all right?" he whispered.

Winter realized Moon was rubbing her temples. He'd forgotten that she must be hearing the thoughts of all the dragons around them. While the baby dragons were bombarding the newcomers with words, they must also be blasting the inside of Moon's head with their thoughts.

"I'm fine, I just need to adjust," Moon said, dropping her claws and shaking out her wings. "We can't sneak away yet — the guards are too focused on us." She glanced at Winter. "I'll keep listening." Her talons went back to her head and she closed her eyes.

"Guess what?" Kinkajou said, lightly bouncing the vines below her. Her claws had all turned dark green to match the wingery so it almost looked as though she had no feet at all if you didn't look closely. "I think I figured it out! I was thinking about Moon's prophecy while you were off chasing Icicle. The 'stalker of dreams' — that must be Scarlet! Using the dreamvisitor to bother people, right?"

"Maybe," Qibli said. "Although there's something a little ominous about 'darkness' and 'stalker' so close to each other in the prophecy. What if there's a connection to that Darkstalker you mentioned, Winter?"

"Pfft," Winter scoffed. "He's been dead for centuries. If the prophecy is about him, it's a little out of date."

Was it his imagination, or did Moon just press her eyes closed even harder?

"Everybody shush," Kinkajou ordered. "I'm *telling* you something. So I thought, if Scarlet is the stalker of dreams, *maybe* the 'talons of power and fire' is that freaky SkyWing everyone's afraid of. What's her name again?"

"Peril," Winter growled. Of course it could be Peril. The dragon who could burn other dragons to death just by touching them. She'd stared at him with her creepy fiery blue eyes, standing there in the entrance hall of Jade Mountain as though she could go wherever she pleased. After everything she'd done and everyone she'd killed. Free and unpunished . . . it wasn't right. "I could believe it. She's murder waiting to happen."

Qibli shook his head. "But she saved Clay's life. I was there; I saw it. I don't think she's working with Scarlet anymore."

"Then you're an even bigger fool than you look," Winter snapped.

"Hey, hey, quit being mean," Kinkajou said. "Maybe that's what 'one who is not what she seems' is about. Peril *seems* like she's changed, but actually she is totally going to betray the dragonets and scorch the earth and kill everyone and all the other bad things at once." She paused. "Suddenly I am not enjoying this conversation as much as I thought I would."

"Did you see anything in Peril's mind?" Qibli asked Moon, nudging her gently. "Was she planning anything terrible?"

"Peril's mind is almost impossible to read," Moon said, opening her eyes. "It's all fire in there, like she's burning from the inside, too. I think — I think she's not a happy dragon, but I'm not sure she's evil. I don't really know, though. I mean, no one is completely evil."

"What are you talking about?" Winter demanded. "Plenty of dragons are completely evil."

"Not when you see what's going on inside them." Moon shook her head fiercely. "Dragons are complicated. Some are kinder than others." She looked up at Qibli, then quickly away. "Or braver than others." Here she glanced mysteriously at Winter, and he shivered. "And some of them do really cruel things. But everyone has both good thoughts and bad thoughts and reasons for what they do, reasons they believe are important."

"*I* don't have bad thoughts, do I?" Kinkajou asked Moon.

Moon laughed. "True, not that I ever heard," she admitted.

"I'd better have them all now, quick while I can," Kinkajou said, touching her skyfire pouch with a grin.

Winter puzzled over Moon's words for a moment. He would have assumed that hearing other dragons' thoughts would confirm that most of them were evil or at least halfway there. How could Moon be immersed in other minds all day and still believe in the goodness of dragons?

She hasn't met very many other dragons, he told himself. *Growing up in the rainforest, hidden away.*

But she'd met the whole NightWing tribe (which *surely* was full of evil), and Peril, and Sora, the dragon who'd tried to kill Winter's sister. And Moon had met Icicle.

"Don't you think Icicle is evil?" he blurted. "I mean — I don't, but —"

"No," Moon said. "That's what I mean. She's doing what she thinks she has to do to save her brother. I wouldn't make the choices she's made, and she needs to be stopped, but I think I understand them. It is very cold and intense inside her head . . . I guess, I think it would be hard, growing up like she did, always knowing your parents are expecting — um, expecting big, um, things of you." She trailed off, giving Winter a sideways glance.

She knows what my parents want from Icicle, Winter realized with a jolt. *She knows Icicle is supposed to grow up to challenge Queen Glacier. But she's keeping that secret . . . perhaps just to show me that she* can *keep secrets.*

Don't trust her, he reminded himself. *NightWings are manipulative. She's probably just saying what I want to hear.*

Moon shifted her wings, turning to look at the playing dragonets, and a fan of sunshine brushed across her scales. *They're not just black,* Winter thought. *They're more of a dark purple, with shades of dark blue and green mixed in.*

"Back to the prophecy," he said irritably, trying to focus. "So perhaps Scarlet and Peril are conspiring. Maybe they're planning to take down Jade Mountain together. What does the old NightWing home have to do with that?"

"We should go there and see," Kinkajou said. "It's not far from here."

"Maybe there's something there we can use to stop them," Qibli suggested.

"The third dreamvisitor," Moon said suddenly. She sat up and flicked her tail over her talons. "Starflight said it was lost when the volcano exploded. Maybe we can find it."

"Then we wouldn't need to hunt for Icicle," Qibli said, turning to Winter. "You could contact Scarlet yourself and ask about Hailstorm."

"I can't," Winter said. "I've never seen Queen Scarlet. Icicle was part of the delegation that went to negotiate for Hailstorm's release — unsuccessfully, obviously. So they met, and that's why Scarlet can get into her dreams. But I couldn't do it, even if I had a dreamvisitor."

There was a pause. Qibli tapped his claws together softly, thoughtfully.

"I might be able to," he said. "I saw her once. From far away, but . . . I think I could dreamvisit her."

"So let's go," Kinkajou whispered. "Moon, how about now?"

Moon tipped her head sideways, then nodded. "I think they're calming down," she said. "But the little ones are still very interested in us. They'll put up a huge fuss if we try to leave."

"Oh, I have a plan for that," Kinkajou said confidently. "Watch, it'll be hilarious." She fluffed out her wings, turned herself an iridescent blue like a dragonfly, and sauntered over to where the baby dragons were arguing in loud whispers about why Winter and Qibli had such weird tails.

"Hello," Kinkajou said to them. "Want to play a game?"

"YES!" they all shrieked in chorus.

"It's basically hide-and-seek," Kinkajou said. "You know, where you try to find the camouflaged dragons. The four of us have a bet that we can each hide better than the others, even though I'm clearly going to win, because I'm the only RainWing." She lifted her talons and dramatically changed them red.

"OOOOOOOOO," went all the dragonets.

"So you all close your eyes, and we'll hide, and whoever finds one of us first, wins!" said Kinkajou. "All right? Make sure you count to a thousand so we have enough time."

"OK!" squealed one of the RainWings, covering her eyes. "One! Two! Three! Six! Seventeen!"

The others all covered their eyes as well and began shouting random numbers along with her.

"Whoops," Kinkajou said, galloping back to Moon. "I forgot about how most RainWings can't count. We'd better move fast."

"Which way?" Qibli asked Moon. "Where are the guards?"

Moon closed her eyes and pointed at six spots around the circumference of the trampoline walls. "And two of them are also watching the sky, to make sure we don't fly out," she added, opening her eyes again.

"So we go down," Winter said. "Over here." He crossed to a corner with more shadows than the others, where a few curiously shaped branches and large seed pods were piled, as if for playing with. He moved them aside and touched the place where the wall met the woven vines. "If we make a hole here, they might not notice for a few minutes — long enough for us to get away."

"I can burn a hole," Qibli offered, small flames spurting from his nose.

"Put those away," Kinkajou said, batting at his snout. "No fire in my forest, thank you!"

"This will be safer," Winter said. He crouched, clenched his jaw, and summoned the cold from deep inside him. It hissed into his throat like a building snowstorm. Finally he opened his mouth and shot a shimmering blast of frostbreath at the web of leaves and branches.

He froze a spot just large enough for a dragon to crawl through, a small icy circle of silver vegetation.

"SIX HUNDRED!" one of the dragonets bellowed suddenly, leaping ahead a few hundred. The others gleefully joined in. "Six hundred and NINE! Six hundred and FORTY-TWO!"

"Quick," Moon whispered.

Winter leaned forward and rapped sharply on the ice with his front claws. The circle cracked and then shattered into tiny frozen splinters, leaving a jagged hole at the base of the wall.

"What was that?" one of the NightWing dragonets asked, but he was drowned out by the others shouting, "Six hundred and NINETY-EIGHT! EIGHT HUNDREDY FIVE!"

"Go, go, go," Kinkajou whispered frantically.

Winter dove through the hole first, catching his wings on a few remaining shards of ice. Moon was right behind him as he shot toward the ground and plunged into a thicket of enormous leaves. A moment later, Qibli and Kinkajou landed beside them with soft thuds. Kinkajou's scales immediately shifted and she vanished like a snowball thrown back into the snow.

Moon was still as an iceberg beside Winter, her wings folded to hide the silver scales that sparkled underneath, her eyes closed and brow furrowed.

He leaned closer to whisper into her ear. "Did anyone see us?"

She shook her head. "But I can't imagine those dragonets are going to believe we're somehow hiding in there for very long."

"You'd be surprised," Kinkajou said. "Hide-and-seek is our favorite game in kind of an obsessive way. They'll search every square inch of the wingery before giving up. I pulled a few things over to hide the hole, so with luck we'll have a few minutes, at least."

"This way," Moon said, slipping off into the trees. Winter tried to stay low and in the shadows as he hurried after her. He spotted the flicker of black wings overhead as one of the guards circled around the wingery, but no one raised an alarm yet.

"How am I going to find Icicle?" he whispered to her. "Before anyone else does?"

She hesitated, giving him a worried sideways look. "I don't know how much you want to hear about what I can do," she whispered back. "I've never had anyone to talk to about it before, except — well, no one really. But I don't want to freak you out."

"It is disturbing," he admitted, "but tell me anyway, if it's about Icicle."

"I can't sense her anywhere." Moon shook her head. "I've been listening as hard as I can since we got to the rainforest, but there's no sign of her."

"Maybe she left already," Winter said. "Maybe she figured out where Scarlet is and went to confront her." He checked behind him and saw only Qibli battling the vines and mud. If Kinkajou was there, it was impossible to tell. What he wouldn't give for camouflage scales. Then he could slip through the trees without Glory or any guards spotting him; he could find Icicle and get her away from here before anything terrible happened.

Anything else terrible, that is.

Are you really wishing you were a RainWing right now? he scolded himself. *Wouldn't Mother and Father love to hear about that.*

Now was the time to ditch these dragons. Before his thoughts got any more entangled. He could fall behind Qibli, wait until no one was paying attention, and then take off. Now that he had the skyfire, Moon wouldn't be able to find him by his thoughts. He'd hunt down Icicle and they'd go get Hailstorm together. Or if he couldn't find her, he'd go back to the Ice Kingdom on his own, like he'd originally planned.

He paused for half a step, letting Moon slip ahead of him. Another minute, and then . . .

Moon suddenly froze, digging her talons into the ground. Instinctively Winter and Qibli froze, too.

"Search party coming this way," she whispered. "We have to hide!" She turned and pushed Winter toward a nearby fallen tree covered with moss and winding yellow flower vines. "Under there — can you fit?"

"I'd rather fight them," Winter objected.

"They'll think you're Icicle and lock you up," Kinkajou's voice said from the air.

"Unless they kill you first," Qibli said. "Which I realize I should be more enthusiastic about, but for some reason I'm not. Come *on*." He tugged on one of Winter's wings, then dove under the tree himself, rolling into a ball in the shadows.

Winter reluctantly followed, crouching until his underbelly was sliding across the wet leaves. Dangling curls of damp moss caught on his horns and something scuttled down his spine as he wedged himself in next to Qibli's warm scales.

"Oh, why are you so glittery?" Kinkajou fretted from outside the hiding hole. "Nothing natural is that color."

"It's all right," Moon whispered back. "Just try to cover us and stay as still as you can."

"I'll have you know I was a hide-and-seek *champion*," Kinkajou started. "No one —"

"Shhh," Moon said, and a moment later, Winter was startled to feel her sliding in beside him. The silver scales by her eyes caught the light for a moment as she turned her head, listening. He could feel the whole length of her body breathing softly, anxiously.

"That's better," Kinkajou whispered. "I can't see him anymore."

Winter covered the skyfire pouch with one of his talons and tried to breathe. Maybe this was what Moon had meant when she said reading his mind was confusing. He couldn't even tell what he was feeling. Furious, trapped, frustrated — grateful, safe, alone, protected — on fire — wanting the wrong things, hating himself — confused, confused, confused.

His mind flashed back to the first time he'd done a rankings test out in a storm with Hailstorm and Icicle. They'd lost him as soon as they could, each striking out on their own. It made sense, even to a one-year-old dragonet struggling through a blizzard. Nobody wanted to risk letting someone else drag down their ranking number.

So what were these dragons doing? Why were they risking the wrath of their queens by helping him?

Moon's scales rippled as she shifted quietly. Was that her heartbeat he could feel, thundering in the places where their wings were pressed together, or was that his own?

He closed his eyes and tried to stop thinking.

A few eternities passed, and then finally Moon whispered, "They're gone."

"Then get out of the way and let me out," Winter said in a strangled voice that came out more harshly than he'd meant it to.

She rolled instantly away, and he wriggled after her until he stood blinking in the green rainforest light again. Qibli emerged, stretching out his wings and shaking his tail.

"Careful with that thing," Winter snapped, glaring at the poisonous barb as it swung back and forth.

"If you ever get stabbed by my tail, I promise it won't be by accident," Qibli said haughtily. "Moon, wait up!" She was already moving away, toward the sound of a waterfall in the distance, and the SandWing hurried after her.

I could leave now, Winter thought, feeling as though his talons were paralyzed with indecision. *I should leave now.* That would be the smart IceWing thing to do.

"The words you're looking for are 'thank you,'" Kinkajou said, materializing suddenly beside him. Winter jumped. "*Thank you*, Moon, for warning me and hiding me and helping me even though I am an enormous super jerk sometimes."

She flounced off into the trees, her orange scales fading back into the green of the leaves.

Winter hesitated . . . and then followed her.

They're still useful to me, he thought. *I have a better chance of finding Icicle if I stay with them. But just for now.*

Soon, he promised himself. *I'll leave soon.*

— CHAPTER 7 —

When Winter caught up to the others, they were gathered at the base of a huge tree beside a waterfall, staring up at a hole in the trunk. There was something immediately and indefinably uncomfortable about this place. It was like a spot of thin ice on a frozen lake, where the cool safety of the upper world came too close to the dark depths below.

"That's the tunnel to the NightWing island," Kinkajou said softly. Her voice was never that quiet or wobbly. Winter squinted at her. Was she afraid of the place for some reason?

"You can wait here if you want," Moon said, brushing Kinkajou's tail with her own. "If it's too — too anything."

"I'm all right," Kinkajou said. She flared the ruff behind her ears and deliberately turned her scales dark blue. "I just haven't been back since the whole . . . thing."

"Whoa," Qibli said, making the connection before Winter did. "I didn't realize you were — you're one of the RainWings they —"

"Imprisoned and experimented on," Moon finished for him.

"It wasn't *quite* as horrible as it sounds," Kinkajou said. "Only *mostly* that horrible."

Winter had to take a deep breath and poke the feeling he was having to be sure he was having it. Respect for Kinkajou? Surprise that a dragon as silly as her could have survived what the NightWings did to the RainWings? He'd heard only rumors, really — stories that had spread after the war ended. Tales of NightWings abducting harmless RainWings, dragging them back to the volcanic island, chaining them up, and forcing them to use their venom so the NightWings could study it.

It sounded unforgivable to him. But Kinkajou did not act like a dragon with a grudge; she didn't seem to hate the NightWings at all. Even though she clearly should. Yet she treated Moon like a best friend . . .

Because Moon is different, whispered his treacherous mind. *Because she would never do what the other NightWings did.*

"But you don't hate them," Qibli said, echoing Winter's thoughts. "That's fascinating."

"Well — they're not my *favorite* dragons," Kinkajou admitted, squirming. "Except Moon, of course, and Deathbringer is usually pretty great. But, you know, they're trying to change. They have to. And with Glory as their queen, they won't do any more awful things."

"We'll see," Winter muttered.

Moon flew up to the hole and stepped inside, then twisted to look back at them. "Winter, come look at this."

Just inside the mouth of the tunnel was a squashed wet leaf shaped a bit like a scavenger's paw. When Winter crouched to sniff it, it felt colder than the tunnel around them.

"Did she go this way?" he asked Moon.

"I don't know," she said. "I still can't hear her, but maybe that's why, if she's at the volcano."

Winter started down the tunnel, walking straight into that unsettling wrong-feeling air. He heard the shuffling wings of the others falling in behind him.

Heat crackled along his scales as he glimpsed the end of the tunnel, and he paused. This was worse than the damp rainforest heat — this was the kind of heat where he wouldn't be able to use his frostbreath. And there was something blurring his sight . . . bits of ash, maybe, drifting through the air.

He took a deep breath and stepped out into a cave, his talons sinking instantly into a layer of ash that covered the floor. It was dark and nearly impossible to see, but a faint gray light scraped the walls on either side of him. Winter took a step forward as Moon emerged behind him and breathed out a small plume of fire.

Sharp claws seized Winter's heart. The shape of a huge dragon loomed overhead, its wings outstretched, its talons reaching toward him.

"He's dead," Moon said quickly. "Whoever he is. He's gone — this is just the shape of him left behind." She edged forward and tapped one of the grasping talons. The dragon didn't move. "I wonder who it was."

Winter's breath slowly returned. He carefully made his way around the petrified dragon, trying not to touch the statue of hardened ash. There was a tunnel he could just squeeze into, although it was clogged with ash and the floor was a field of cooled lava that was still too hot for Winter's liking. It was a relief when he reached open air and was able to spread his wings and fly.

This, then, at last, was the secret home of the NightWings.

He circled, studying everything below him, and felt his triumph dimming.

The island was smaller than Winter could have imagined. It made him feel instantly claustrophobic, even with (or perhaps because of) the vast ocean lurking in all directions. Dense black ripples of lava flows covered everything he could see, still glowing orange and yellow in places where liquid fire was spilling through the cracks. A mountain cut jaggedly into the sky — the volcano itself — but it looked as if the top had been smashed in, leaving a smoking hole.

Had the air been this impossible to breathe before the volcano erupted? Thick gray clouds, heavy with ash and smoke and sizzling with lightning, stretched across the sky. Everything smelled of sulfur and fire and death.

Winter couldn't imagine anyone actually living here. What did the NightWings eat, in a place so empty of life?

How could they sleep, with the promise of fiery death smoking and muttering over their heads all the time? Who would raise their dragonets in such a hideous place?

It felt like a whale smacking him in the face, how suddenly and completely he understood Moon's mother and her decision to hide Moon in the rainforest. The stranger question was why other NightWings hadn't done the same.

Afraid to disobey their queen, probably, he guessed. IceWings followed Queen Glacier's orders with unquestioning obedience as they were handed down through the levels of the aristocracy. It was like obeying your parents; no one would ever think to do otherwise.

But IceWings had the entire Ice Kingdom, the safest and most purely beautiful place to live in all of Pyrrhia. It was the polar opposite of this nightmare. Queen Glacier took care of them. The NightWing queen could not have cared about her subjects at all, if she kept them rotting in a place like this.

"Oh!" Kinkajou gasped, soaring up beside him with Moon and Qibli. "Look, their fortress — it's totally destroyed!" She pointed to the smoking volcano.

Winter hadn't even noticed the outline of walls poking through the lava. But now that he looked, he could see the clear shape of the wrecked structure. One of the towers looked eerily like his own flight training tower in Glacier's palace.

"I had no idea," Moon said. "I mean, I've seen the island in their heads, but I never felt this — Mother never said — it's so horrible."

"Holy smoking vipers," Qibli said. The SandWing swooped down toward a river of molten lava and then back up to Winter. "If I ever had nightmares, they'd be about this place from now on."

"I think this might take care of my nightmares," Kinkajou said. "Imagine having your home devastated like this. Poor NightWings."

"Poor NightWings!" Winter exploded. He would not — *would not* — feel sorry for NightWings. "Are you serious? What is wrong with you? Don't you remember what they were doing to your tribe — to *you*? How they planned to steal the rainforest and probably kill you all?"

Kinkajou flinched away from him, covering her eyes. "I know," she said in a small voice, "but isn't it still sad?"

"They deserve this," Winter spat. "After everything they've done, the NightWings *deserve* to lose their home like this."

"How can you say that?" Moon asked. "How could any tribe deserve this?"

"Seriously," Qibli said. "What did they do to the IceWings to make you hate them so much?"

Winter twisted away from them, flying toward the volcano. His training had never covered this. He'd grown up knowing the old stories about NightWings, and he'd always assumed everybody else did, too. They were a part of his bones and the bones of every IceWing. *We hate NightWings. They stole from us. They are all liars and back-stabbers and monsters.*

Was it a secret, the story of what they'd done to the IceWings so long ago? Or did other tribes not know about it because they didn't particularly care? Or because the NightWings had covered it up over the years, layering their own lies on top of the truth? That was certainly something they were particularly good at.

A blast of sulfurous smoke came from one of the vents below and he dodged around it, coughing.

He'd always imagined the NightWings lounging around their secret home in perfect security, feasting and laughing and reveling in their superiority. He'd imagined them living among marvels, perhaps deep underground somewhere, smugly enjoying what they'd stolen from the IceWings.

Not this — not anything like this hellscape.

He banked to the left, searching the ground for any sign of Icicle.

"Winter?"

He turned and found Moon following him. "Please tell me," she said. "I really don't know what the NightWings did and I think — I think I need to." She flicked her tail anxiously. "Does it have something to do with Darkstalker?"

"It does," Winter said, watching Qibli and Kinkajou flying over to join them. Well, if it was a secret, someone should have told him to keep it that way. The truth was, it was better for everyone to know so they'd understand never to trust the NightWings. "But it begins with his thrice-cursed mother, Foeslayer. She approached the IceWings under the guise of peace, to offer us an alliance against the SkyWings, and instead she abducted our prince."

"What for?" Qibli asked. "You know, all the IceWing princes I've met have been kind of grouchy. Why would someone want one around enough to steal him?"

Winter glared at him. "Because Prince Arctic was our last animus."

They all gazed back blankly, as though they'd completely missed the thunderbolt he'd just thrown at their feet.

"*Our last animus,*" he growled. "Don't you know anything? Not every tribe has animus dragons. IceWings haven't had any in centuries . . . and you know why? Because the NightWings stole that power from us."

"That's crazy," Qibli protested. "You can't steal a power like that."

"You can if it's genetic," Winter said. "The NightWings never had an animus dragon until they took Prince Arctic. Now they have them, and we don't." He took off, flying in a wide circle around the volcano as he eyed the lava-strewn slopes. He kept hoping to see a flash of white scales, but the only colors on this island were black and red and gold and gray.

"Wait," Moon said, catching up to him. "What are you saying? That Foeslayer . . . and Prince Arctic . . . they had eggs together? A NightWing and an IceWing?"

"Sounds twisted, doesn't it?" Winter hissed, ignoring the stab of guilt he felt at the thought. "Especially when you realize that Arctic would never have agreed to it — would never have betrayed the royal family that way — unless Foeslayer threatened him with something terrible. But whatever she did, it worked."

Moon's wings missed a beat and she nearly fell out of the sky. "Winter," she cried, "are you saying Darkstalker's father was an *IceWing*?"

"Not just any IceWing," Winter snarled. "Prince Arctic, the very last animus ever hatched in the IceWing tribe. Father of the Darkstalker, the first NightWing animus. They planned it that way."

"That's . . . complicated and devious," Qibli said.

"Congratulations, you've just summed up NightWings," Winter said to him.

"But couldn't Arctic go home after that?" Kinkajou asked. "I mean, once they had his eggs, couldn't the NightWings let him go? Why didn't he go back to the IceWings and have more eggs there?"

Winter saw Moon falter again and realized that somehow she knew the answer.

"Because Darkstalker killed him," Winter said. "His own son murdered him to make sure the IceWings never got their stolen power back."

"That's not —" Moon cried, and then checked herself. "I mean — that's not the reason I heard."

"Well, it's the truth," Winter said. The volcano rumbled threateningly and spat a small shower of sparks into the air. They were flying over the far side of the island now, and there was still no sign of Icicle.

"But," Qibli said cautiously, "is it that big a deal? I mean, I hear animus dragons are more trouble than they're worth. Don't they go crazy after a while?"

"That's true," Moon said. "I read about a SeaWing animus who murdered almost his entire family."

"But we knew how to handle them," Winter scoffed. "We *perfected* the use of animus power. IceWings were the first tribe to figure out that too much use can damage the dragon's soul. So we were very careful with our animus dragons. We bred them into the royal line, watched each potential animus from hatching, and trained them carefully so they would understand their limits.

"Each IceWing animus spent years planning his or her one great enchantment. They could use their power just once, to create something that would benefit the whole tribe. Prince Arctic was only days away from his gifting ceremony when the NightWings kidnapped him."

"Wait," Qibli said. "What happened if an animus didn't do what he was told? What if he wanted to use his power for something else? Or what if he didn't want to marry whatever princess was chosen for him?"

"I don't understand the question," Winter said. "It is obviously an honor to marry into the royal IceWing lineage."

"But if you take away all of a dragon's choices . . ." Qibli trailed off.

"Stop being obtuse," Winter shouted. "You are missing the point entirely. Prince Arctic was *our* animus heritage, and everything would be different if the NightWings hadn't stolen and killed him."

"I'm just wondering if there's another side to the story," Qibli suggested, shrugging his wings.

"No," Winter said. "There isn't."

"What *I'm* wondering is why you're *still* so mad about it," Kinkajou interjected. "It sounds like it happened hundreds and hundreds of years ago. Isn't it time to move on? Who cares about all that ancient history?"

"It's not ancient history to us," Winter growled. "We still live with the consequences every day."

"But you can't blame the NightWings who are alive now — it wasn't *their* idea," she argued. "And it's not like you can get your vengeance on Foeslayer or Darkstalker."

Moon dropped suddenly down toward the fortress. Startled and irritated, Winter had to wheel around in midair to follow her. When they caught up, she was sitting in the mouth of a half-caved-in tunnel, peering into the darkness.

"I don't think this is right," she said as they all landed next to her. "This isn't the lost city of night in the prophecy."

"It isn't?" Kinkajou said. "Why not?"

"There was a city before this one," Moon said. "The NightWings used to live somewhere on the continent, back in Darkstalker's time. But they fled their city after he was — once he was gone — and they came here. To hide from him, in case he ever came back." She cast an odd, worried look at Winter. "I think *that's* the city we need to find. The ancient one, the one that's really lost."

"Oh," Kinkajou said. "You couldn't have maybe mentioned that a bit sooner?"

"Sorry," Moon said. "I was hoping this would work."

"So we don't have to go look for a dreamvisitor in there?" Qibli said, nodding toward the tunnel. "Because I am all in favor of *not* going into the creepy smoking lava-filled tunnel."

"Me too," Moon agreed, "except that I thought I heard . . . maybe . . ."

"Icicle?" Winter demanded. "You think she's in there?"

"I'm not sure," Moon said, but at almost the same time, they all heard a strange *scrrrrrrape* sound from deep inside the volcano.

"Oh dear," Kinkajou whispered. "Now I'm really wishing we had saved the ancient evil dragon stories for somewhere less spooky."

Scrrrrrrrape.

Scrrrrrrape.

Scrrrrrrape.

Winter was sure a moment before Moon turned to him with wide eyes. He saw the glint of silver-pale scales shimmering toward him as a figure crawled slowly out of the dark tunnel.

It was Icicle. They'd found her at last.

CHAPTER 8

"She's not all right," Moon whispered to him. "Her mind is all scattered and foggy. I don't know why."

A talon of ice trailed down Winter's spine as he watched his sister stagger into the gray light. Her arctic blue eyes were bloodshot, crackled with dark blue veins, and the scratches she'd gotten in the fight at Jade Mountain still hadn't healed. She was streaked with mud and blood — not just her own dark blue blood, but splatters of dark red that must have come from the NightWing she'd killed.

Icicle's scales had always been whiter than everyone else's: her claws sharper, her teeth gleaming, and her spikes pristine even after clubbing a walrus to death. She plunged into the frigid ocean six times a day because she believed an IceWing who glittered like diamonds was a more menacing IceWing. In Icicle's view of the world, grubby, dull dragons deserved to be Seventh Circle.

Winter could never have imagined her looking this wretched.

She clutched the edge of the tunnel with her front talons, leaning against the rocky wall and glaring at him.

"Icicle?" he said. "Are you —"

"Why are you here?" she spat. "To ruin yet another of my plans? You don't feel satisfied that you've already guaranteed Hailstorm's death?"

"What's wrong with you?" Kinkajou blurted. "You look terrible."

"Could be worse," Icicle snarled. "I could look like you."

"I want to help you find Hailstorm," Winter said. "If he's really still alive —"

"I don't need *your* help, of all dragons," Icicle said with a hiss, limping forward a step. "You don't have the claws to do what needs to be done." She touched her head, wiping away a trickle of blood from one of her horns. "And she's probably killed him by now anyway."

"What did Scarlet say?" Winter asked. He spread his wings, blocking her path. "When she found out Starflight and the others were still alive?"

"I haven't spoken to her." Icicle swayed a little on her feet. "I can't — I don't want to see her — to admit I *failed* — your fault — but what if she kills him in front of me — or what if he's already dead . . . and she shows me his body . . ."

She took another staggering step and Winter reached out to catch her, but she recoiled, snapping her teeth at him.

"But how have you —" he started.

"She hasn't slept," Moon said wonderingly. "Not since Jade Mountain."

"If I don't sleep," Icicle muttered triumphantly, "then she can't get to me. She can't visit my dreams if I don't have any. Ha ha!"

"But it's been days!" Kinkajou cried. "You haven't slept in *days*? Don't you feel *awful*?"

"I don't need to sleep," Icicle said. "Whenever I get tired, I lie down beside the lava until the pain wakes me up." She spread her wings, and Winter saw with a shudder that she had blisters and small burns bubbling in spots across her scales.

This he *could* imagine, too easily: his fearless, stubborn sister angrily burning herself, slashing pain across the body that betrayed her by daring to be tired.

And he understood what she was going through, too. He'd lived with the guilt of losing Hailstorm for the last two years.

"Icicle, we need to know if she's killed him," he said.

"I'd wager a few camels that she hasn't," said Qibli. "He's more use to her as a bargaining chip than as a corpse. Not very useful, corpses, as a rule. All right, shutting up now," he added, catching the look Moon was shooting him.

"Do you have any idea where she is?" Winter asked Icicle. "If we can get to her and find him —"

"If it were that easy, I'd have done it," Icicle snapped. "I've considered all the options, trust me. There's only one way to save him, and that's killing the RainWing queen."

"I'm not going to let you kill Queen Glory," Kinkajou said stoutly.

Icicle barked a ragged laugh. "And how are you going to stop me, you preposterous pink dragon?"

Kinkajou lunged at Icicle, flying past Winter in a red-and-orange blur before he realized what was happening. The little RainWing knocked Icicle over onto her back and wrapped her talons around the IceWing's throat.

"Nobody threatens my queen!" Kinkajou shouted.

"Hey!" Winter shouted.

"Get off me!" Icicle raged. She swung her tail at Kinkajou's wings but missed. Her vicious claws went up, the serrated edges glittering dangerously, ready for a killing blow at Kinkajou's underbelly.

"Kinkajou!" Moon cried, jumping toward them.

But before she could reach them, before Icicle could strike, before Winter could do anything, something small came whistling through the air and thunked into Icicle's neck.

Icicle let out a gasp and jerked back. Kinkajou jumped off of her with a yelp and looked up at the sky.

Winter followed her gaze to the clouds and then watched as the gray melted and shifted, like dragonets bursting out of the snow, into nine dragons in shades of red and gold and green.

"Icicle of the IceWings," Queen Glory announced, "you are under arrest for murder and attempted murder."

"No!" Icicle roared, clawing at her neck. She rolled over and shoved herself upright, but her legs wobbled and her head was starting to droop. "What have you done to me? What is happening?"

"It's only a tranquilizer dart," said Deathbringer, winging down to land beside them. "We find it makes transporting prisoners much simpler. You'll wake up just fine in a few hours."

"*No!*" Icicle shrieked. "I can't sleep! Don't make me sleep!" She hurled herself at Winter, dug her claws into his shoulders, and shook him with all her fading strength. "Winter, stop them — help me — tell them I can't — she'll find me! She'll tell me he's dead and then it'll be over and he'll be gone! Winter, keep me awake!"

"It's too late," Deathbringer said, studying her with a puzzled expression. "It's not that bad, the dart sleep."

Icicle slowly collapsed forward onto Winter, her talons clenching open and closed as if she was trying to claw herself back to waking. "She'll come for me," Icicle whispered.

"So let her come," Winter said. He crouched as his sister's weight pressed him down, bringing his mouth close to her ear. "Go ahead and sleep, Icicle. You can't stay awake forever anyway. Talk to Scarlet and tell her she can still get what she wants."

"But she can't." Icicle's voice was barely a mumble now. "I'll be — prison —"

Winter glanced up at the faces around them. Nobody could hear what he and Icicle were whispering to each other. Not unless they could read minds.

Well, this was one way to find out if the skyfire really worked.

He leaned closer to Icicle, close enough for the skyfire pouch to touch her scales as well as his own. And then, as his sister's eyes closed, he whispered, "Tell Scarlet if she can prove that Hailstorm is still alive . . . I'll kill Glory for her myself."

──── CHAPTER 9 ────

The healers' pavilion near the RainWing village was large, quiet, and sunlit, with curtains of green vines shielding the interior from curious onlookers. And there were plenty of curious dragons — ones Winter could see and ones he could only hear, murmuring and twittering like a council of invisible birds in the trees. The rainforest was starting to give him the suffocating, spine-crawling feeling that he was always being watched.

Only RainWings were allowed to carry the unconscious prisoner. Glory ordered all the NightWings to stay away and sent Deathbringer to make sure none of them came looking for her. She also didn't object when Winter pushed his way into the pavilion and stood next to his sister, glowering around defiantly.

"I'm staying right here," he said.

"Understood," Glory said with a nod. She turned to survey the others as they edged through the curtain and stood back against the wall, out of the way.

"Your Majesty — how did you find us?" Moon asked hesitantly.

Glory glanced at Kinkajou, her scales shifting to starbursts of royal purple against deep blue.

"I left her a trail to follow," Kinkajou admitted, looking guilty. "Sorry, Moon — but she's our queen. I wanted her there in case we really did find Icicle."

Moon nodded thoughtfully, looking back at the sleeping IceWing. "I guess it's lucky you did," she said.

Winter wanted to disagree, but he remembered the desperate rage on Icicle's face. She had been seconds away from killing Kinkajou. And even though Kinkajou was just a RainWing, he had to admit (only to himself) that he didn't want her dead.

Besides, whatever she has planned for my sister now, Queen Glory would have been much less merciful if Icicle had killed her friend.

So it was lucky for Icicle, too, that Glory had found them right then.

A pair of sky-blue RainWings was moving quietly around Icicle, cleaning her wounds. Another one, pale pink, stood by her head with a blowgun and darts at the ready in case she woke up.

Icicle's chest rose and fell in long peaceful movements, and her face was as still as Winter had ever seen it. The tortured expression was gone, for now. He hoped she would get a few hours of real rest before Scarlet came hunting through her dreams.

"It's odd," one of the RainWing healers murmured to the other. "Look how much this scratch has bled, Bullfrog."

"She wasn't letting herself sleep," Kinkajou told them. "She hasn't slept in four or five days."

The healers both made alarmed clicking noises with their tongues and bent over Icicle again, inspecting her more closely. "Why would any dragon do that to herself?" said the one named Bullfrog. "It's worse than refusing to eat. Another day of it and she'd probably be dead. At least she'll be able to heal now that she has to sleep."

"Going even twelve hours without sleep is one of my nightmares," said the other.

"Remember that RainWing a few years ago who couldn't sleep? That was the saddest case I ever saw." Bullfrog shook his head and his tail turned a glum shade of gray.

"A RainWing who can't sleep?" Glory echoed. "Isn't that kind of like a SeaWing who can't swim?"

"It was worse than that," said the pink dragon. "He couldn't change his scales either."

"*Because* he couldn't sleep," said Bullfrog. "We figured out he had a snout deformity that kept him from sleeping for more than an hour at a time. But there was no way to fix it. It was awful."

"*He* was awful," said the pink dragon. "Sometimes I would wake up from my suntime nap and he'd just be standing there *staring* at me. And he couldn't camouflage himself, and you could never tell what he was feeling by looking at his scales."

"Brrrrrrrrgh," said the other healer, shuddering from talons to tail.

"It's like he wasn't even a RainWing at all," said Bullfrog. "He was a lot grumpier than a real RainWing, too."

"So what color was he, if he couldn't change?" Qibli asked curiously.

"Kind of an ordinary lime green all over," Bullfrog answered. He held out one talon and shifted the scales along his arm to demonstrate. "Very boring."

"And unattractive," agreed the second healer. She gathered the damp leaves stained with Icicle's blood and bustled off.

"That's our cautionary tale of what happens when you don't sleep," said the pink dragon. "Ahem. Your Majesty."

"I *do* sleep," Glory protested. "Maybe not as *much* as other RainWings, but I've been doing suntime *every day,* no matter how busy I am. So quit your scolding, Jambu."

"I'm just saying." Jambu resettled his wings, looking pleased with himself.

"What are you planning to do with my sister?" Winter asked Glory. "I can take her back to the Ice Kingdom. I promise Queen Glacier will see that she's punished."

Glory circled Icicle's bed, studying the sleeping dragon. "She's too dangerous," said the queen with a flick of her tail. "She killed one of my subjects —"

"On the way to killing you," Kinkajou interrupted to point out.

Glory waved this away with one talon. "I can't let her just fly out of here," she said to Winter. "I need to be a true queen to the NightWings, and that means letting them see justice. But I also don't want to start a war with the IceWings, and I believe a queen should have a say in what happens to her subjects. So I'll send for Queen Glacier, and together we can decide what happens to Icicle."

That was more fair than Winter could have hoped for, and yet it made his stomach twist in a painful, anxious way to think of his queen coming here to judge him and his sister. *The rankings,* he thought, and, *What will Mother and Father think?*

I need to find Hailstorm before she arrives, he thought. *If I can free him, Queen Glacier will understand why Icicle did what she did.*

"In the meanwhile" — Glory sighed — "we'll have to keep her tranquilized so she doesn't try to escape or hurt someone else."

"Wait, what?" Winter rose to his feet and got his wings caught in a woven-leaf hammock that was hanging from the ceiling. He wrestled it off with a growl of frustration. "I need to talk to her."

"And *I* need a decent prison," Glory said, snapping her tail back and forth. "The RainWings don't have *anything*. Where am I supposed to put misbehaving dragons?" She turned to an older RainWing who was sitting in the corner, watching with stately composure. "Has no RainWing in history ever required punishing?"

"We don't imprison, we banish," said the older dragon with an elegant shrug. "What could be worse than being thrown out of the rainforest?"

"You see what I'm dealing with," Glory said to Winter. "I have one prisoner right now — a NightWing — and we basically had to stick him in a quicksand pit. Every few hours his guards haul him out just enough so he doesn't die, and then he starts sinking again."

"Yuck," said Kinkajou. "But he deserves it, actually."

"And there are two others I should deal with, but Queen Thorn has agreed to keep them in her SandWing prison instead, until I decide what to do with them." Glory's sloth poked its head out from behind the queen's shoulder and started climbing slowly up her neck. "I'll figure out something else eventually," Glory said. "But I'm guessing Queen Glacier wouldn't appreciate it if I stuck one of her dragons in quicksand, so I'm afraid Icicle has to stay asleep for now."

"Your Majesty," said a peach-and-plum-colored dragon, poking her head through the curtain. "Deathbringer would like a word."

"Excuse me," Glory said to Winter with a small bow. The older dragon followed her out, leaving Jambu on guard and Bullfrog still gently cleaning Icicle's scales. Winter inspected Icicle's face with concern. A small furrow had appeared between her eyes — was she speaking with Scarlet at that very moment?

He watched her for a long minute, but she didn't move or speak or give any other sign of what her dreams were about.

Finally he turned and stalked to the wall where Moon and Kinkajou were sitting together, their tails entwined. Qibli was pacing around the healers' pavilion, poking his nose around curtains to see the other patients, sniffing piles of medicinal leaves, and scaring clouds of small yellow butterflies out of the rafters.

"Now what am I supposed to do?" Winter hissed at him. "It was your bright idea to come here. But I'm no closer to finding Hailstorm *and* it's my fault my sister's been caught by a bunch of RainWings."

"We are closer to finding Hailstorm," Kinkajou objected. "We've found the only dragon who's spoken to Scarlet and knows the whole story."

"And she's fast asleep," Winter said. "Which does me any good how?"

Qibli stopped next to Moon, brushing her wings with his. Winter's claws twitched and he clenched his jaw.

The other RainWings weren't paying any attention to them, but Qibli lowered his voice anyway. "Didn't you say you overheard Icicle and Scarlet conspiring?" he asked Moon. "Does that mean you can get into dreams, too?"

A shock like lightning ran through Winter's veins. "Is that true?" he demanded. "Can you listen in when Scarlet finds her?"

"I will try," Moon said, leaning a little closer to Kinkajou. "I *am* trying. It's all darkness in Icicle's mind right now — she's too deep in sleep for dreams."

Three moons, Winter realized. *If Moon hears their conversation, she'll know what I told Icicle. She'll probably have Glory arrest me, too. I'll have to be ready to fly the moment she tells me what I need to know about Scarlet.*

"So we wait," Kinkajou said. "For Scarlet to come."

It seemed as if a long time passed, as the shadows slowly lengthened and night came creeping into the pavilion. Winter arranged himself in the IceWing guarding stance, but after a while all his training failed and he fell asleep.

Moon jolted him awake by touching one of her talons to his.

"She's here," she whispered. "She's in Icicle's mind. Shhhh."

The pavilion was dimly lit by a few beams of moonlight and several jars hanging from the ceiling that appeared to be full of fireflies. Qibli and Kinkajou slept peacefully, curled next to each other on the floor. Winter blinked into the shadows and saw that Bullfrog was still in the pavilion, asleep in a hammock next to a snoring RainWing patient. Jambu had been replaced by another RainWing, who was watching Icicle, her blowgun at the ready.

He stepped quietly over to Icicle's bed and saw that his sister was sleeping very differently now. All her muscles were tensed as if she wanted to run but couldn't, and her claws were twitching violently.

"Do you think she's about to wake up?" the RainWing guard asked Winter. "She just had another dart an hour ago, so she shouldn't, but I've never seen anyone fight sleep like that. She looks like she's eaten some kind of toxic fern."

"I don't think she'll wake up," Winter answered. He meant it, but he was still surprised when the RainWing nodded and sat back. Why would she trust the prisoner's brother to tell her the truth? RainWings really had no sense at all.

"Winter," Moon whispered, his name in her voice like a spell that ran warmth through his bones. He hurried back over to her. "I need paper," she said, grabbing one of his talons without opening her eyes. "And something to write with. Quickly."

Winter searched all the corners and boxes and niches. He even checked under all the beds. He ransacked the entire pavilion and didn't find a single scroll.

"I'll be right back," he whispered to Moon, hurrying past her to the outer curtain. She just nodded, her brow wrinkled with pain. He paused for a second, watching her where she crouched in the moonlight. Did it hurt, listening to other dragons' dreams? Or was it particularly bad listening to Scarlet and Icicle?

He pushed through the vine curtain and stared out at a very dark rainforest. In the Ice Kingdom it was rare to find this kind of darkness; the gift of light had been passed along to every inhabited part of the kingdom, and there were moon globes everywhere. His home also had so much open space, and the three moons always glittered on everything — the snow, the ice palace, the frozen lakes, the glaciers.

He wished he had a moon globe. He wasn't used to flying into pitch-black like this, especially when he couldn't tell where any of the RainWings were. He could *hear* some of them snoring, amid the nighttime rainforest cacophony, but he couldn't actually see any other dragons, even in the spots where moonlight could reach.

He thought of Hailstorm trapped in some kind of secret SkyWing prison, probably in complete darkness for the last two years.

"Wait," a voice called softly behind him. Kinkajou pushed through the curtain and stood next to him. "You stay here," she said. "I'll get Moon some paper. I know where to go — the new RainWing school is close by."

"I should come with you," he said.

"No, thanks." Kinkajou nudged him out of her way. "You'd probably wake the whole village, thrashing and flailing around. Stay and make sure Moon is all right."

She flashed away, vanishing quickly into the dark. And, he had to admit, more or less soundlessly. He wondered if RainWings had better night vision than other tribes. The tribes with fire would just use that when they needed to light up the dark, he guessed. What about SeaWings? Could they see in the dark? If he were still at school, he could probably get someone to let him test that theory by studying his fellow students.

But I'm not still at school, and I'm not going back, and I shouldn't — I mean, I don't *care what other tribes can do anyway.*

He returned to Moon and found her in a curtained-off corner of the pavilion, next to the only window with a view of the starry night sky. A small blue frog with darker blue speckles was sitting on one of her front talons, and they both seemed to be listening to the chorus of frogs and birds and insects and whatever other mysterious creatures were making all that noise outside.

Winter paused beside his sister for a moment. Icicle looked as though she was slowly relaxing back into real sleep.

"Scarlet's gone," Moon said as Winter approached.

"Was it terrible?" Winter asked. "Is Icicle all right? What did Scarlet say about Hailstorm?"

Moon gave him an odd, searching look. Her teardrop scales caught the moonlight on one side and the firefly lamp on the other, gleaming as though one was ice and the other was gold.

Winter realized this was the first time they'd been alone together — apart from the sleeping dragons around them — since he found out she could read minds. Or was it the first time they'd ever been alone together? He felt the weight of the skyfire rock pouch around his ankle.

"Scarlet says your brother is still alive." Moon turned her talon over, gently sliding the frog onto the windowsill. "Icicle asked for proof, but Scarlet only laughed at her. I wish I could read Scarlet's mind, but she's too far away and it's not really her in Icicle's dream, only a projection of her. So I can't tell what she's thinking or whether it's true about Hailstorm. I'm sorry." She gave him that quick, confused look again. "Icicle offered her a deal."

"You don't have to —" he started.

"I'm not," she said. "Worried, I mean. I know you won't kill Queen Glory."

"Do you know that?" he asked. "How?"

"Because I think she's the kind of dragon you respect," she said slowly. "And I think you wouldn't want to start a war between the IceWings and both of her tribes. I think you can imagine what killing her would do to Pyrrhia, and you know it would be bad. Also, you're her guest; she's welcomed and trusted you. You aren't the kind of dragon who betrays someone's trust."

Winter studied her profile as she wound a vine between her claws. "That's a lot of thoughts," he said. "Weren't you paralyzingly shy at one point? What happened to that unobtrusive, quiet dragon?"

"It turns out it's actually much easier to talk to you when I can't hear what you're thinking," Moon admitted, smiling.

He stared into her dark eyes for a long moment. "But all of that about Queen Glory . . . are you sure you're not still reading my mind?" he finally asked, quietly.

"I don't have to," she said. "I've already been in there, for one thing — I know you. And I've watched you. I saw you put out the fire in the history cave. I saw you save me and Starflight from your own sister. I think you can think bigger than just one tribe against another — you can think about what's best for all the tribes. I guess I just — I trust you."

"You seem very sure of certain things about me," Winter said. "That I would never hurt a dragonet. That I would never kill Queen Glory. That I am somehow honorable and brave."

"I am," said Moon. "I am sure of those things. Even when everything else inside you is confusion and mirrors and pain, those things are true."

He lifted the vine from her claws and wrapped it around his own talons, lowering his voice even more. "Sometimes I'm only sure of one thing," he said. "That I hope I never hurt you."

She gazed up at him in surprise. "Me? But I thought you hated me."

"Then you're not much of a mind reader, are you?" he said with a half smile. "I mean, I should. But for some reason I can't."

He took another step closer, tilting his wings forward to brush hers.

"Well, good," Moon said, looking at their wings instead of his face. "I'm — I'm glad you can't hate me."

"Got it!" Kinkajou's voice said eagerly behind them. "Moon? Where are you?"

Winter let out a breath he hadn't known he was holding.

"Here," Moon said. She touched one talon lightly to Winter's chest, then went past him and through the curtain. Winter pressed his talons together, trying to stop them from shaking, and then followed her. Kinkajou was in the center of the pavilion, under one of the firefly jars, spreading a blank scroll on the floor. She nudged an inkpot toward Moon with her tail.

"What is this for?" Kinkajou asked.

"I saw something," Moon said, crouching beside her. She took the long thin reed that Kinkajou was holding and dipped it in the ink. "Behind Scarlet — I got a glimpse of what was behind her, and I think it was a mountain. It was kind of an unusual shape." She started drawing. "Maybe we can find it."

Winter watched the lines appear under Moon's claws, swooping and turning back, crisscrossing and diving like flights of dragons in the sky. This was a real clue. A clue that might lead them to Hailstorm.

It looked like a wall at first — tall and sheer, with silvery waterfalls trailing down it like dragon tails. Along the top of the wall was a ridge of sharp peaks that looked like an

IceWing's spine, leading up to one peak that looped up and back on itself, almost in the shape of an eye.

Moon lifted the reed and studied the picture. "That's close anyway," she said. "Does it look familiar to either of you?"

Winter shook his head. "I haven't spent much time in the Sky Kingdom, though," he said. "Assuming that is the Sky Kingdom."

"I've never been anywhere but the rainforest and Jade Mountain," Kinkajou said with a helpless shrug. "And the NightWing island, of course. Hey, Qibli, wake up and look at this."

The SandWing came instantly awake as Kinkajou poked him, jumping to his feet as if he was ready for a battle. Moon held the sketch out to him and explained where she'd seen it.

Qibli studied it for a while, then shook his head. "Never seen it," he said. "But someone must have. Great work, Moon."

"Yeah, thanks," Winter added hastily.

"I didn't really do anything," she said, taking the drawing back. "It's only — I mean, I'm just —"

"Lucky," Kinkajou finished. "I wish I had a cool power like that."

"Lucky?" Moon said wonderingly. Above her head, three fireflies escaped their jar and darted off in a flicker of surprised sparks.

"Well, it's no use asking any RainWings where this is," Kinkajou said, flicking her tail at the sketch. "None of us leave the rainforest if we can help it. Because it is *awesome* and *perfect* here," she added with a stern look at Winter.

"Let's try Deathbringer," Moon suggested. "He's been all over the continent."

Qibli shot a sideways look at Winter. "Is that all right?" he asked. "He's not exactly your favorite dragon."

"I'll survive," Winter said. "If he can help me find Hailstorm, that's what matters."

It was hard to focus on hating the NightWings now that there was real hope in front of him. A chance of finding Hailstorm before Scarlet killed him — if he'd bought enough time with his lie about killing Glory for her. If he moved fast. If Moon had truly seen where Scarlet was, and if Hailstorm was there, too.

If . . . if . . . if . . .

If I can make this happen . . . I might really see my brother again after all.

PART TWO

IN THE CLAWS OF THE CLOUDS

CHAPTER 10

Deathbringer didn't recognize the mountains Moon had drawn, but he knew who might.

"The Talons of Peace," he said. He breathed out another small flame to study the drawing. "Find them — or what's left of them — and ask one of their SkyWings to help you." They'd found him on guard outside the royal treehouse where Glory slept. The darkness was not as thick up here, close to the treetops, where more moonlight could filter through the leaves. The small glowing lights of phosphorescent insects trailed up and down the branches, and Winter spotted a few eerie glow-in-the-dark moths nestled in the pale night orchids.

"All right, then," said Qibli. "We'll go ahead and track down a shadowy underground group who move every few weeks and weren't caught for the entire war. Easy."

Deathbringer swatted at him and Qibli jumped out of the way with a grin.

"They're not all that shadowy *now*," Deathbringer said.

"And nobody said you were coming," Winter said to Qibli. "I don't know what this 'we' business is all about."

"Ignore him," Qibli said to Deathbringer. "We're growing on him, I'm pretty sure. Why do the Talons of Peace even still exist, now that the war is over?"

"Many of them aren't welcome back in their tribes, so they have nowhere else to go," Deathbringer said. "Their goals are shifting, though. I know the dragon who's taken over the group. I can help you find them, if Glory doesn't mind you leaving."

"Oh, how nice of you to check," Glory said, materializing suddenly out of the darkness. Winter jumped, wondering how long the RainWing queen had been there. And why she was camouflaged — because she was following him, or because she was spying on Deathbringer?

"As it happens," Queen Glory went on, "I don't mind what Qibli and Prince Winter choose to do — I'm not their queen. But I *do* have a few reservations about allowing two of my favorite subjects to gallivant around the continent chasing Pyrrhia's most dangerous dragon."

"Did you hear that?" Kinkajou said, nudging Moon so vigorously she nearly knocked her over. "*Favorite.*"

"The part you were supposed to hear is 'dangerous,'" Glory said. "With Blister and Burn both dead, Scarlet is probably the scariest dragon left alive — and she certainly hates us the most. Explain to me how it is a good idea to send a quartet of young dragonets after her."

"No quartet necessary," Winter said. "Just the one. That's me. IceWing prince over here. Going to save my brother. Without the entourage. Please order them to stay here; it would make my life a lot simpler."

"We're not going after Scarlet," Moon said to Glory. "We're going to find Winter's brother."

"WE are doing no such thing," Winter said firmly. "*I* am going to find him. JUST ME."

"That's right," Qibli said. "Just him and the three of us, his best friends in the world."

"I can't even dignify that with a snort," Winter said, looking down his nose at the SandWing.

"If we can figure out where she's got him locked up, maybe we can set Hailstorm free without Scarlet even seeing us," Moon said.

"Besides," Kinkajou said, "we're not *that* much younger than you and your friends were when you set out to save Pyrrhia from all the bad dragons."

"We'll be careful," Moon said. "We promise."

"Don't listen to them," Winter said. "I don't *want* them to come with me. In fact, if you could stick this SandWing in some quicksand while I get away from him, I will personally bring you a walrus to express my gratitude."

"Ew," said Kinkajou.

"His very best friends," Qibli said sincerely.

In the moonlight, it was hard to tell what the colors were that were shifting across Glory's scales. She curled her tail around the branch underneath her and sighed deeply. "Deathbringer?"

"I think you should let them go," Deathbringer said. "I went on my first mission when I was four, and I turned out fine."

"Well, that's debatable," Glory said. "And if I wanted to go, you'd have an absolute heart attack."

"Yes, because you're the most important queen in Pyrrhia," said Deathbringer. "And also because I couldn't live without you, not that you care, torturing me with your recklessness all the time."

"That's true," Glory said. "You'd be an absolute mess, the way you were before you met me."

"I was only half a dragon before I met you," he declared. "And I would be even less if I lost you now."

"All right, settle down," she said affectionately. She turned to Kinkajou and Moon. "You may go, but here are my orders: Do not interact with Scarlet. Stay as far out of her way as you can. Don't let her know you're there. Don't fight with anyone, don't make any queens mad, and most importantly, don't you dare die. Understood?"

The two dragons nodded, and Kinkajou clapped her front talons together with excitement.

"Am I speaking a language only IceWings understand?" Winter demanded.

"Listen," Glory said, fixing her green-eyed gaze on Winter. "I used to think I could do everything by myself, too. I didn't want help from anyone. But I wouldn't be here now if it weren't for my friends, and I have a feeling you'll be saying the same thing a year from now."

"That might apply if these dragons *were* my friends," Winter objected, "but they're actually strangers who happened to get thrown into a group with me. They're not even IceWings. Why should they care what happens to Hailstorm?"

"They care what happens to *you*," Glory said.

"For some reason," added Deathbringer.

"Entertainment value," offered Qibli.

"So," Glory said, shooting a quelling look at the SandWing, "I strongly suggest you stop fighting and take them along. You might be surprised to find how useful dragons from other tribes can be."

Winter growled softly. He didn't want to give in. He wanted to prove to his family that he could save Hailstorm alone. And he really didn't want to admit how much he would rather have these dragons with him when he faced Scarlet. Moon's mind reading, Kinkajou's camouflage, and Qibli's aggravating intelligence . . . yes, he could imagine how they'd all be useful.

What was wrong with him? Where was his IceWing pride?

But it would waste time if he tried to keep arguing.

And saying yes meant a few more days with Moon . . .

Which should have been a reason to say no.

"Very well," he said finally. "Tell me how to find the Talons of Peace."

The Winding Tail River began high in the Claws of the Clouds mountains and ran down past Jade Mountain to the sea. Near a bend in the river, north of the rainforest and west of Queen Moorhen's lake, there was a scavenger den that was believed to be the biggest in Pyrrhia. Unlike most scavenger dens, this one was not hidden away; instead, it was well fortified with stone walls and defended fiercely by the little creatures who lived in it.

"I know some dragons who've hunted there," Deathbringer had said, "but most of them say it's not worth it. You'll just end up getting jabbed with sharp things and pelted with heavy things. There's much easier prey in the river and mountains."

This was the new spot the Talons of Peace had chosen for their signals, apparently, now that Jade Mountain was being watched by too many dragon eyes. The scavenger den was fairly high up, built on a cliff overlooking the forest, and any dragon flying over it would be visible for miles in every direction.

Which wasn't Winter's favorite feeling, to be honest, but that was how it worked. The Talons of Peace were out there somewhere, with someone watching the skies in case of a signal like this, and he needed to find them.

The four dragonets reached the area shortly after midday, landing on one of the clifftops below the scavenger den. A brisk wind buffeted their wings and tossed hawks around far overhead with piercing hunting cries. The sun was brilliant yellow-white in a perfectly clear sky, much like the day Hailstorm had been captured.

"We could wait until night," Moon suggested. "Then Qibli and I can fly up and signal with fire — trails of flames in the night sky. Deathbringer said that would work."

"They're not just watching for fire-breathing dragons, though," Winter said. "I can take care of this part, don't worry." He flung himself into the air before anyone could argue with him.

The wind caught his wings and lifted him in a wheeling spiral, up and up and up toward the blue dome overhead. It was such a relief to be out of the rainforest and away from all the clinging damp vines and weird ripe-fruit smells. Winter felt as though his wings were six times larger out here, with room to stretch and soar.

He flew as high as he could, circled over the other dragonets, and then plummeted swiftly down like a meteor slicing through the sky. He zoomed over their heads, banked upward, and caught a wind where he could float like a leaf.

Now for the signal. Winter angled his wings to catch the sun. He'd swum in the river and polished his scales this morning so they glittered even more than usual, wintry blue and white. The sunlight reflected off him as he tilted his wings, flashing like a mirror to any watching dragons below.

He twisted slowly, making sure he could be seen from any direction, although he guessed the Talons of Peace were somewhere in the long range of mountains that split the land like jagged claws pushing out of the ground. He could see the twin peaks of Jade Mountain far away to the south. To the west, the pale rolling dunes of the desert filled the horizon beyond the mountain range. And below him, to the east and north, were the swamps of the Mud Kingdom.

Was Hailstorm out there somewhere? Did he know the war was over? Did he know how Scarlet was using him now? Was he crouched in darkness, wishing someone would come save him?

Winter shook those thoughts away, turning his attention to the scavenger den. It was cleverly chosen. The scavengers had found a spot where a huge overhanging ledge sheltered much of their home from the sky, shielding them in one direction from flying predators. Cave entrances dotted the cliffside and odd little structures were carved out of the rock, each probably large enough for nine or ten scavengers to curl up inside. A wall of thick stones ran around the den, ending at the cliff on each side, barricading them in.

He could also see several patches of greenery that looked almost like gardens — could scavengers think far enough ahead to plant gardens? Next to the ledge, a waterfall cascaded cheerfully down the cliff, right past the den. Some kind of wooden contraption was built out into the spray, catching buckets full of water and spinning them back toward the safety of the walls.

Winter hovered, watching the scavengers. Several of them were darting about, calling to each other in their squeaky chirps. They seemed very active — much more so than Bandit — almost like a pod of dolphins flurrying about after you accidentally drop the remains of your whale carcass on them.

A few were peering over the wall at the nearby cliffs. He saw one point to the ledge where Moon, Qibli, and Kinkajou were sitting in the sun together, resting their wings, black and pale yellow and iridescent blue-purple-green side by side.

Are they worried about dragons so close to their home? Winter wondered. That was cute. Of course, this particular group of dragons was possibly the least likely to eat a scavenger of any dragons in Pyrrhia. But if they'd wanted to, what would the scavengers do about it?

The scavengers were rolling something up to the wall now . . . something made of pieces of wood fitted together, with ropes and metal bits as well. The sharp pointed end of it slid into a slot in the wall and poked out the other side.

Winter swooped lower, trying to figure out what they were doing. It didn't seem as if they'd noticed him yet, in the sky above them.

A scavenger with long fur swooping off its head like a tail climbed nimbly onto the wall and leaned over, holding a torch that flickered with fire at the end. It lowered the torch to touch the end of the contraption that was sticking through the wall. The flames caught and licked around the point, and immediately the scavengers on the other side of the wall started bustling around, twisting the ropes and pulling things and pointing the device —

— *at the dragons below.*

It was a weapon! These scavengers had some kind of fiery projectile weapon — and they were about to shoot it at Moon and the others.

Winter folded his wings and plummeted toward the den as fast as gravity could take him. There was a shout from one of the scavengers. Suddenly the weapon fired, and a spear as long as a dragon came hurtling out of the wall, dancing with flames and wickedly sharp. It plunged down, straight toward Qibli's heart.

"LOOK OUT!" Winter roared. He wasn't close enough to reach it but —

He called up the cold from inside him and blasted a spray of frostbreath at the spear.

The fire went out instantly as ice crystals appeared all along the weapon. The extra weight and the force of his breath knocked the spear off course. It crashed into the cliff underneath Qibli's talons, and then dropped to the earth far below instead.

Kinkajou shrieked and Qibli leaped aside, spreading his wings to shield Moon.

Winter wheeled over their heads and landed beside them. "Time to move," he barked.

"The scavengers are shooting at us!" Kinkajou cried. "That's so mean! We didn't even try to eat them or anything!"

"But other dragons have," Qibli pointed out. The four of them swiftly arrowed into the sky, far out of range of the scavengers' weapons. Winter glanced back and saw the small furry faces peering out to watch them fly away.

"Is it weird that I'm kind of impressed?" Moon asked. "I had no idea they could come up with something like that."

"I'm sticking with outraged," Kinkajou said. "Hello, I'm a vegetarian! There is SO no need to shoot ME, of all dragons! I should go down there and ROAR at them." Her scales were vibrantly, alarmingly orange, much brighter than any SkyWing's scales could be. Winter guessed that if the Talons had somehow missed his mirror signal, a dragon this weirdly colored might still catch their eye.

"What in the world was it?" Qibli asked. He soared in a tight circle, trying to see down into the den. "How did it work? How did they make it? Could we make one? I mean, not us, not right now, but maybe one day for Thorn's palace?"

"I've never seen anything quite like it," Winter admitted.

"Can you draw it for me?" Qibli asked.

"Um . . . sure."

They found a place to wait for the Talons, above the scavengers, out of their sight this time, near the river that led to the waterfall. Kinkajou and Moon went off to find food, while Winter tried to sketch the weapon in the sandy banks beside the river.

"But did this pull it back?" Qibli kept asking. He poked the drawing, scattering sand over Winter's claws. "Did this part fit into here? Wouldn't they need a piece like this?"

"I have no idea!" Winter finally erupted. "I was a little busy saving your scales!"

"That's true," Qibli said, sitting back and giving him a delighted smile. "You totally saved my scales. I *knew* we were best friends. Did I say thank you yet?"

"No," Winter grumbled.

"Thank you," Qibli said, entirely too sincerely for Winter.

"Well," Winter said, "I would have done the same thing for anyone, you know."

"I know," Qibli said. "I like that about you."

Winter saw, with surprise, that he meant it. Qibli was as bad as a RainWing, flapping his feelings all over the place all the time.

"You would get eaten alive in the Ice Kingdom," Winter pointed out.

Qibli shrugged. "Maybe not. I survived the Scorpion Den," he said. "And my family. They would not have saved me in this situation, if you're curious. More likely they'd have grabbed the spear and stabbed me themselves."

"Mine would have waited to see if I could save myself, and then stood there shaking their heads in grave disappointment when I didn't," Winter said. "Taking notes on all the things I did wrong. 'Stood in the wrong place. Allowed spear to penetrate scales. Bleeding too much.' And so forth."

Qibli laughed. "They sound great."

"They are," Winter said quickly. "That's how IceWing parents are supposed to be. I'm very lucky."

Qibli gave him a strange look. "I guess they did something right," he said after a moment. "I mean, for you to be so determined to rescue your brother. If I were in a SkyWing prison, my brother would definitely not come to rescue me. To be fair, I wouldn't go rescue him either. Pyrrhia would be much better off with him locked up where he can't hurt anyone."

A breeze sent ripples across the surface of the river. Winter stepped over his sketch and waded into the water, rinsing the sand off his claws. Tiny golden and silver fish darted around his talons. The water was bracingly cold, like a fleeting reminder of home.

"I have a sinister older sister, too," Qibli offered.

"Icicle's not older than me," Winter said. "We were in the same hatching. And sinister is a bit of an exaggeration."

"Mmm-hmm," Qibli said skeptically.

Winter sighed. "My parents will probably be so proud of her. Up until the part where she failed — which they'll see as my fault — and then got caught by RainWings — also my fault. Going home is going to be excellent in all the ways. I can't wait."

"It'll be all right, because you'll be bringing Hailstorm with you," Qibli said confidently. "So they'll have to forgive you."

Will they? Winter wondered. Would they be proud of him if he succeeded? Or would they be too horrified by his methods and his company?

His sharp ears caught a quiet splash nearby. Alertly he spun in a circle and scanned the river.

Suddenly he spotted a dark shape swarming through the water toward him, moving faster than a shark.

Before he could cry out, a dragon lunged out of the water and straight for his throat.

— CHAPTER 11 —

Winter let out a roar and swung his claws in a ferocious arc.

The attacking dragon stopped himself at the last moment, just out of range of Winter's talons. He yelped in surprise and fell back with a splash.

"Hey!" the new dragon said indignantly. "Rude! You could have taken my nose off!"

"And you'd deserve it for jumping at me like that," Winter snarled.

"I was *practicing* my *stealth approach*," the dragon grumbled, standing up and shaking off his wet green wings. He was a SeaWing, a bit older than Winter, but much scrawnier. "I wouldn't have actually hurt you."

"That's true, because I would have ripped off your tail and beaten you with it first," Winter said.

"Nice," Qibli said from the shore. "Not the face this time. Very creative."

"Squid!" someone shouted above them. "Didn't you hear my orders?" A sky-blue SeaWing with dark blue horns came soaring down from the clouds and landed next to the first with a splash. This dragon was bigger, and frowning.

"Whaaaaaaaaaaaaaaaat," Squid whined.

"I very clearly said, *Nobody approach the strangers until I've had a chance to speak to them*," said the new SeaWing. "What you're doing? The opposite of that."

"I was being STEALTHY," Squid said, smacking the water with his wings. "Dad said I should *practice*. He thinks I'm *really good* at it. He said maybe I'll be an amazing *spy* one day."

The other SeaWing looked as though he had reached the farthest horizon of his patience. "Squid, take your lurking and snooping and harassment *somewhere else*. Right. Now."

"Fine fine FINE." Squid floundered out of the water, flapping his wings and grumbling. "You know, my dad *used* to be the leader of the Talons of Peace. I don't know why he lets *you* boss him around. When he wanted to step aside, he could have let *me* take over, I mean, what was wrong with *that* plan . . ." He took off into the sky. They could hear him muttering and whining for a while as he flew away.

Winter and Qibli exchanged an amused glance. The blue SeaWing took a deep breath and exhaled slowly.

"I apologize," he said. "Let's pretend that never happened. My name is Riptide. I saw your signal . . . Are you looking for the Talons of Peace?"

"Yes," Winter said, climbing out of the river onto the grass. "Deathbringer said we should come to you. We need a SkyWing to help us with something."

"We don't have a lot of SkyWings," Riptide admitted. "Ruby pardoned almost everyone who'd had a disagreement with her mother, so all the fugitives who'd been hiding from Scarlet went home. But we still have a couple who don't feel safe going back — I can ask one of them."

He let out an odd high-pitched whistle and two more dragons emerged from the trees. One was a MudWing with a crooked tail; the other, Winter realized with a shock, was an IceWing, glittering silvery-white with pale purple under-scales. But it was an IceWing he'd never seen before — and how was that possible? Winter had an excellent memory for faces, and he thought he'd met every dragon in the tribe at least once.

"Please ask the SkyWings to come here," Riptide said to the MudWing, who nodded and flew away.

"Who are you?" Winter asked the IceWing, who was regarding him with cold, snakelike eyes.

"Cirrus of the IceWings," the strange dragon hissed. "And you?"

That was even stranger. Every IceWing knew the royal family, surely?

"I'm Prince Winter," he said slowly. He realized he didn't know what his current ranking was, which was a very unsettling feeling now that he was facing another IceWing. Could he still say "Second Circle" and hope it was true? But then, Cirrus hadn't offered his circle number either. *Because he wouldn't have one,* Winter had to remind himself. *He'd have been thrown off the list when he abandoned his post and joined the Talons.* "Why don't I know you?"

Cirrus flicked his dark blue tongue between his teeth. "It's a big tribe," he said.

"Not really." Winter eyed him from horns to tail. Even without ranking circles, Cirrus still should have known to bow to a prince. But it didn't seem like a good fight to start — Cirrus was quite a bit bigger than Winter and fiercely thin, with claws that looked even sharper than normal IceWing claws.

"Cirrus has been with the Talons of Peace for a long time," Riptide said. "Much longer than I have. He probably left the Ice Kingdom before you were hatched."

That somewhat explained it — although Winter was still surprised he'd never heard of Cirrus. He hadn't realized there were any IceWings in the Talons of Peace. What kind of IceWing would choose banishment from the kingdom? To never return to the snow and the ice palaces — to give up your place in the rankings forever — Winter couldn't imagine it.

"Did you know my parents?" he asked Cirrus. "Tundra and Narwhal?"

Cirrus glanced up, tracking a rose-colored butterfly with a malevolent gaze, as though he was considering eating it. "Perhaps," he said. "Long ago."

He *had* to know that Narwhal was the queen's brother.

How could anyone have grown up as an IceWing without learning the royal lineage?

Before Winter could ask any more questions, he heard snapping branches and turned to see Moon and Kinkajou returning. Kinkajou was carrying a small pile of peaches and plums between her talons, and a pair of rabbits dangled from Moon's jaws.

"They're with us," Qibli said quickly as Riptide and Cirrus both bristled.

"Really?" Riptide said. "Never thought I'd see a NightWing and an IceWing traveling together. Or a RainWing outside the rainforest, for that matter. How did you all come together?"

Winter glanced over at Cirrus again and found him glaring at Moon and Kinkajou with an expression of searing hatred, so intense that Winter wanted to run across the clearing and fling up his wings to shield Moon from it. Cirrus had left the IceWings, but his loathing of NightWings clearly still ran deep.

"We're from the Jade Mountain Academy," Qibli said to Riptide. "I'm Qibli, and that's Moon and Kinkajou. Guys, this is Riptide and Serious."

"CIRRUS," the IceWing snarled.

"That's what I said." Qibli smiled disarmingly, but Winter could tell by now when the SandWing was deliberately trying to annoy someone.

"Jade Mountain?" Riptide echoed, his whole face lighting up. "You must know Tsunami. How is she? Did she send you? Was there a message for me?"

"No," Winter said. "I mean, Deathbringer sent us. Tsunami doesn't know we're here."

"Oh." Riptide's wings drooped.

Moon took a nervous step toward him, opened her mouth, closed it, and then blurted, "But she thinks about you all the time." She made a face, as though she wasn't sure she should have said that.

"Really?" The SeaWing's phosphorescent scales flashed as he turned to look at her.

"Yes. She — she wants to hear from you."

"I'm not so sure about that," Riptide said. "I should probably wait until she contacts me. Oh, here's Pyrite and Avalanche."

There was a rustling in the trees, and then the MudWing was back, this time with two SkyWings following behind her.

The bigger SkyWing had red scales, smoke rising from her ears, and a bad-tempered expression. There was something about the way she glared at them that made Winter's spine prickle. He followed her gaze and realized that her hostility was directed at Qibli; she almost looked as though she wanted to rip the barb right off his tail. *Does she know him, or does she have a problem with SandWings in general?*

Well, if she does know him, that would explain why she wants to kill him. Ha ha.

Winter let himself be amused for a second — but he also found himself hoping she wouldn't be the one who helped them.

The second SkyWing was smaller and her wings twitched constantly, as if she might take off at any moment. Her scales were an interesting orange color that was close to yellow, like the inside of a peach, and her eyes were a darker shade of orange, like the amber earring Qibli wore. Around her neck was a small brown pouch on a gold chain, tight as a choker, and she also had a gold nose ring on one side of her snout, which was a jewelry decision Winter had never seen before.

"Hi," she said, and then launched abruptly into a speech. "Listen, whatever it is you need, I don't think I can help you. It's not that I wouldn't like to. I *would* like to, really, I wish I could do all kinds of things, but the truth is I'm not very good at anything and I'm sure I'm not the dragon you're looking for, so . . ." She trailed off, staring at them and twitching.

"We're not asking much," Winter said. "We just want you to look at a sketch and see if one of you recognizes it — and if you do, maybe you could give us directions on how to get there."

"Why should I help you?" the red SkyWing demanded.

"Because we're at peace now," Riptide said sharply. "And dragons at peace help each other. That is kind of the entire premise of the Talons of Peace."

She growled deep in her throat, sending more smoke out her nostrils.

The other SkyWing touched the little bag on her necklace, rolling it anxiously between her claws. "I don't know, I mean, I have a terrible memory," she said. "And an awful sense of direction."

"Just give it a try, please, Pyrite," Riptide said. There was something in his voice that gave Winter the impression he'd spent a lot of time managing this particular dragon.

Moon took the mini-scroll with her sketch out of the satchel around her neck and spread it out on a flat boulder, revealing the odd mountain shapes she'd drawn.

Avalanche stomped over and glowered at the drawing for a moment. "Doesn't look familiar," she muttered.

"All right," Moon said with a sigh. "Thank you anyway."

"Can I go now?" Avalanche demanded, squinting at Riptide. He nodded, and she leaped into the sky, flapping away with noisy, powerful wingbeats.

"Pyrite?" Riptide said, indicating the scroll.

The thin SkyWing edged up to Moon, glanced quickly at the paper, then shook her head, saying, "Sorry, sorry, sorry. All trees look the same to me."

"It's not a tree," Moon said firmly, pinning Pyrite with

her gaze before the SkyWing could retreat. "It's a mountain, and you *do* recognize it. Tell us where it is."

Pyrite gave her a surprised, guilty look. Winter wondered whether he should warn Moon to hide her mind reading a bit better.

"Oh . . . I suppose it's a bit familiar," Pyrite said, squinting at the sketch again. "I'm sorry, I don't usually, um, do anything useful, so . . ."

Winter already wanted to smack this dithering dragon. Hailstorm was out there somewhere, alone and trapped. If fidgety Pyrite thought she was going to be the one thing standing in Winter's way, he had a tail full of spikes ready to convince her otherwise.

"It's all right, don't be nervous," Kinkajou said, her scales shifting to a warm golden color similar to Pyrite's. "Anything you can tell us would be helpful."

"Well — I suppose it's not too far away," Pyrite admitted. "If I remember right, it's southwest of the Sky Palace. Ish."

"Hmm," Qibli said. "Can you be any more specific?"

"Maybe you could help us find it," Kinkajou suggested.

"Oh dear, no," Pyrite said, stammering and shuffling backward. "I couldn't, I'm sure."

"Why are you looking for this place?" Cirrus suddenly demanded. Winter had almost forgotten he was there, but he'd somehow crept around until he could see the sketch over Pyrite's shoulder. "What do you really want?"

"It's a fair question," Riptide pointed out. "If you want Pyrite to go with you, we should all know what she's flying into."

Winter liked the way Qibli looked to him, waiting for Winter to decide whether to reveal the truth.

"We think this is where Queen Scarlet is hiding," Winter said cautiously.

Riptide sucked in a startled breath. Cirrus sank lower to the ground and hissed, his tail lashing furiously.

But Pyrite turned shining eyes to Winter. "Queen Scarlet? She's all right?" She picked up the drawing and held it close to her chest. "And you think she's here? I'll take you there if she's there."

"I'm not sure that's wise," Cirrus growled.

"Why would you get a vote?" Winter demanded. "She can help us if she wants to." He had to admit to himself that he did not love the idea of a fervent Scarlet loyalist leading them to the queen. What if she betrayed them along the way? But perhaps if they kept their true mission a secret, they could still use her.

"I can try," Pyrite said. "I mean . . . I might get us lost, but . . . I'll do my best, for Queen Scarlet. I always do my best for her. Did, I mean."

She let out a little sigh, settling her wings.

"Thank you," Winter said.

"I don't like this," Cirrus interjected. "What good could come of finding Queen Scarlet? What are you planning to do if she is there?" He suddenly gave Winter a sharp look. "Did you say *Prince* Winter?"

"Mind your own business," Winter snapped.

"It's all right, Cirrus," Pyrite said. Twisting her claws together, she gave Winter an apologetic smile. "He kind of takes care of me. He's just being protective."

Add that to the pile of weird mysteries about this IceWing, Winter thought. *Why would he be so concerned about this rather annoying SkyWing? He can't be in love with her, can he?* Cirrus didn't have anything loving about his demeanor. He didn't even seem to particularly like Pyrite; he barely glanced at her when she spoke. He certainly didn't look at her the way . . .

. . . the way I look at Moon.

Winter glanced across the clearing and finally admitted something to himself.

Or the way Qibli looks at Moon.

Did Moon look at either of them that way? He couldn't tell. It didn't matter — neither of them could be with her anyway. Not if they wanted to remain loyal to their queens and tribes.

Stop thinking about this and focus on getting Hailstorm back.

He stepped over to Pyrite and reached for the drawing in her claws. As she held it out, their talons briefly touched — and Winter felt a sudden weird shifting of the world, like something tugging apart his muscles from inside him.

He froze, staring into the SkyWing's innocent amber eyes. He'd felt something strange like this once before — at the tunnels in the rainforest, where magic had made the world not quite right.

And if he felt the same twisting of magic when he touched her talons, that could only mean one thing.

Pyrite must be an animus.

CHAPTER 12

Winter didn't have a chance to tell the others his theory about Pyrite that day; as it turned out, she was not only a very nervous dragon, but she was also extremely clingy. As soon as Cirrus and Riptide were out of sight, she attached herself to Winter's tail and followed him around as though he were made of delicious bear meat.

Why he'd been chosen for this particular honor, Winter had no idea. Kinkajou and Qibli were much nicer to Pyrite than he was, and yet she got all flappy and anxious whenever they talked to her. Maybe she was simply used to having an IceWing watch out for her.

And maybe Cirrus knows exactly what she is, Winter guessed. *Maybe that's why he's so interested in her whereabouts. Maybe he's planning to use her power for something.*

But what? What sort of sinister plans could a lone IceWing be hatching, brooding among the dwindling numbers of the Talons of Peace?

Was he planning to deliver her to the IceWings — an

animus to replace their long-lost Prince Arctic? In exchange for letting him back into the tribe?

Cirrus didn't seem to be in any hurry to get back to the Ice Kingdom, though. There must be a reason he left.

What was he up to?

It was also strange that Pyrite could possess such enormous magic and not be more sure of herself. Didn't she know she was an animus? Had she ever used her power? How often, and what had she done with it?

He glanced over his shoulder at where she was flying, barely a wingbeat behind him, casting fearful looks at the mountains below them. The first animus he'd ever met. She was not at all what he would have expected.

"So, Pyrite," Qibli said in a friendly voice, swooping up on her other side.

Pyrite jerked away from him and nearly bowled Winter out of the sky. Her wings thwacked around his snout for a moment, and once again he got that twisty, ill feeling.

He shoved her off him and righted himself. "Watch it," he snapped.

"Sorry, sorry, sorry," she mumbled. She flicked her tail at Qibli. "You *startled* me."

Qibli made a "what is wrong with this dragon?" face at Winter. "I was just wondering how you ended up with the Talons of Peace," he said. "You don't exactly seem like the type to desert your wing and strike out into the wilderness on your own, looking for a band of rebels to join."

"Oh, no," Pyrite said. "No, I'm not like that at all. I'm completely loyal. I would have kept fighting for Queen Scarlet as long as she needed me." She stretched her long neck and scanned the ground below them again, then twitched her wings to steer them a little more westward. "But when Ruby took the throne, she made everyone swear an oath to her, and I couldn't do that, you know? I'm completely loyal to Queen Scarlet. Always and always and always."

Winter noticed that Moon was frowning at Pyrite as if she were a book written in the language of narwhals. Had she also figured out that Pyrite was an animus? Could she see it in Pyrite's mind?

But if Scarlet had a "completely loyal" animus under her claws, why didn't she use her to win the war?

"So I left the Sky Palace and joined the Talons of Peace." Pyrite sighed. "Sometimes I have dreams about Queen Scarlet telling me to come to her. But Cirrus always says to ignore them. He says it isn't safe for me to go flapping around the continent looking for a dragon in exile, and that dreams don't mean anything." She smiled hopefully at Winter. "But this isn't a wild-scavenger chase. You really think she'll be there, right?"

"I do," Winter said, suddenly wondering if this was a terrible idea. Bringing Queen Scarlet a pet animus? How many ways could that go horribly wrong?

Would Pyrite get in the way if they tried to save Hailstorm? What would she do if she knew that was their goal?

They stopped to rest for the night in a valley dappled with clumps of small white flowers that made it look as though someone had been tossing down snowballs from the peaks around them. Qibli started a fire and cooked the squirrels Moon caught, while Winter got himself a fish from the stream and ate it raw. He couldn't quite understand why anyone would want to scorch up their food before eating it, although it still sounded more appetizing than the wild cherries and plums Kinkajou had for dinner.

Pyrite picked halfheartedly at her squirrel, her scales glowing in the firelight. Every time Winter looked over at her, he was sure she'd edged a little closer to him. She didn't say much and barely seemed to be listening to Qibli as he told the story of the dragonets defeating Burn and Blister and giving the SandWing throne to Queen Thorn. He'd been there and seen the whole thing, and he was a compelling storyteller, too. Moon and Kinkajou were rapt, although they must have heard it all before.

Finally everyone curled up to sleep, including Pyrite. Winter volunteered to keep the first watch, which was a concept that seemed to endlessly puzzle Kinkajou. Why did anyone have to stand guard, she'd asked the first night. Who would attack sleeping dragons? What did they have to fear, now that the war was over? And other such inane, typically RainWing-type questions.

Darkness lay quietly over the valley. One of the moons was a sharp crescent just over the peaks, while the other two were a little more full and higher in the sky. Winter waited until Pyrite's breathing was slow and steady, and then he carefully eased himself around the others to gently nudge Moon.

She stretched her front talons and made a soft noise in her sleep, curling farther into her wings. He felt an almost unbearable longing to press himself against her scales and fall asleep with her star-speckled wings over his.

"Moon," Winter whispered, shaking her shoulder again.

At last she opened her eyes and sat up, yawning. "What's wrong?" she whispered.

"Is Pyrite truly asleep?" he asked as softly as he could.

She listened for a moment, then nodded. Winter beckoned for her to follow him out of earshot of the others, to be safe. They stopped below a tree wrapped in blooming vines of moonflowers, pale ghost petals shivering in the breeze.

"I think Pyrite is an animus," Winter said, coming straight to the point because he was afraid of what else he might say to Moon alone in the dark.

"Oh . . . that's interesting," Moon said. "If she is, she doesn't know it, or she never thinks about it. Wouldn't that be strange? To know you have the most powerful magic in Pyrrhia and not think about it once all day? I'd imagine an animus would constantly be thinking, 'I could just enchant this one thing and it would make my life easier.' And, 'but what if I go too far and lose my soul? Is this one thing worth it?' All day, I would think, it would go back and forth.

Maybe that's just what my brain would do, though. In any case, I didn't hear anything like that in Pyrite's head."

"What do you think of her?" Winter asked.

"Well . . . I feel sorry for her," Moon said. She ran one claw lightly down the vine-wrapped trunk of the tree. "Her brain is very odd. It's like her thoughts are stuck in a circle. I don't know if she's been hit on the head really hard or something, but they just go round and around: *I'm completely loyal to Queen Scarlet. I'm not very good at anything. I'm glad I'm a SkyWing. I'm clumsy and not very bright and generally useless.* And then back to, *I'm completely loyal to Queen Scarlet.*"

"Maybe she *isn't* very bright," Winter suggested.

"Or she's worried about the same things so much for so long that her thoughts have worn grooves in her mind, where they keep spinning and spinning," Moon said. "I don't know. I haven't read anyone like her before. It's very . . . okay, this sounds weird, but it's very shallow in there."

"Really," Winter said. "You've been surrounded by RainWings but never met anyone shallow before?"

Moon poked him with her tail. "That is a really narrow-minded view of RainWings," she said. "You must have noticed that Kinkajou and Glory are anything but shallow." She paused, then added with a small laugh, "Well, all right, there's Coconut. I suppose he isn't much deeper than Pyrite. But it still feels unusually weird in her head."

"Maybe because she's an animus," Winter said. "Maybe she's using some kind of magic to hide her power from other dragons."

A flurry of snowy petals swirled down from the tree and over their wings. Moon shivered. "That makes her sound very ominous," she said.

"That's exactly what I'm worried about." Winter reached out and brushed a petal off Moon's shoulder. "What if she's a lot more dangerous than she seems? What if she can hide even from you? How can we trust her?"

They both turned to look back at the slumbering shapes beside the fading embers of the campfire.

"Beware one who is not what she seems," Moon whispered, sending a trail of ice along Winter's wings. "Could that be Pyrite?"

"We need her help, though," Winter said gruffly. "It's not like we can just fly off and ditch her." He was starting to wish they could, though.

"I guess we just have to be careful," Moon said softly. She tilted her head to the side. "We should tell Qibli and see what he thinks."

"I'll tell him," Winter said, hoping he didn't sound as ungracious as he felt. It was true it would be smart to get the observant SandWing on the case, keeping an eye on Pyrite. But he found himself picturing Qibli standing here, under this tree with Moon, and it made him feel hollowed out, like an ice cave. "When I wake him for the next watch. You can go back to sleep."

"All right," Moon said. She hesitated, then took a step closer to Winter so that their wings were nearly touching. He felt his breath catch in his throat. She was made for moonlight, all silver and ebony, or moonlight was made for her. He could imagine her in the Ice Kingdom, silhouetted against the vast whiteness, dark as the ocean and glittering like the moonlit snow.

Except if she set one talon in the Ice Kingdom, someone would probably kill her, or at the very least throw her into Glacier's dungeon, where the cold would take care of her just as thoroughly.

And his family would do the same, no matter where she was, if they had any idea how Winter felt about her.

He would never let that happen.

"Go on, sleep," he said, his voice coming out rougher than he meant it to. "We might need you to find Scarlet tomorrow."

She dropped her gaze. "Thank you for telling me about Pyrite," she said. "Good night."

And then she was gone.

Winter took the second watch as well, knowing sleep would be a long time coming for him tonight.

CHAPTER 13

Qibli was the first to spot the eye-shaped spire in the distance, early in the afternoon the next day. Gray clouds had rolled in, covering the sky in soggy blankets and threatening to rain at any moment. Winter's wings felt like giant seal flippers hanging off his back, heavy and ponderous. He had barely slept, and his eyelids wanted nothing more than to slam shut and drag him into slumber.

But when Qibli called, "Over there! I think I see it!" a burst of energy jittered through Winter's muscles. He soared over to Qibli's side and squinted in the direction the SandWing was pointing.

"I don't see anything," Kinkajou said.

"That's because you're a RainWing," said Pyrite. "*I* see it. SkyWings can see much better and farther than you do."

So can IceWings, Winter wanted to add, but he didn't want to sound anything like Pyrite.

"I don't see it yet either," Moon said to Kinkajou. "But if it's over there, let's go!" She put on a burst of speed and shot ahead of the others.

"Race you to that peak!" Kinkajou yelled, zipping past her.

The two of them swooped away, their laughter echoing back off the mountains. Kinkajou's scales were dappled gold and silver today, like some metallic treasure version of a dragon. She'd chatted happily with Pyrite over breakfast, and Winter had felt a pang of guilt that he hadn't woken her up to hear his theory, too. Were RainWings even capable of regarding other dragons with suspicion?

"Terribly undignified," Qibli said in a haughty voice, tipping his snout at the racing dragons. "We would never allow such higgledy-piggledy shenanigans in the Ice Kingdom."

"Was that supposed to be me?" Winter asked him. "Terribly unimpressive, if so. I haven't once said 'higgledy-piggledy' in my entire life. We would never allow such linguistic imprecision in the Ice Kingdom."

Qibli barked a delighted laugh and did a loop in the air.

In their shadowy conversation last night, Qibli hadn't quite believed that Pyrite could be an animus. He'd pointed out that SkyWings hadn't had one in centuries, possibly as long as the IceWings — which was something Winter should have remembered for himself.

But he had agreed that there was something not quite right about the skittish SkyWing. Winter found himself oddly comforted by the idea that Qibli was watching her. If anyone could figure out Pyrite's secrets and strangeness, it was probably Qibli.

I wonder if this is how MudWings feel, working in teams all the time. He'd read about the MudWing sibling bond, and how they lived and fought and died together. *Father said it made them weak because a MudWing warrior would listen to his brothers and sisters instead of his commander. Mother said they'd always be worrying about what might happen to the soldier next to them, instead of focusing on the battle. That's why it should be easy to defeat the MudWings, they said.*

But it hadn't been that easy, as many, many battles had taught them over the years of the Great War.

Maybe I'd rather have allies like Qibli and Moon, making their own decisions and trusting each other, than a commander telling me what to do, Winter thought. Was that treasonous? Did it make him less of an IceWing?

If he kept having thoughts like these, would he be completely ruined by the time he got home?

They reached the spire not long after that and found the jagged mountain wall that matched Moon's drawing. It overlooked a hidden valley where the three waterfalls turned into rivers that led into a crystal-blue lake. The lake bent and squiggled around the edges like a new-hatched dragonet's drawing of a circle. Winter and the others landed on the northern shore, staring up at the eye-shaped rock formation far overhead.

"I don't like it here," Kinkajou said at once. She shivered, flicking her tail and turning a sort of pale jade green. "It feels like we're being watched. I mean, as if the mountains themselves are watching us."

"And the rivers are whispering about us," Qibli said. Kinkajou thwacked him with one of her wings and he jumped back, looking injured. "I was *agreeing* with you!" he yelped.

"Oh. Well, try to sound less sarcastic next time," Kinkajou scolded. "My point is, it's creepy here."

Moon glanced around to make sure Pyrite wasn't listening. The SkyWing had waded into the lake and was scanning the sky and trees hopefully. "Sounds like the perfect place for Scarlet to hide," she whispered.

A sudden flutter of wings made them all spin around, but it was only a group of crows taking flight from a nearby tree. *A murder of crows,* Winter thought with a shiver.

"There's something over there," Pyrite said, waving her tail toward the far side of the lake.

They hopped over the water, following her, and found what appeared to be the wreckage of a rough structure. Long branches stripped of their leaves were scattered across the ground, and vines still tied in knots lay in crushed piles, as if they had been trampled by angry talons. The entire mess was covered in ripped-up flower petals, rose and violet and daffodil-yellow shredded scraps everywhere. The only remaining intact piece was a canopy woven from vines that tilted lopsidedly in the tree overhead.

"Yikes," Kinkajou said. "Someone was not pleased about something."

Winter glanced over at Moon, for the nine thousandth time that day, and found her frowning up at the ridge that loomed over them.

"What is it?" he asked her.

"Just a feeling," she said, letting a shiver run out to her wingtips. "I don't know, exactly."

"I do know," said Kinkajou. "Creepy, being-watched feeling, as I have already mentioned."

Pyrite let out a gasp and pounced on a stack of broken twigs. Caught on the point of one of them was a dark orange scale.

"It's Scarlet's!" she cried. "I know it is. I'd recognize her color anywhere." She looked around desperately. "But where is she? What happened here? Did something terrible happen to her?"

"There's no sign of violence," Qibli said, moving one of the branches aside to look underneath. "No blood, no claw marks on the surrounding trees. It looks more like she destroyed her shelter in a temper and left."

"Perhaps she somehow found out we were coming," Winter said. Dread crept slowly under his claws and up along his spine.

"What? How would she know that?" Kinkajou said in alarm.

Winter, Qibli, and Moon all looked at Pyrite. The orangey-yellow SkyWing was overturning bits of foliage and scraping through the moss as though she expected to find Scarlet buried in it somewhere. Preoccupied with muttering and hissing and grumbling, she didn't notice their attention on her.

"Pyrite," Qibli said. "Did you happen to see Queen Scarlet in your dream last night?"

She glanced at him and shook her head doubtfully. "I don't think so. I don't really remember. I think I had a weird dream about snow, maybe? But that happens whenever I sleep near Cirrus, too."

"It's still possible," Moon said. "Even if she doesn't remember it. Scarlet could have interrogated her in her dream and found out what she was doing and where she was going."

"It doesn't matter," Winter said. "What matters is that Scarlet's gone and so is Hailstorm." He ripped a large branch off the nearest tree and hurled it into the forest. *Gone* — their one chance of finding his brother. Scarlet could have taken him anywhere in Pyrrhia by now.

Or she could have killed him, if she figured out that Winter was not, in fact, in the rainforest trying to assassinate Glory for her.

It was strange to Winter that Hailstorm's death could still hurt *so much* every time it happened. He would have thought the first time would be the worst — the night a spy had burst into the royal dining room, shouting that all of Scarlet's IceWing prisoners were dead. "The NightWings killed them all!" he'd shrieked. It made no sense — why would NightWings enter SkyWing territory to kill prisoners? But it felt true nonetheless, like something NightWings *would* do.

If they could have attacked the Night Kingdom that very moment — if they'd known where it was — they would have. All the IceWings in Queen Glacier's domain would have risen up to avenge their murdered comrades.

Winter's parents hadn't spoken to him for a month after that report, and he didn't blame them. He didn't want to speak to himself either; he couldn't bear to see his own pathetic face in the icy reflections everywhere. Until then, there'd been hope that they could still negotiate Hailstorm's release or carry out a rescue plan.

But there was no hope. He was gone, as dead as all the other lost IceWings.

And now Winter had the same crumbling feeling inside, except instead of a snowdrift caving in, this was a whole avalanche cascading heavily down into his bones. This time it was even more his fault. He had failed his brother and then failed him again and again and again.

"Stop, *stop* it," Qibli said, suddenly in front of Winter, taking his shoulders and shaking him. "I see you going to the giving-up place in your head. Get yourself out of there right now. We do not know he's dead any more than we did an hour ago. What we have to do is keep searching, because he's only definitely dead if we give up and sit here like moping camels. You are not allowed to mourn until you see a dead body, do you understand me?"

"What else am I supposed to do?" Winter snarled. "What's your next brilliant idea? How can he still be alive?"

"Who are we talking about?" Pyrite asked, wrinkling her snout. "What he? I'm confused."

"We split up and search the whole valley," Qibli said, ignoring her. "I'll go with Kinkajou and you go with Moon. Look for clues about how long Scarlet was here and where she might have gone. Look for a cave or something else that could have been used as a prison. Figure out where and how she actually kept him and see if we can guess how she's transporting him. Were there other SkyWings helping her? Or how else was he guarded? Is she traveling in a group? With a chained IceWing behind her? Because that's going to be a little obvious, don't you think? Look for messages she might have left behind. Look for *anything* that will actually tell us *something*."

Winter stared at him, breathing so hard his tail spikes were rattling. Qibli stared back, deadly serious.

What kind of moons-dazzled dragon would do all this for a stranger from a different tribe? Why hasn't he given up? Why isn't he letting me *give up, when it means he could go back to Jade Mountain and carry on with his life?*

"Come on, Kinkajou," Qibli said, flicking his tail at her. "We'll take the valley south of the lake; the rest of you go north."

"You bet," Kinkajou said with ridiculous enthusiasm.

He's letting me go with Moon, Winter realized. *On purpose, even though he wants to be with her as badly as I do. But he knows — or he hopes — that searching with her will keep me going.*

Am I that obvious?

"I'll go with Winter," Pyrite declared. "Not that anyone asked. But. I figure. That's ok, right? Although . . . what are we looking for?"

"Signs of Scarlet being here," Winter told her. "Anything that looks like the detritus of dragons."

She accepted this with a puzzled shrug.

He led the way back over the lake and they started into the woods, methodically covering every square of ground all the way back to the mountain cliff ahead. Winter's eyes raked the dirt and trees and shrubs and streams and all the small corners around them.

"Can you hear anyone?" he whispered to Moon when Pyrite was out of earshot.

She shook her head. "Only Pyrite. Sorry, Winter."

Qibli had a point, though. Where had Scarlet been keeping Hailstorm for the last two years? Was he guarded? Chained up? Had he been moved here from somewhere else? Who had fed him and kept him alive while she was trapped in Burn's stronghold? How did she keep him from trying to escape?

The brother Winter knew would have fought tooth and claw to be free. If he'd been imprisoned anywhere near here, there should be clues — claw marks scored along the walls of a cave, or a tree with indentations of chains crushed into its trunk.

Or most likely of all, something Hailstorm had used his frostbreath on. They should look for signs of something that had been frozen.

But there was nothing. They spent the rest of the daylight searching, with no success. The only sign of life in the whole valley was Scarlet's scale in the destroyed structure. Otherwise, the grass waved peacefully, and the trees quietly filled with fruit, and it seemed as though no talons had ever disturbed the stillness.

Winter couldn't imagine a prison here anywhere. There were no suitable caves for keeping prisoners in — at least not close to the valley floor.

"Perhaps Hailstorm's prison is higher up in the mountains," Winter speculated around their campfire that night. He was keeping his distance from the flames; the heat made his scales feel all melty and sticky.

"We'll search up there tomorrow," Moon said. "We'll find something." She shivered. "It's so quiet out here."

Winter actually found it distractingly noisy, compared to the Ice Kingdom. For one thing, it sounded like two rival cricket symphonies were competing at top volume. The owls were hooting so much it was a wonder they had time to fit prey in their mouths as well. Things flapped overhead and small splashes came from the lake. The night felt extremely *populated*.

Then it occurred to him that Moon might be talking about the noise *inside* her head. With all of them wearing sky-fire, the only voice she could hear in there was Pyrite's, presumably still treading in its odd boring circle.

That must be strange for her, he realized. *To give that all up and trust us with her secret . . . would any other NightWing do that? Would any other dragon in Pyrrhia do that?*

He wanted to believe that he would — that if he had the power to read minds, he'd tell other dragons right away instead of invading their minds in secret. But would he really? With a rare weapon like that, wouldn't he be tempted to use it?

That night he let Moon take the first watch. All he wanted to do was turn off the world and his brain for a while. He gazed up at the shadowy, hulking forms of the mountains as sleep drifted through him, slowly leading him into odd half dreams about his brother in a cave up there, watching the valley below for two lonely years.

He wasn't sure how much time had passed, wandering through a half-seen labyrinth of stone passages, when he turned a corner and suddenly the dream sharpened around the edges.

An orange dragon stood before him, wearing veils of dark smoke that poured from her snout and from the fire beside her. Blood and ice dripped across her face and wings, until she shifted, and he realized it was only rubies and diamonds embedded in her scales, catching the firelight.

She pinned him with her yellow gaze, sharp as talons.

"Tell me who you are," she ordered.

"Don't you know?" he asked. "I know who you are."

"Very flattering," she said in a slithering voice. "So perhaps then you can also gather why I am not pleased to see you." She took a step toward him, and the dream-cave trembled around them. Something wavered across her face, like a mask slipping to reveal a glimpse of another, disfigured face underneath. "You're a long way from the rainforest, prince of ice. There's no one who needs killing around where you are now."

He was silent for a beat too long, and she began to laugh. "Oh, you mean me?" she said. "Is that your clever plan? Find the most deadly queen in Pyrrhia, kill her, and take back your brother?" She leaned toward Winter, every muscle taut with glee. "Even if you could kill me, you would never find your lost IceWing. *Never.* The prison I've got him in is far too clever for that."

"Where is he?" Winter demanded. "Is he all right?"

"He *was* all right," she said, her face twisted in a strange smirk of triumph and fury. "But he won't be after this conversation. I gave your sister one last chance. She swore to me that *you* would kill Glory — and yet, here you are, and I know that backstabbing, face-melting queen still lives." Queen Scarlet sighed hugely and shook her head with a mockingly disappointed expression. "I suppose if I want more dragons dead, I'll just have to kill someone myself. And let's see, who do I have right in my clutches . . ."

"Don't kill him!" Winter cried. "What else do you want? Queen Glacier's treasury is vast — she would pay you his weight in diamonds for his safe return."

Scarlet snorted. "What use are diamonds to me? If I want something, I don't pay for it; I *take* it. And right now, groveling prince, I only want two things: my throne back — and vengeance."

Her eyes narrowed to slits and her tail lashed dangerously. "Here's some interesting information for you. Your queen doesn't want her nephew back as badly as you think. I visited her dreams with a proposal: help me drag my conniving daughter off *my* throne, and she could have him. Would you believe she turned me down? She said he'd been mourned already, and her duty was to the yet-unlost lives of her subjects. Doesn't that make you furious, ice dragon?"

Winter stared down at his claws. Was Scarlet lying? Had she really tried to negotiate with Queen Glacier? And had his queen decided to leave Hailstorm to die?

He realized he could believe it. The IceWings had just survived twenty years of war over another tribe's throne — and with nothing to show for it except too many dead warriors. Queen Glacier would not be eager to plunge them back into another conflict, especially on behalf of a dragon she couldn't trust and wouldn't want to see in charge of the Sky Kingdom again anyway.

"So you're his only hope," Scarlet taunted him. "Or at least, you *were*. It's all over now, though. I can see that you're far too useless to kill anyone for me. My only remaining pleasure is watching your face as I tell you your brother will be dead by morning."

Winter's head jerked up. *Wait* —

He backed away from Scarlet, blinking rapidly. *I have to wake up.* He dug his claws ferociously into one shoulder, but felt nothing. The dream-cave still held him, and Scarlet's yellow eyes watched with menacing amusement.

"Perhaps you'd like to hear *how* I plan to kill him," she mused. "I could slowly burn him to death. That would be lengthy and painful."

Winter turned and stumbled out of the cave. Was there a way out through the passages? He tried to visualize snapping awake. Opening his eyes. Sitting up and finding himself in the valley.

It wasn't working. Scarlet's mocking laugh followed him through the narrow maze, echoing off smooth stone walls that all looked the same.

"Maybe I'll gouge out his eyes first!" she called. "Maybe I'll stuff live goats into his throat until he suffocates!"

Winter stopped running and fumbled for his ankle. He felt the weight of the skyfire pouch there, solid and heavy.

"Don't you want to beg?" Scarlet shrieked. "Don't you

want to offer to do *anything* for me? What if I told you to kill the RainWing who's with you? What else could you throw at my feet, desperate prince?"

With trembling claws he ripped at the cord binding the pouch to his scales. Finally he yanked it free and dropped it on the ground.

MOON! he yelled in his mind. *Wake me up! Wake me up RIGHT NOW!*

Barely a moment later, he felt talons on his shoulders, shaking and shaking him until finally the dream world tore away like wet paper, and he was sitting up on the grass, eyes popping open, wide-awake.

Moon let go of him and took a shaky breath. "Are you all right?" she whispered. Behind her was Qibli, rubbing his eyes sleepily.

They all looked down at the skyfire pouch. Winter had really managed to tear it off in his sleep, and now it lay between them . . . leaving Winter's mind exposed.

Moon immediately picked it up and handed it to him. "Tell me what happened," she said.

"Queen Scarlet was in my dream," Winter said, tying the pouch back on.

"Well, no wonder," Qibli said. "You've been thinking about her all day."

"No," Winter said. "I mean, it was really her. *Dream-visiting me.*"

They both got it at the same moment.

"That means she's seen you," Qibli said, completely awake now. His tail curled up into attack position. "In order to visit your dream, she must have seen you. *Today*, or she would have done it sooner."

"Scarlet saw you today," Moon echoed. She jumped to her feet, turning in a circle. "In this valley. Where we are right now."

"Exactly," Winter said. "Which means . . . Scarlet is somewhere close by."

── CHAPTER 14 ──

A breeze whipped through the trees, hurtling wet droplets over their wings. The low embers of the fire made a hissing sound, and Pyrite shifted in her sleep with a grunt.

"Scarlet is close enough to watch this valley," Moon said again. "Kinkajou was right; we *were* being spied on."

"She said my brother will die in the morning," Winter said. He took a deep breath, trying to shut up his hammering heart. "She said now that she's seen me, she knows I'm not going to kill anyone for her." *How could she tell, just by looking at me?*

"That's a *good* thing, that you're not that kind of dragon," Moon reminded him, nudging his side.

"Did you see any clues?" Qibli asked. "About where she is now?"

Winter shook his head. "We were in a cave, in my dream. It looked like any other cave, underground or in a mountain somewhere. Except . . . at one point, her face seemed to change in front of me, and the face I saw underneath — apart from being horrible — it looked like it was lit by moonlight."

Qibli looked up at the sky, his black eyes darting from the moons to the peaks. "Half the mountain range is in shadow right now," he said. "We fly to the other side and search. Everywhere in view of this valley. We go now."

Moon took a step toward Kinkajou, and Winter reached out to stop her. The RainWing slept peacefully, a half smile on her face, her scales dappled in silver splotches like the moonlight that fell through the leaves and across her wings.

"This is what your queen said not to do," Winter reminded Moon in a low whisper. "We're going to confront Scarlet. She could rip Kinkajou apart in a heartbeat. Glory would want her to stay out of it — and you too."

"I'm *not* staying out of it," Moon said fiercely. "You need me if you're going to find her. I'm not going to hide. I don't do that anymore."

"Then keep at least half your promise to your queen," Winter said. "Leave Kinkajou asleep and safe."

"He's right," Qibli said. "Glory would definitely not want you both marching off to find Scarlet."

Moon blew out a breath that ruffled the tree branches around them. "She's going to *kill* me," she whispered, glancing back at her sleeping friend.

"Better that than Scarlet killing her," Winter pointed out.

"All right," Moon said. She shook her head. "All right. Let's go."

Winter was in the sky by the end of her sentence, winging toward the eye-shaped rock formation. From there they could sweep south and around the circumference of the valley, checking the mountain crags and crannies. It was a lot of distance to cover, and perhaps Scarlet had flown off as soon as she saw him, ending up hundreds of miles away by now.

But now that he'd seen her thirst for vengeance firsthand, he had a strong suspicion she was still nearby. She'd want to watch Winter's despair the next morning, and whatever panicked action he took next.

So if she was close — and if Moon could catch Scarlet's mind — maybe they had a chance to stop her while Hailstorm was still alive.

If he even is still alive, and she isn't just torturing us.

"Let Moon go first," Qibli said, soaring up beside him. "No offense, but you're glowing like a fourth moon up here, and I'm not exactly the most shadowy dragon myself. She's practically invisible in the night sky. That's kind of the point of her whole tribe, after all."

Winter twisted around and had to admit to himself that Qibli was right. It took him a minute to even see Moon behind him; she faded perfectly into the dark, and her silver scales looked exactly like distant stars.

But *he* wanted to lead the way. *He* wanted to find Scarlet first and sink his claws into her neck. *He* wanted to be the one who rescued Hailstorm, the hero who brought him back, the dragon who surpassed all his parents' expectations.

His wings wavered in the air. His luminous, treacherous

wings, which reflected the moonlight to anyone below who might chance to look up.

This is not about your place in the rankings. It's not about what Mother and Father and the queen think of you.

It's about saving Hailstorm.

He fell back, lifting up into the cloud cover. The dense, rain-soaked clouds around him made it hard to see the land below, but they would also hide his gleaming blue-white scales from anyone watching.

Moon shot out ahead, sweeping low over the mountain ridge. Her head tilted from side to side, listening, and she flew in long glides, keeping her wingbeats quiet and spaced apart. Qibli and Winter followed, imitating her.

The folded, crooked peaks whooshed silently past below them.

Winter felt the minutes ticking by with awful urgency. What if Scarlet guessed they were coming and left? What if she killed Hailstorm now instead of waiting until morning? How soon was morning? Was the sky getting lighter in the east?

He remembered her awful yellow eyes fixed on his. He tried to remember his brother's eyes instead. Bluer than Winter's or Icicle's. Crinkled around the edges when he grinned, which was all the time, because Hailstorm was the only IceWing Winter had ever met who could laugh about what other dragons thought of him.

Of course, it must be a lot easier to laugh from the top of the rankings.

He'd never forgotten Hailstorm's last words to him. Had he truly meant them? Had he always been disappointed in his little brother?

Would he feel differently if Winter came flying in to rescue him?

Moon suddenly checked herself, flaring her wings to come to a stop in midair. Winter and Qibli did the same, farther up in the clouds. Winter's heart was thudding so loud he thought they must be able to hear it in Glacier's palace.

He scanned the area — a stretch of rocky slope leading up to a peak, where several flat ledges and outcroppings directly overlooked the valley. From here he could see the dim flicker of the fire they'd left behind, although Kinkajou's and Pyrite's sleeping shapes were obscured by the tree cover. But if Scarlet had watched from up here all day, she would have clearly seen Winter traversing the open spaces below. Clearly enough to guess who he was and then walk straight into his dreams.

Moon beckoned them down to her and they all dove under a narrow shelf of rock that hid them from the ridge above.

"She's up there," Moon whispered. "Her and someone else."

"Hailstorm?" Winter clenched his talons, holding in the wild prickles of energy that were stabbing through his scales.

"I don't think so," Moon said. "It doesn't have the bright glare of an IceWing mind, although it feels a little familiar. I can't actually read it — like there's a wall of humming between me and it."

"Someone with skyfire?" Qibli asked.

She shook her head. "A bit like that, but not exactly the same. It might just be the distance. They're near the top of this mountain." She put one talon over Winter's suddenly, making a *shh* gesture.

Winter forced himself to sit in silence as she listened.

"They're arguing," Moon said. "Scarlet's mind is loud and angry and all over the place. I think we can get closer without her noticing."

"Lead the way," Qibli said.

She flowed silently over the ledge above them and began creeping up the hill, vanishing almost instantly into the night-shrouded undergrowth. Winter hurried after her, trying to be as quiet as she was. It was almost impossible; his talons were shaking with impatience and tension.

Halfway up the slope he began to hear voices.

"I absolutely hate these narrow-nosed IceWings," spat a voice that was unmistakably Scarlet's. "This one was worse than his sister! He barely groveled at all. I don't think he ever had any *intention* of murdering anyone for me! The nerve!"

"You couldn't convince him otherwise?" said a second voice. "Usually you are very . . . convincing."

"He was obviously a lost cause," Scarlet said with a snarl. "Kept making this hero face at me, like *I'm* the bad guy and he's coming to right all the wrongs. *Excuse me*, who got attacked by her own artwork and then kidnapped by her ally and then blackmailed by her champion midrescue while meanwhile her own daughter was stealing her throne? Who's the one with the hideous face-maiming? Whose throne is currently OCCUPIED by a PRETENDER who could NEVER have beaten me in a challenge before? WHO had her whole life RUINED and demolished and shattered by those STUPID HORRIBLE DRAGONETS?"

There was a pause, but before the other dragon could answer, Scarlet shouted, "ME, THAT'S WHO! *I'm* the victim here! Someone should be all heroically trying to help ME right all the wrongs! Where's *my* rotten cavalry of loyal idiots?"

"Well . . . you have me," said the voice, with a notable lack of enthusiasm.

"You barely count," said Scarlet. "You're weird. And unreliable."

"Ahem," the voice bristled. "I believe my talents have proven to be *very* useful to you."

"Not as useful as if you were a proper animus," Scarlet grumbled. "One limited power is not going to get me back my throne."

An animus? Winter thought. *Like Pyrite? Does Scarlet have two animus dragons loyal to her?*

By now they had crept close enough that Winter could see small spurts of flame coming from Scarlet's snout. She was pacing on a moonlit ledge, while her companion stood in the shadow of the mountain, hidden from view.

Moon tugged him behind a tangle of boulders and shrubs. He crouched beside her and Qibli crept up on her other side. Moon carefully spread her black wings over them, hiding as much of their pale scales as she could. Her wing across Winter's back was warm, like a polar bear fur wrapped around your shoulders after a swim in the arctic ocean.

"You are welcome to dismiss me from your service," said the stranger in a cold voice. "Once you have paid me everything I am owed, of course."

Scarlet growled low in her throat. "What do I do now?" she demanded. "I have this IceWing pawn who should be thrillingly useful, and it turns out *nobody* will do what it takes to get him back. ALL I AM ASKING FOR IS A LITTLE VENGEANCE. Is that so much to expect?"

"Perhaps a new strategy is in order," said the stranger drily.

Scarlet let out a huffy sigh. "I suppose I do have to kill him," she said. "Now that I've promised to about eight times. It will serve all of them right. Or maybe it won't, since nobody even seems to care enough to commit just a LITTLE murder for me. THREE MOONS."

She fumed in silence for a few minutes. Smoke curled from her nostrils up to the sky.

"So?" the stranger said after a while. "Are you prepared to kill the prisoner?"

Scarlet flung a rock off the edge and watched it bounce and clatter down the hill. Winter held his breath, pressing closer to Moon's side. She hooked her front claws in the bush in front of them and leaned forward, eyes closed, head tilted toward the arguing dragons.

"Yes," Scarlet said. "Very well. Bring me Pyrite."

— CHAPTER 15 —

Moon's eyes flew open and her bewildered gaze met Winter's.

Pyrite???

What does she have to do with Hailstorm?

Did she do something to him? Does she know where he is?

If she does, we have to get to her first.

Winter started to scramble to his feet, but Moon pushed him back down with her wing, pointing up at the ledge.

A moment later, a dragon leaped off it and spiraled up into the sky, banking toward the valley. Winter only caught a glimpse of his scales as the firelight flickered over them, but he was sure of what he saw.

Scarlet's ally was a NightWing.

"Who is that?" he demanded.

"I have no idea," Moon whispered back. "But if he's a NightWing, maybe that's why I can't hear him think. Maybe he's been trained to shield from mind readers or something."

"We have to get to Pyrite before he does," Qibli whispered from Moon's other side.

He was right. They didn't have time for the mystery of a NightWing who worked for a deposed SkyWing queen. Winter slid out from under Moon's wing and started crawling back down the mountainside as fast as he could, looking for a spot where he could take off without Scarlet seeing him. Pebbles bounced past him as Qibli and Moon followed.

"Now," Moon breathed suddenly. She launched herself off the mountain and Winter hurtled after her. He arrowed down toward their camp, his eyes fixed on that small flicker of firelight.

"The NightWing won't go straight there," Qibli panted behind him. "He'll want to sneak up and take Pyrite while the rest of us are sleeping. He'll land and approach the camp quietly. We'll get there first."

"Only if you shut up and fly," Winter growled.

Qibli didn't say another word as they shot down the cliffs and over the trees. Winter plunged through the leaves and landed with a skidding crash beside Kinkajou.

"Yikes!" the RainWing yelped, leaping to her feet.

For a wild, breathless moment Winter thought Pyrite was gone. But then she sat up on the other side of the fire, rubbing her face.

"What's all the noise?" she mumbled.

"Yeah, really," Kinkajou said, flaring the ruff behind her ears. "Is someone on fire? Why are you smashing around waking up perfectly happy sleeping dragons? YEEP!" she cried as Moon and Qibli came thudding down behind Winter, trailing broken branches, with leaves and twigs caught in their wings and tails.

"You!" Winter leaped over the fire and bowled Pyrite to the ground. She screamed, flapped her wings at him, and tried to wriggle away, but he leaned all his weight on her back and pinned her down with his deadly IceWing claws. Even though she was bigger than him, she stopped resisting quickly. Her talons twitched in the grass and she twisted her neck to look back at him.

"This is mean," she protested.

"What do you know about my brother?" he demanded.

"Nothing at all," she said. "Now can I get up?"

"You know *something*," he said in a low, dangerous voice. "He's an IceWing named Hailstorm. A couple of years older than me. The bravest dragon in Pyrrhia. Scarlet's prisoner for the last two years." He shook her roughly. "You know where he is!"

"All right, all right!" she whined. "But you don't have to attack me; I would have told you if you just asked! Queen Scarlet's prisoners are kept in an arena in the Sky Palace. I can draw you a map of the place if you want. I don't think there are any IceWings there anymore, though. And Ruby traded back almost all the prisoners of war."

Frustration surged through Winter and he dug his claws in just a little, making Pyrite wince. Across the fire, Kinkajou was watching them with wide, bewildered eyes.

"Don't toy with me, SkyWing," Winter hissed. "Scarlet needs you in order to kill Hailstorm. So why is that? Where is he? Did you use your magic on him?"

"What *magic*?" Pyrite protested. "I don't have any magic! I never did anything special for Queen Scarlet!"

"Winter, I think she's telling the truth," Moon said. She had her front talons pressed to her head and an expression of pain scrawled across her face. "She has no idea what you're talking about."

"What she said!" Pyrite yelped. "No idea!"

"She's blocking you somehow," Winter said furiously. "She *is* magic, I can *feel* it." With the SkyWing pinioned below him, the muscle-wringing sensation of powerful animus magic was beating through him stronger than ever. He glared down at the dragon and spotted the necklace tangled around her neck. "Maybe with her necklace — maybe she enchanted it to hide her mind from you." He reached for the chain.

"Don't touch that!" roared Pyrite, surging to her feet and throwing him off with sudden powerful violence.

Winter was flung straight into the fire. The burning embers sizzled against his scales and back talons, and he leaped away with a howl of pain.

It took a moment for his head to clear, but when it did he saw two shapes grappling through the smoke of the scattered fire. Qibli's tail was poised like a scorpion's as he wrestled Pyrite. Her arms were longer than his and her claws slashed at his underbelly while her wings beat him away from her.

The SkyWing's teeth were bared and her face was a grimace of fury and determination.

Winter's burns were sending fiery bolts of pain along all the nerves in his body, but he staggered forward to help Qibli.

And then Kinkajou shrieked, and a black dragon was suddenly there, appearing from the shadows. He pounced on Kinkajou, striking her three times with swift brutality and then slamming her out of the way with a powerful blow from his tail. The little RainWing was thrown into a tree trunk with a sickening *crack*. She crumpled to the ground, her scales fading to white.

"Kinkajou!" Moon cried. The black dragon turned on her and she roared a jet of blazing fire straight at his face. He reared back, covering his eyes, and she leaped at him, slashing furiously at his wings and neck. A bright gash of red appeared along his throat and he roared, seizing Moon's talons. Blisters were starting to bubble along the edges of his mouth and nose and he kept shaking his head as though it was hard to see, but he was strong and huge, and he flung Moon to the ground with ease.

Winter didn't remember choosing, although there must have been a moment when his head said, "Go after Pyrite; she's the key to finding Hailstorm," while his heart shouted, "No, *help Moon*!" But as far as he could tell, there was no conscious thought involved. He was just there, barreling into the NightWing before the monster could stamp his sharp talons down on Moon's neck.

The two of them rolled across the clearing, black and white scales clashing, both of them roaring at full blast. Winter felt metal tangle and clatter around his claws; the NightWing was wearing a mess of dark jewelry and things that felt like compact iron boxes on chains as they smacked into Winter's jaws and knuckles.

He ducked his head as the NightWing shot a burst of flames past his ear. The ice was rising in his throat. He twisted to bring his mouth up to the NightWing's face and hissed frostbreath straight into the dragon's eyes.

The NightWing slammed his eyes shut at the last second, but ice immediately began spreading across his snout, sealing his eyelids in place and melting into the burns Moon had given him.

The black dragon's bellow of agony was like nothing Winter had ever heard before. He threw Winter off him and bolted into the sky. For a moment Winter could see him, weaving and dipping from side to side as he tried to fly without sight. And then the NightWing's black scales vanished into the dark and the heavy storm clouds.

At some point it had started to rain, scattered fat droplets that plopped into the dying fire with dragonlike hisses. The raindrops were soothing on Winter's burns as he dragged himself back to Moon.

She was crouched beside Kinkajou, shaking the little RainWing gently.

"Please be all right," Moon whispered. "Kinkajou. Please

wake up." Her voice snagged into a sob. "I can't hear her. I can't hear anything from her mind at all."

"She's just unconscious," Winter said, but he wasn't sure. The dragonet looked as if she'd been dropped from a great height, crumpled and still.

"He went for her first," Moon said. "Did you see that? He could have attacked any of us, but he started with Kinkajou on purpose. Why would anyone do that? Why target a tiny RainWing, the smallest of us?" She straightened one of Kinkajou's crooked wings and smoothed it back into place.

"Maybe he was worried about her venom," Winter said. "Scarlet has probably talked about RainWing venom quite a lot, given her experience."

Moon lifted and dropped her wings with a doubtful expression. Her eyes never left Kinkajou's pale face.

Winter turned and saw, finally, what should have been his first thought: Qibli had subdued Pyrite and was standing over her on the other side of the clearing, his venomous tail suspended over the midpoint of her spine.

Winter limped over and looked down at the traitorous SkyWing.

"That NightWing could come back with Scarlet any minute," Qibli warned him. "We should get out of here as fast as we can."

Winter nodded. He reached for Pyrite's necklace.

"*No*," Pyrite said with a hysterical edge to her voice. "Please. I'm not supposed to take it off *ever*. It's life or death. I need to wear it. Please leave it alone. Don't take it. Don't —"

He ripped it off her neck, yanking three times before the chain finally snapped.

The SkyWing let out a cry of despair. Winter felt the pouch crinkle between his claws; whatever was inside was very light and crunched like a talonful of snow.

He was about to open the pouch when Pyrite's scales began to slide off.

At least, that was Winter's first impression. It looked almost as though she was melting and growing and snapping into place at the same time. Her snout narrowed and lengthened. The orange color bled swiftly out of each scale. Sharp spikes shoved up through the skin all along her back and at the tip of her tail.

Qibli leaped off her with a shout of surprise.

It was over in a matter of seconds.

The dragon who was no longer Pyrite arched his back, unfolded his long white wings, and opened eyes as blue as the arctic sky. He coughed and stared around him in utter bewilderment. His gaze landed on Winter and Qibli.

"Winter?" he said in a shaky, hoarse voice.

Winter stared up at him, his talons rooted to the earth, his wings prickling with fear. He was too shocked to speak.

"Holy snakes," said Qibli. "Is that — are you — ?"

Pyrite was gone. Standing in her place . . . was Hailstorm.

— CHAPTER 16 —

"Hailstorm?" Winter whispered. "But how? You were just —
you were a *SkyWing*. I *saw* you. How did you — ?"

"What happened to the throne room?" Hailstorm asked,
his voice getting stronger. "And *what* have you been eating
to get so big?" He stopped, swaying in place and rubbing his
eyes. "Wait, I have to find the queen . . . why are my scales
the wrong color?" He held out his talons and then recoiled
from them with an expression of terror. "What have you
done to me? Why am I so cold?"

He seized Winter's front claws in a grip that sent shock
waves of desperation along Winter's arms. "*Who am I?*"
Hailstorm demanded.

"You're my brother," Winter said. That was clear. That
was true. They could deal with spells and lingering side
effects later. He leaned into Hailstorm's grasp, locking their
eyes together. "And we have to get you out of here before
Scarlet finds you."

"Queen Scarlet," Hailstorm corrected automatically. "She
wouldn't hurt me. I am completely loy —" His face twisted,

horror warring with despair and confusion. "What am I saying? Winter, *what am I saying*?"

"We'll fix it, but right now we have to fly," Winter said. Qibli darted across the clearing and said something to Moon. She immediately slid her talons under Kinkajou and tried to hoist the RainWing onto Qibli's back, struggling as Kinkajou's tail flopped sideways and overbalanced her. The unconscious dragon's wings whapped Moon in the face and her head lolled awkwardly on her long neck.

Winter took a step toward them, but Hailstorm wouldn't let go of him.

"Are you real?" the tall IceWing asked. "Is any of this real?"

"Hailstorm, snap into it," Winter barked. "We need to help my friends and get out of here."

"Friends?" Hailstorm echoed. He squinted over at the tangle of dragons on the edge of the dying firelight. "But Winter, I think there's a *NightWing* over there."

Winter's guilt came slamming back through him, along with a second wave of guilt that came from remembering how much Moon had done to help him.

"She's on our side. She's helping me rescue you. Hailstorm, *move*." He finally got his claws free and ran over to the others.

He reached Moon's side in time to catch Kinkajou as she slid sideways off the SandWing. Qibli had his teeth gritted and his eyes closed, his legs bowed under her weight.

Kinkajou was small, but not *that* much smaller than Qibli, who was wiry and narrow-shouldered. Winter couldn't imagine how the SandWing could even take off with her on top of him, let alone keep up a breakneck escape pace. And Winter couldn't do it either; he was broader than Qibli, but not any bigger.

But what's the alternative? Leave her here?

He was astonished to find that he couldn't even consider that possibility. He wouldn't abandon her, not even to save Hailstorm. He could feel his brother watching him, the needles of centuries of IceWing judgment pricking along his spine.

"We need someone as big as Clay," Moon said ruefully, resting Kinkajou's head in the crook of her shoulder and wing.

Hailstorm might be big enough, but he's too confused. And he has no love for RainWings, either as Pyrite or as himself. I don't know what he might do with her midflight.

If only Qibli and I could carry her together . . .

Winter darted over to the trees, leaped up, and wrenched the canopy loose from the trunk it was bound to. The weave of branches and vines was thick enough to keep out rain; if they were lucky, it would be strong enough to hold Kinkajou.

He spread it out beside Moon, who understood without words what he was doing. Awkwardly they shifted Kinkajou onto the makeshift stretcher, curling her tail close around her body and tucking in her wings. There was no sign of life from her as they did this, although Winter thought he could feel a pulse in the palm of her talons.

The pouch was still crushed in his claws. He needed to look at it more closely, but not right now. And he wasn't about to risk wearing it, after seeing what it did to Hailstorm. Carefully he tucked it beside Kinkajou, snagging the chain securely around several branches.

Qibli took one side of the canopy in his front talons. Winter reached for the other, but Moon interceded.

"I'll do it," she said. "You take care of your brother."

She hooked her claws in the web of branches and nodded at Qibli. Beating their wings together, they lifted up into the air, wobbling and lopsided for a moment. Winter jumped to catch Kinkajou in case they dropped her, but they righted themselves and flew higher, their wings finding the same rhythm. They shot up into the clouds as the rain began cascading down harder and harder.

Winter ran back over to Hailstorm. "Fly!" he shouted. "Follow me!"

"Maybe I should wait here for Queen Scarlet," Hailstorm said uncertainly. "She could probably explain what's happening to my head."

"No!" Winter shouted. He shook his wings furiously, which did not help dry him off at all. "She is the enemy! Come on!" He couldn't believe Scarlet wasn't here already. How long could it take the NightWing to fly back to get her?

Even with his face burned and frostbitten? Maybe he'd gotten lost, unable to see . . . but Scarlet still should have heard the noise of the battle. She could be flying down to investigate right now.

He launched himself into the air, and to his relief, Hailstorm only hesitated a moment before following.

The rain smashed down on them, harder and harder. Winter wished it were snow instead — he tried imagining the drops as light, fluffy flakes of comforting snow, but it didn't help. Lightning flashed overhead and he caught a glimpse of the odd flapping shape that was Qibli and Moon and the sagging canopy. They were flying west, hopefully out of the mountains and toward the Kingdom of Sand.

And beyond that, the Ice Kingdom, Winter thought. He glanced sideways at Hailstorm, now keeping up with long, powerful strokes of his wings. *I did it. I found him. I can take him home.*

He looked forward again, at the dragons winging their way over the mountain range, and felt a strange stabbing feeling in his chest.

Home.

Where none of my friends can go.

Where I must be — I mean, where I can *be a true IceWing once again.*

* * *

They flew without stopping for the rest of the night. Winter and Hailstorm soon caught up to the others and then slowed to match their speed — although Hailstorm gave Winter a puzzled look as he did. After a while, Winter moved in to take the canopy from Moon and she let him; a short time after that, she took it from Qibli, and the three of them traded off turns silently for hours, saving their breath for flying.

Hailstorm did not offer to help, but he stayed with them, to Winter's relief.

Finally they flew out of the edge of the storm, straight into a cool gray morning somewhere in the borderlands between the Sky Kingdom and the Kingdom of Sand. The mountains were behind them, and the sun had not yet climbed high enough to make it past the peaks, but everything was lit in that barely dawn, colorless way that makes your eyes tired. A small herd of springboks turned graceful, antlered heads to the sky, spotted the dragons, and bounded instantly away, their white tails flickering as they fled south.

"We can rest at the river," Qibli called. "Almost there."

Winter hefted his side of the sling, trying to adjust his aching talons. The entire front half of his body felt numb, as though he had turned to stone and someone had decided to hang a RainWing off his petrified arms. His head was fuzzy with exhaustion.

Soon he saw the Great Five-Tail River ahead of them, a vast green-brown-blue vein stretching from the desert to the delta. According to the history scrolls, this was the most disputed piece of territory in all of Pyrrhia, as the SkyWings and SandWings had fought over ownership of the river for centuries. Winter wondered if Burn had promised it to the SkyWings in exchange for their alliance in the War of SandWing Succession. He wondered if it was only a matter of time before Queen Ruby and Queen Thorn resumed the battle that had raged for so long.

But for now, the banks of the river were peaceful. Near the delta, the SandWing settlement on the west side had slowly merged with the SkyWing village on the east over the last twenty years, so that now, red and orange and sandy-yellow wings dotted the sky and the streets side by side. A wide white stone bridge had been built across the river, lined with shops where dragons traded and bartered all day.

Winter knew this from reports he'd heard in the throne room. IceWing reconnaissance had kept a close eye on the tentative peace that was forged between Burn and Scarlet. Would it last beyond the war? Where would that leave the IceWings . . . the next border where the SandWings might look for new territory?

But he had only ever flown over the Great River; he'd only seen the growing town from a distance. Now, seeing it take shape ahead of them, he realized that was Qibli's destination. Winter had expected to stop in a clump of trees somewhere, but the SandWing was clearly leading them to the town itself.

"Wait," he said, and Qibli immediately circled back to take Kinkajou's stretcher from him. Winter shook out his talons, feeling the blood slowly tingling back into motion. "Where are you taking us? Shouldn't we hide somewhere?" He gestured at the wild landscape below them: the sand dotted with palm trees that stretched away south, the muddier banks farther north, the thicker greenery near the town and the delta. There was something about bringing Hailstorm into a crowded settlement that made him nervous.

"Possibility is the best place to hide," Qibli argued. "There are hundreds of dragons there, from all the tribes these days. We'll blend right in — and Scarlet won't dare show her face in the town, with so many of Ruby's dragons patrolling the streets. Besides, Kinkajou needs a doctor."

As usual, Qibli's nine thousand very good points were impossible to counter. Winter glanced at Kinkajou's still, white face and nodded.

"The town is called Possibility?" Moon asked. Her voice was strained, but when Winter reached for her side of the canopy she flicked her wing at him. "No, take a longer break," she said. "I can handle it for another few minutes."

"When the two sides merged, neither wanted to take the other's original name," Qibli said. "This was about seven years ago. They talked and disagreed and talked some more, throwing around names like Hope and Peace and Union, but finally they put it to a vote, and the majority of the citizens chose Possibility."

"I like that," Moon said. "The possibility of hope and peace. But it's not guaranteed; they still have to work for it."

"You know someone here?" Winter asked Qibli.

"A lot of someones," Qibli said. "I met practically the whole SandWing tribe after Thorn became queen, as everyone came to pay tribute — and to see if they could support her as queen. Which they can and do, of course, because she is amazing. Anyway, several of them were from Possibility. I just have to find one who can help us."

They flew down to land on one of the islands in the river as the sun clambered over the peaks, scattering warm yellow light that outlined the palm trees in gold. A hippo was planted in the mud on the island's shore. It gave the dragons a resigned look as they landed, like *Fine, go ahead and eat me, I knew it would happen eventually.* But they were all too tired to kill anything, and after a moment the hippo splashed loudly into the river and submerged, probably congratulating itself on its impressive stealth.

Moon climbed onto the canopy as soon as it was spread out on the ground. She picked up Kinkajou's talons, trying to rub warmth into them.

"I'll be back as soon as I can," Qibli promised. He darted off to the bridge, not far away, where merchants were already unrolling carpets and setting out trays of food that exhaled clouds of steam. Winter could see Qibli in the gaps between the stalls, pacing along the length of the bridge and speaking to dragons here and there.

"This is weird," Hailstorm said behind Winter. "All those dragons from different tribes, just . . . acting like it's totally normal to be together. Not as weird as you bonding with your strange little trio, though."

Winter turned to look up at his older brother — although it wasn't as far up as it used to be. Hailstorm looked so exactly like he had the day he'd been captured. There were no new scars, no signs of starvation or beating or anything Winter would have expected him to go through in a SkyWing prison.

But then, if Hailstorm hadn't been himself all this time . . .

"What do you remember about being Scarlet's prisoner?" Winter asked.

Hailstorm shook his head. "I was never her prisoner," he said. "I've been a loyal soldier to her for . . . I thought it was my whole life but now . . . all my memories of being a SkyWing dragonet are fading. I think I hatched as an IceWing."

"You *did*," Winter said. "You're my brother Hailstorm. You've always been an IceWing."

Hailstorm shuddered in a big, bone-wracking way. "But I *know* I've been fighting for Queen Scarlet in the war," he said. "I remember bowing to her. Worshipping her. I fought — I killed IceWings for her." He drew his wings in closer and clenched his talons. "Or was it a dream? Maybe

I'm still myself and I'm only hallucinating memories of being an IceWing." With trepidation he held out his claws, saw that they were still white, and slammed his eyes shut.

Winter's veins felt as if they were iced over and cracking, bits of him splintering off inside his body. Hailstorm looked the same, but inside he was nothing like the brother Winter remembered. This lost dragon, torn in two, who had killed some of his own tribe in service to a queen he hated — it was worse than all the things Winter had imagined Scarlet doing to him.

"Hailstorm, focus," Winter said, flicking his brother's tail. If he treated him like their parents did, sharp and demanding, maybe Hailstorm's real personality would come back. "You are my brother Hailstorm. You were under some kind of enchantment, but you're back. Just forget about Pyrite and be you again."

"But which me?" Hailstorm protested. "I look at that river and think, *I can't swim.* But I remember diving into dark green oceans studded with drifting pieces of ice. I look at my claws and think, *I'm clumsy and useless.* But I remember winning every competition — I remember being at the top of the rankings. I feel like the air is too warm and I think I can't wait to go home and roll in snow, but I imagine being surrounded by IceWings and I immediately want to kill them all to protect my queen." He made a noise of despair and pressed his forehead as though he were trying to keep his brains from spilling out.

Winter exchanged a glance with Moon, who looked as horrified as he felt. Was it even safe to bring Hailstorm back to the Ice Kingdom? Had he been too badly damaged by living as a SkyWing for so long?

Would he ever truly be Winter's brother again?

— CHAPTER 17 —

A trio of red and orange dragons flew overhead, the wind from their wings sending ripples across the river to wash up on the shore near Winter's talons.

Hailstorm squinted up at the sky, as if he was thinking about following the SkyWings.

"You just need some time," Winter said, although it sounded stupid as soon as it escaped his mouth. "The longer you're Hailstorm again, the more you'll feel like yourself." At least he hoped that was true. He looked down at his claws and picked a piece of wet reed off one of them. "How long were you like that? Trapped in the body of a SkyWing?"

"I have no idea," Hailstorm answered. "The SkyWing patrol took me straight to Queen Scarlet, I think. And then there was a yellowy-orange dragon who . . . did something to me. Wait." He dropped his talons and frowned at them. "She looked like *me*. How did I do that to myself?"

"I bet Pyrite is a kind of mask," Moon offered. She was still watching Kinkajou, so she didn't see the look of repugnance that Hailstorm shot at her — but Winter did. "Not a real dragon at all. I bet the other dragon was wearing the Pyrite mask when you saw her, and he or she put it on you." She looked up at Winter. "Maybe it was that NightWing. Scarlet's ally. Scarlet had a lot of confused thoughts about what he could do for her, changing dragons into other dragons . . . I couldn't understand them because I had no idea this was even possible."

"Your SandWing is coming back," Hailstorm said, nodding at the river, where Qibli was swooping toward them.

"Directions to a doctor," he said as he landed, brandishing a small scribbled map. "Meerkat is going to fly ahead and tell her we're coming." He took the side of the canopy again as Moon climbed off it.

Winter took the other side, checking as he did that the necklace and pouch were still securely tucked beside Kinkajou. They were the key to whatever had been done to Hailstorm. They must be animus-touched.

So the NightWing is an animus, but Pyrite wasn't. The magic he'd felt when he touched her must have been the spell on Hailstorm. Had he felt anything like that from the NightWing? It was hard to remember in the confusion of the fight, but he thought so.

Their little group got a few odd looks as they flew through the town, but not as many as Winter would have expected. Most dragons were still asleep, and those that were up were busy getting ready for the day. The smell of bread baking and meat cooking wove through the streets, and Winter could hear the *tink-tink* of small hammers, the clattering of mugs, and voices calling to each other within the walls of the houses. Some kind of stringed instrument greeted the sunrise with musical scales and hints of half-played melodies.

They were on the west side of the river now, originally the SandWing side, but Winter wouldn't have been able to guess which tribe had settled here first. The structures were spread out in a haphazard, lazy way, some with gardens planted around them, some pressed up against a crowded row of other buildings. Some were magnificent towers that could have fit into any queen's palace; others were barely more than mud huts. He saw cascading fountains and several bejeweled statues of stone dragons; he also saw a discarded, bloated crocodile carcass gathering flies, and a brackish puddle with a red tint that looked like blood. (Not IceWing blood, at least.)

"What a strange place," Winter said to Qibli. "There's no order to it at all." Not like the Ice Kingdom, where your ranking on your seventh hatching day determined where you would be assigned to live. The highest-ranked lived within the walls of the palace itself, like Winter's parents. After you turned seven, you were shifted to the adult rankings, where if you worked hard enough and moved high enough, you might be able to request a transfer closer to the center of power.

"Let me guess, all your igloos look exactly the same?" Qibli asked.

"We don't live in *igloos*," Winter said, looking down his nose at Qibli. "Not *aristocrats* anyway."

"Oh, that's right," Qibli said. "Didn't you say you're related to someone important?"

"Very funny," Winter said.

"Yes," Hailstorm interjected at the same time, a little too loudly. "We're *Queen Glacier's nephews*. EVERYONE knows that." He lifted his chin and regarded a pair of passing SandWings with enormous disdain.

To his credit, Qibli managed not to laugh, although Winter was glad that Hailstorm didn't notice the mischievous glint in the SandWing's eyes.

"So, your not-igloos don't look like this?" Qibli asked.

"Our cities are all very carefully planned," Winter explained. "It's always clear where the power and the wealth is, and who has it, and who can influence it."

Hailstorm was nodding, which Winter found reassuring. Maybe his IceWing memories were taking over.

"Order and clarity are built into our architecture," Winter said. "The only thing that seems to be built into the architecture here is absurdity."

"I love it." Qibli inhaled deeply. "It smells like freedom. Freedom to be whoever you want to be, not who someone tells you you *have* to be."

"It smells like rotting water buffalo," Winter said. He couldn't help but notice the way Moon was looking at Qibli, as if what *he* said made more sense than what Winter had said. Was that what she wanted? Freedom at the expense of order?

Didn't everyone want to know where they fit into the world?

A few young dragonets burst past them, laughing — two SkyWings, two SandWings, and a MudWing — and veered toward a bigger building with pictures of tumbling, acrobatic dragons painted on the side.

"Does Sunny know about this place?" Moon asked Qibli, her eyes on the group of dragonets. "It seems like her dream come true."

"Well, it's not quite as utopian as that," Qibli said. He pointed to an alley where someone had scrawled DESERT-MUNCHERS GO HOME! in red paint. A few doors down, a MudWing sat on a corner with one leg wrapped in bandages and his wings drooping. A hollow coconut half shell sat next to him, into which someone had dropped a pitiful couple of fried grasshoppers.

"But it's the right idea," Moon said. "Dragons from different tribes living together and getting along, for the most part."

"That's true, and Sunny does know about it," Qibli said, checking his map. "But I don't think she's been here yet. Look, that's the house." He nodded at a compact structure with walls of whitewashed bricks and a roof of dried reeds. A small green flag stuck out of the wall by the door, with the word DOCTOR neatly printed on it.

A young, handsome SandWing came bustling out the door as they approached and reached for Winter's side of the stretcher.

"Hello, I'm Meerkat," he said with a friendly nod. "Wait out here."

"We're staying with Kinkajou," Winter insisted.

The SandWing shook his head. "Sorry, there's not enough room in there for seven dragons. Mayfly is very strict about her space. Extra visitors can wait in the garden." He pointed to the back of the house, where a riot of greenery was trying to vault over the roof.

"Mayfly?" Winter said. He kept his grip on the canopy, his claws tingling suspiciously. "Your doctor is a MudWing?"

"The best in Possibility," said Meerkat.

Winter would not have thought there were any MudWings smart enough to be doctors, let alone the best in town. Maybe there wasn't much competition. Or maybe this was the wrong place to bring Kinkajou.

"One of you can come in with her," Meerkat said. He reached out again, and this time Winter relinquished his grasp. What choice did they have? Where else could they take her?

But he reached in and fished out the animus-touched pouch first. He wasn't letting magic like that out of his sight.

Qibli opened his wings to let Moon take the stretcher from him and she disappeared into the house with Meerkat and the unconscious dragonet.

There was an awkward pause. Winter, Hailstorm, and Qibli glanced sideways at one another, shuffled their wings, and squinted thoughtfully at the sky.

"I'll be in the garden," Qibli said finally, edging away.

Hailstorm stomped over to stick his nose in the neighbor's pond, muttering something like, "Don't even know why I'm here."

This seemed like a good time for pacing.

Which Winter did, until he realized he had accidentally trampled some bright yellow flowers poking up around the base of the house. He stepped back and tried to keep still.

Maybe he could see something through the windows.

He explored around the side of the house until he found a window open and large enough to poke his head in. From here he could see a round sunlit room, clean and uncluttered. The only furniture was a large, plain white table in the middle and a few shelves on one wall that held neatly labeled bottles and jars. Kinkajou was lying on her back on the table, looking smaller than ever with her wings flopping helplessly to either side.

A brown dragon with a wide, flat face was examining Kinkajou. Her talons moved professionally over the dragonet, checking her wings, her bones, her head. She paused for a moment, glancing from Kinkajou's tail to her snout. "Is this a RainWing?"

"Yes," Moon answered. "Her name is Kinkajou."

"Interesting," said the doctor. "Never seen one before. The white scales made me think IceWing at first."

"She looks nothing like an IceWing," Hailstorm exploded with great indignation, poking his nose over Winter's shoulder and making Winter jump.

"Get out of my window!" the doctor snapped with a hiss. "Stop blocking the light! Shoo!" She flapped her wings, taking a few limping steps in their direction.

Winter realized that the doctor's back left leg and half her tail were covered in unmistakable frostbreath scars — blackened and blistered, with two claws missing. She'd been in a battle with IceWings, within the last year, if he had to guess. Which meant she probably didn't feel too kindly toward ice dragons in general.

"Sorry! Sorry," he said, pushing Hailstorm back.

"Go sit in the garden!" she barked, slamming a jar down on the windowsill that smelled like something was stabbing his eyeballs.

"Garden, yes, absolutely," Winter said. He grabbed Hailstorm's tail and tugged him toward the back of the house.

Winter didn't have a lot of experience with gardens, but he suspected they didn't usually go *up* quite as much as this one did. Seven trees ringed the small plot of land, each of them exploding with different fruits and flowers. Vines scaled the back wall of the house, covered in blue and gold flowers, and various ferns and shrubs took up almost all the ground space. In the center of everything there was a tower that looked as if it was made of glass, with overflowing flower-pots and seed trays on each level, piled up to the height of the trees.

Qibli was flying around the top of the greenhouse tower, studying a plant that looked like dark purple dragon tongues, but he flew down when he saw them step through the trees.

"Kind of a great idea," he said, flipping one wing at the ascending levels of glass. "I'll have to remember to tell Thorn."

"Excuse me," Hailstorm said bossily to Winter, ignoring Qibli. "Why are we obeying a MudWing's orders?" This sounded so much like his real brother that Winter's spirits rose — until Hailstorm added, "*They* report to *SkyWings*, not the other way around."

Qibli regarded him thoughtfully. "He's really confused, isn't he?"

"You think?" Winter growled.

"Imagine being a totally different dragon all of a sudden," Qibli said. "With completely different memories. That would be very . . . unsettling."

"Oh, really?" Winter said. "Do you think that's what's wrong? What a useful insight, I hadn't thought of that."

"All right, grouchy," Qibli said, giving Winter an affec-tionately exasperated glare. "I'm just expressing *sympathy* over here. I realize that's an unfamiliar concept for IceWings."

"I don't need a SandWing feeling sorry for me," Hailstorm said stiffly.

"It seems like an awfully complicated spell, though," Qibli said after a moment. "What kind of animus would agree to waste his power — and lose bits of his soul — just to hide a prisoner? Why wouldn't Queen Scarlet demand something more dramatic? Come to think of it, if she has an animus NightWing, why isn't she queen again right now? She could use him to get rid of Ruby in a million different ways."

Winter had no idea. It didn't make sense to him either. He opened his talons and looked down at the crumpled pouch and chain that Hailstorm had been wearing.

At the sight of them, Hailstorm shuddered violently. "I'm supposed to wear that!" he cried. "It can't ever come off! I'll die if it does!" He stopped, felt his throat for a moment, and covered his eyes with a groan. "All right. I hear myself."

"What's in there?" Qibli asked, leaning closer to study the necklace.

Winter carefully picked at the knot that tied the pouch closed. He wished his claws were a little smaller. The knot was very tight — whatever was in here was never meant to come out.

Finally he was able to hook one claw under the knot and slice it loose. The rope fell away and he poked the pouch open, shaking the contents into his other palm.

A small folded piece of paper fell out, crumpled around the corners. He peeked into the pouch and shook it a bit more. There was nothing else in there.

"Careful," Qibli said, his talons twitching toward the paper. "Don't rip it."

Unfolding the paper was an even more delicate operation than opening the pouch, but at last it was done, revealing words scribbled in a dark red ink. Some of them were faded or caught in the wrinkles and hard to read. Winter found a patch of sunlight where he could smooth it out on a flat rock.

"What does it say?" Qibli asked. Hailstorm was watching curiously now, too. Maybe if he heard the spell, he'd realize that it wasn't real and be able to stop thinking about Pyrite.

"Ok," Winter said, puzzling over the note. "I think it says:

Enchant this paper so that when any dragon wears it in the form of a necklace, he or she shall fully become a female SkyWing named Pyrite, with the following conditions:

(1) Completely loyal to Queen Scarlet and the SkyWing tribe

(2) Insecure and weak

(3) No memory of his or her former identity

(4) Compelled to wear this necklace at all times with life-or-death urgency."

The writing was cramped and filled every inch of the paper, front and back. Winter suspected that everything from "with the following conditions" on had been added after the first part. As though it had been tailored specifically — and spitefully — for Hailstorm.

"Wow," Qibli said. "That is *weird*. I thought animus dragons just — *thought* their spells to enchant whatever they wanted to animus-touch. I didn't know they ever wrote them down." He leaned over to tap the edges of the scrap of paper. "This looks like it was torn from a larger piece — maybe a scroll since it still wants to roll that way."

"Did you hear that?" Winter asked, turning toward Hailstorm. "See? Pyrite was just a spell. Now you're your own real self."

It was staggering to him how unconvinced Hailstorm looked. Here was evidence, written proof that his life as Pyrite was all a lie. And yet Hailstorm kept sneaking looks at his claws as if they might change back at any moment.

Winter folded the paper back up and crammed it into the pouch. He took the chain, threaded it through the pouch strings again, and tied a knot with the broken links.

"What are you doing?" Qibli asked, in a tone of voice that suggested he knew perfectly well what Winter was doing. "I sense a terrible idea coming on."

"I need to see what it feels like," Winter said. "While you're here to — while I'm not alone."

"But it'll turn *you* into Pyrite. Who, let's face it, is no great loss to the world. I mean, it's a tough call, but I'm pretty sure we'd rather have you. Reasonably sure. Like, eighty percent sure."

Winter whacked one of Qibli's wings with his own. "This isn't a joke. I want to know how it works. I want to know what Hailstorm felt like, being her. I think . . . well, maybe it'll help me understand what he's going through."

"I get it," Qibli said, nodding slowly. "It just seems like a risk. I mean, look at him. What if it messes you up the same way?"

"That's not going to happen," Winter said. "I'll only wear it for a moment. But that's what you're here for — to take the necklace off me, because I won't be able to do it myself. Don't let me be a SkyWing for more than three minutes, all right? I don't want her in my head any longer than that."

"Hang on — let me see the paper." Qibli held out his talons and Winter passed over the necklace. The SandWing fished the scrap out of the pouch and read it over, and then, before Winter realized what he was doing, Qibli carefully tore a tiny piece off the bottom.

"What did you just do?" Winter demanded, flaring his wings.

"I ripped off number four," Qibli said. "The part about needing to wear the necklace all the time. Let's see if that makes it possible for you to take it off yourself." He stuffed the spell back into the pouch.

Winter accepted the necklace back, disgruntled. It hadn't even occurred to him to try changing the spell. What if it didn't work now?

He realized, though, that he wasn't *really* upset. A large part of him didn't expect the spell to work on him anyway. Even with a "Pyrite mask" on, as Moon had called it, he'd still be Winter underneath.

"All right," he said, taking a deep breath. "Here we go."

He dropped the necklace over his head.

━━ CHAPTER 18 ━━

Whoa. Where am I?

Pyrite looked around, blinking. Was this a garden? Why did everything smell like peaches and the ocean?

Hadn't she been in the mountains just a minute ago? At night?

Her brain was so useless. There were so many things she couldn't remember. Because she wasn't any good at anything; three moons, it was awful being so pathetic.

"What just happened?" she asked, turning in a lumbering circle. *There go my stupid talons, getting in my way as usual. I wish I weren't so clumsy and useless.*

The SandWing was standing nearby, watching her in a super weird way. "Did we find Queen Scarlet?" she asked.

A surge of powerful emotion rolled through her scales. The Queen! Her Most Wondrous Majesty! Queen Scarlet always knew what to do. She was such an amazing dragon. Pyrite missed her awfully. When she'd lived in the Sky Palace, she'd found a way to see the queen every day, even if it was just from a distance.

I'm glad I'm a SkyWing. She looked up at the clouds — streaked with pink and gold in a blue sky. She could be soaring up there, her wings fully extended, diving and spinning like she used to with the other SkyWing dragonets. They were freer than any other tribe, more loyal to one another, and more independent. Queen Scarlet trusted them to make decisions in battle without her. They were the smartest, fastest dragons in all of Pyrrhia.

I am completely loyal to Queen Scarlet. One day she would see her queen again, and then everything would be all right. It would feel like coming home. It would feel like flying.

"Pyrite," the SandWing said slowly. What was his name again? "How do you feel?"

"Oh, fine," she said. Her memory was a little fuzzy, but that wasn't worth mentioning. "Where are the other three?"

"Do you remember anything about Winter?" he asked.

"You mean, like that he's an enormous grump?" Pyrite said. She saw silvery scales moving out of the corner of her eye and turned, but it was a different IceWing, bigger than Winter, staring at her. What was his problem? He looked as if she was his mother back from the dead or something. Like he knew her, although she was sure she'd never seen him before. Eeeuyuck, IceWings.

"Can I look at your necklace?" the SandWing asked.

Pyrite glanced down and realized she had some kind of pouch on a chain around her neck. "Huh," she said. "Sure, I guess." As she reached for it, she felt a twinge of *should I do this?* And then she was lifting it over her neck —

— and then she was gone.

Winter dropped the necklace as if it were made of lava and leaped away from it.

"YAAAARGH!" he shouted. He clawed at his head. "Get her out, get her out!"

"Winter, it's over," Qibli called, catching his talons. "You're you again. She's not real."

But Winter could still feel Pyrite's scraping, banal thoughts like a damp mildew lingering around his mind. No wonder Hailstorm was so disturbed — Pyrite's thinking was not just different from his own personality, but it had an insidious dullness to it that left a miasma after only a few minutes. He couldn't imagine living with it for two entire years and then trying to shake it all off.

Except for the part about being a SkyWing, loyal to Scarlet — that part was crystal clear in a shiny way that was equally horrible. Winter had known, with a logical part of his mind, that other dragons were loyal to their own tribes. But obviously they were wrong; IceWings were the greatest tribe in Pyrrhia, and that was a fact.

Except now he had this memory of believing the same thing about SkyWings, and believing it with all his heart.

Was that really how SkyWings felt?

And SeaWings and RainWings and even NightWings?

He did not want to try turning into any other dragons to find out.

He turned to pick up the pouch again — perhaps to destroy it, to rip the scroll and Pyrite's very existence into tiny shreds — and found Hailstorm reaching for it.

"No!" Winter shouted, snatching it out of his grasp. "Hailstorm! Don't even touch it!"

"Maybe I should change back," Hailstorm said, his face twisting as though crocodiles might come crawling out of it. "At least when I'm Pyrite I only have one set of memories, right? That's what the scroll said. And I was happy as a SkyWing. It was easier than being an IceWing — no rankings, no one comparing me to everyone else all the time. No Mother and Father expecting me to be perfect. And I had fire — fire was amazing. Winter, please let me change back."

"That is completely insane," Winter said. He tried to make his voice as cutting as their mother's. "When you're fully yourself again, you'll recognize that there is *nothing* preferable about being a SkyWing. No one would ever choose to be anything but an IceWing."

Qibli cleared his throat significantly, and Winter shot him a glare.

The problem was, he felt it now. Not the desire to be Pyrite, but the appeal of being a SkyWing.

He couldn't let Hailstorm see that, though. He needed to be strong so that Hailstorm could be, too.

"You will never be Pyrite again," Winter said. "Get that through your frozen head."

Hailstorm growled furiously, and for a moment Winter wondered if he would actually attack his brother to get the necklace back. But finally Hailstorm spun on his heels and marched to the far end of the garden, where the trees gave way to a street that was starting to be crowded with dragons and rolling carts.

"Good speech," Qibli said. "Well, kind of mean, but in a convincing way."

"I need to be alone for a moment," Winter said.

Qibli raised his wings and stepped back with a little bow of acknowledgment.

Winter needed to straighten out his own brain. He'd wanted to step into Pyrite's talons so he could understand Hailstorm — but he didn't want to understand him *this* well.

He sat down under a fig tree and closed his eyes, taking deep breaths.

I am Winter the IceWing. I have always been an IceWing.

Slowly the Pyrite-ness began to clear.

I am Winter the IceWing. I am loyal to Queen Glacier. I will reach the top of the rankings one day.

What would life have been like as a SkyWing? Would he really have loved the tribe of sky dragons that much?

I am Winter the IceWing. Be strong, be vigilant, strike first. Trust nobody.

His father's mantra didn't quite sit right in his mind anymore, but that wasn't because of Pyrite. It was because of Qibli and Kinkajou and, most of all, Moon.

As he thought of her, he heard a door close and opened his eyes to see her emerging from the back of the doctor's house.

I am Winter the IceWing. I do not make friends with dragons from other tribes.

I am not in love with a dragon I am sworn to hate.

"Is Kinkajou all right?" Qibli asked Moon. Winter stood up and went over to join them. He glanced over at his brother as he did and saw him standing under a tree with round orange fruit, banging his head on the trunk. Winter sighed.

Moon shook her head, curling her tail around her talons. "She has a skull fracture and three or four broken ribs," she said. She sounded as though she was trying to imitate the doctor's professional delivery, but her voice wavered as she spoke. "Also a hairline break near one elbow and bruising all along her spine and left side. The doctor says she needs to stay completely still for probably a month, maybe longer."

"Is she awake?" Winter asked.

"No." Moon ducked her head, shaking back tears. "The — the doctor doesn't know when Kinkajou might wake up."

Mayfly stuck her snout out one of the back windows and beckoned to Moon. "I need your authorization on this," she said, brandishing a small scroll and an inkpot. "To have her transferred to the clinic. They'll take care of her. Although they'll want to know what really happened to her."

"I told you," Moon said with a hint of exasperation. "A dragon attacked her."

"Are you sure?" the doctor asked. "She wasn't hit by an avalanche? Or thrown off a cliff? Or trampled by a herd of hippos? That really happened to a patient of mine once. There's no shame in admitting it. Hippos can happen to anybody."

"Just a dragon, knocking her into a tree," Moon said firmly. She took the scroll and inkpot, dipped her claw into the black ink, and signed her name. "I promise."

"I saw it, too," Winter agreed.

"He was really big," Qibli offered.

"With superdragon strength?" Mayfly muttered skeptically. She took the scroll back from Moon and stomped back inside. Moon looked around, then carefully set the inkpot on the windowsill.

"Oh, good," Qibli said. "So our new mystery NightWing friend has inexplicable animus powers AND unusual strength. Super."

"Also, now he hates us, don't forget," Winter added.

"But you saw what we did to his face," Moon said. "Between my fire and your frostbreath, he's probably much less dangerous now."

The creeping spider legs feeling under Winter's scales suggested otherwise. In his experience, no good could come of adding vengeance to a dragon's list of reasons to get up in the morning.

"Eagle!" Hailstorm shouted suddenly, sending a jolt of alarm through Winter. He whirled around to see his brother at the back gate, craning his neck to see over a SeaWing pulling a fish-laden cart.

"Eagle!" Hailstorm called again, his voice full of excitement. "Eagle! Over here!"

"Uh-oh," Qibli muttered. Winter bolted over to his brother's side as a large SkyWing the color of raw tuna shouldered his way through the crowd and stared down at them. Two more burly SkyWings stepped up behind him, glowering.

"How do you know my name?" the SkyWing demanded. "Who are you?"

"I'm —" Hailstorm faltered. "But don't you — I'm — we fought together under General Ruby —"

"She's Queen Ruby now," Eagle snapped. "And I don't remember fighting any IceWings and leaving them alive." He eyed Hailstorm up and down. "I suppose if I did, that's a mistake that could be corrected."

"But how did 'e know your name?" asked one of the other SkyWings.

"Right," Eagle said, his eyes narrowing to slits. "Explain that, whale-eater."

"He doesn't —" Winter started.

But Eagle growled low in his throat, cutting him off. "Let the lizard speak."

Hailstorm stammered for a minute and finally mumbled, "I — I — I thought we were friends." He rubbed his eyes miserably.

The two flanking SkyWings looked incredulous. Eagle swelled with fury. "What?" he roared. He lashed out, reaching over the gate, and grabbed Hailstorm by the throat. "How dare you? I would *never* be friends with an IceWing! Is this a joke? Did someone pay you to make a fool out of me?"

"He didn't mean it!" Winter yelled, trying to pull Eagle's talons off his brother. "He's just confused!"

Qibli darted up on Hailstorm's other side and grabbed the SkyWing, too. "He was hit on the head," Qibli explained quickly. "A war injury — his memory is all messed up —"

"Please don't hurt him," Winter cried. Hailstorm's face was turning bluer than usual.

"Drop that IceWing right now," said another voice behind Winter. He turned and saw Meerkat standing in the garden beside Moon, arching his venomous tail menacingly. "I order you by the authority of the Enclave."

To Winter's surprise, Eagle immediately let go of Hailstorm. The IceWing collapsed back against the tree, gasping for breath.

"Sorry," the SkyWing said to Meerkat, all the rage gone from his voice. "Didn't realize he was with you, Meerkat." He took a step back. "He was saying some mighty stupid things, that's all."

"Head injury," Qibli said again. Winter crouched beside his brother, but Hailstorm pushed him away.

"Oh. Another wounded veteran," Eagle said. All three SkyWings were nodding. "I've seen plenty of those. Hope he recovers." He jerked his chin at Winter, then turned and shoved his way back into the throng, half of whom had stopped to stare at the fight.

"Moving right along," Meerkat said, waving at the audience until they all started moving again.

"It was just a mistake, Hailstorm," Winter said to his brother in a low voice. "You've only been out from under the spell for a few hours. Give it some time. You'll forget all about Pyrite once you're surrounded by IceWings again."

Hailstorm shook his head; Winter didn't know if that meant disagreement or despair.

"Winter," Hailstorm croaked softly. Winter leaned closer to hear, and Hailstorm turned hopeless blue eyes up toward him. "Winter — I want to go home."

— CHAPTER 19 —

"You're leaving now?" Moon asked, dismayed.

"I have to get him back to the Ice Kingdom," Winter said, glancing over at Hailstorm. His brother was sitting at the base of the greenhouse tower, with his wings folded close around him and his face hidden. "I feel like he won't be safe until he's with our tribe again. And then he'll remember he's really an IceWing . . . I hope."

"But Kinkajou . . ." Moon started, then trailed off.

"There's nothing I can do for her," Winter pointed out. "Right? We're just waiting until she wakes up?"

Moon looked down at her claws, leaving the "*if* she wakes up" unsaid.

"None of you can come with us to the Ice Kingdom anyway," Winter said. "You should go back to Jade Mountain."

"No way," Qibli said, and Moon glanced up at him in surprise. "We have to find the lost city of night. Remember the thunder and ice? Earth shaking, ground being scorched, all of that? I don't know about you, but I'm in favor of that prophecy *not* coming true. Now that we've found Hailstorm,

I say it's time to get on top of the whole saving-the-world thing."

"That's what I was going to do!" Moon cried. "I've been having these awful nightmares every night — I mean, worse than ever. I've *got* to figure out the prophecy . . . but I wasn't sure if anyone would want to come with me."

"Um, me," Qibli said, waving a wing at himself as though that was as obvious as the sun. "Sign me up."

Moon turned hopeful eyes toward Winter. "Maybe after you take Hailstorm home?" she asked. "Then you could come back and we could all look for the lost city of night together."

He wanted to say yes. He wasn't even sure which reason was strongest. Was it because he believed the world needed saving? Because he wanted to protect Jade Mountain?

Or because he couldn't stand the idea of Moon and Qibli searching Pyrrhia, alone, together?

"I . . . I can't," he said.

Ah, that was why: because he hadn't wanted to watch her face do this, this crumbling into disappointment.

But there were fifty thousand reasons why he couldn't say yes — reasons like Moon's safety if Winter's parents found out about her; reasons like needing to prove his loyalty to the IceWings and struggle back into the rankings. Reasons like his own sanity.

"I *can't*," he said again. All at once he was aware of Hailstorm standing behind him, listening. Hailstorm's blue eyes, watching Winter's next move. "Listen, get this into your head. I'm an IceWing." He hated that it came out sounding almost like a question. He wasn't like Hailstorm; he knew who he was.

"I'm an IceWing," he said again, firmly. "That means I belong in the Ice Kingdom with my own tribe. I should never have gone to Jade Mountain. This prophecy, if it's even real, has nothing to do with me, and *I* should have nothing to do with *you*."

"But," Moon said, "I thought —" She reached toward him, her dark eyes puzzled and hurt.

"What, that we were friends?" Winter spat, shoving her talons away. "We can't be friends." *We can't be anything. We can never, never be what I dream of us being.* "You're my sworn enemy, NightWing. I never asked for you to follow me around."

"Hey," Qibli said. He sounded genuinely angry. "Don't talk to her like that. She helped you find your brother and she risked her life to do it. What is wrong with you?"

"It's all right," Moon said, brushing Qibli's wing with her own. Her eyes flickered to Hailstorm, close behind Winter. "He's striking first, that's all. Winter, I believe that you're one of the best, bravest, truest dragons in Pyrrhia. I'll never be your enemy, no matter what you say. But go ahead and leave, if that's what you want."

It's not what I want. His chest felt as if it might burst, spilling shattered ice everywhere. *It's how things have to be.*

"We'll wait for you," Qibli said. "Right here, in case you

change your mind and realize that stopping a big world-destroying prophecy is what you were hatched to do."

"Don't bother," Winter said, hoping his cold snarl was still as intimidating as he'd once been able to make it.

"One week," Moon said, glancing at Qibli for confirmation. "We can wait one week, and then we're leaving."

"Then you're idiots! I don't care!" Winter nearly shouted. Why did it have to be so impossible? How could they still even want to be his friends when he was pushing them away so hard? "Three moons! Leave me alone!"

He turned to Hailstorm. "Let's go."

As he spread his wings and leaped into the sky, Qibli called, "Don't be a stranger."

And he thought he heard Moon say, "We'll miss you."

Hailstorm soared into the lead, his wings glittering silver-and-white with reflections of rose from the setting sun ahead of them. He grinned over his shoulder at his little brother — the first happy expression Winter had seen from him all day.

Winter forced himself to look forward. He would not look back at the garden, at the black and pale yellow dragons watching him go.

He would not admit to himself that he would miss them, too.

He would ice over the hole in his chest, the way he'd cleared out the Pyrite memories.

Ahead were his parents and Queen Glacier, and he would need to be perfect again before he faced them.

The Ice Kingdom was waiting for him.

PART THREE

BENEATH THE ICE

— CHAPTER 20 —

Winter and Hailstorm reached the southern border of the Ice Kingdom the next day at twilight. A few stars and one claw-shaped moon were already glimmering in the violet sky. Winter could see the Great Ice Cliff that marked the border, stretching from one horizon to the other in a sheer unbroken line.

Hailstorm squinted at it as they approached. "Is that a wall?" he asked. "What's the point of that? A wall can't keep out dragons."

"You don't remember the Great Ice Cliff?" Winter replied, startled. "It's probably our oldest animus gift."

Hailstorm shrugged. "Seems like a waste of magic," he said. "We're going to fly right over it."

"Right, because we're IceWings," Winter said. "But if we were from any other tribe, the Great Ice Cliff would shoot icicle spears at us and most likely kill us. It's secret defensive magic — the other tribes don't know about it. Usually no one else ventures this far north anyway. But if they did, they'd get a chilly, pointy surprise."

Hailstorm balked in midair. "What if it doesn't let me past?" he cried.

"It will," Winter said, a little irritated. "You're an IceWing, Hailstorm. The wall will recognize that . . . and so will everyone else."

His brother did not look convinced. But some of his old bravado seemed to be coming back; even if he was scared, he was clearly determined not to show it.

Of course the wall did not react as they flew over it. Winter remembered the last time it had gone off, a year and a half ago when one of Blaze's SandWings had apparently decided to wrap herself in a few blankets and explore the mysterious Ice Kingdom. They'd found her what must have been days later, on the north side of the wall. She was half buried in a snowdrift with a spear through her heart, her sky-colored blankets frozen to her scales, so at first they thought she was a SeaWing.

Other than that, the wall had been quiet for Winter's entire life. The other tribes didn't know about it, but they did know about the subzero temperatures and freezing wind in the Ice Kingdom. Even during the War of SandWing Succession, no one had dared send troops into their territory. It would have been a complete massacre if they had.

Which made Winter think about the animus who had built and enchanted the wall thousands of years ago. The gift of defense, it was called. Was it worth it at the time? Were there more attacks on the kingdom back then? Were there dragons from other tribes who had figured out how to survive in the arctic cold, long enough to stage an invasion, at least?

Or perhaps the animus was looking forward, not back. Perhaps he anticipated a day when some other tribe's animus might craft heat-generating armor that could carry soldiers into the farthest reaches of the north.

(But even if someone did that — why conquer a land you couldn't possibly live in?)

In any case, if Winter were an animus dragon, building a wall like that would not have been his major contribution to IceWing society.

The Ice Kingdom didn't need defensive magic; what it needed *now* was something to help them conquer other tribes. If they still had animus dragons, they could have won the War of SandWing Succession in no time at all, and then all the territory Blaze had promised Queen Glacier would now be theirs. More important, no IceWing soldiers would have had to die . . . and Hailstorm would never have ended up as Scarlet's prisoner.

It all goes back to Foeslayer. If she had never stolen Prince Arctic, imagine how powerful we could be now. We'd have another two thousand years of animus gifts. We could have been the rulers of all Pyrrhia! We'd definitely have something that helped us in battle — exploding snowballs that kill every dragon they touch, or maps that tell us exactly where all our enemies are, or diamonds that hypnotize every other queen into surrendering to us.

When he thought of the IceWing lives lost in the war, and for *nothing* in the end, he wished he could climb back through time, find an animus IceWing — maybe the one who wasted her gift on defense — and force her to make something that would wipe out all the NightWings at once.

Uneasiness whispered through his bones at that thought . . . a thought he'd had a hundred times before. But now he could picture the NightWings in their ramshackle rainforest village, trying to rebuild after the horrors of the volcano. He could remember the shivering dragonet in the wingery and the protective parents he'd seen, including Moon's mother.

It was actually completely terrifying to think that any dragon with magic could easily wipe out an entire tribe with just one enchanted object.

It was even *more* terrifying to realize that your own tribe no longer had that magic — but your worst enemies did. Why hadn't the NightWings used animus power to destroy the IceWings long ago? Did they have so little control over their animus dragons — or so little vision of what their stolen magic could do?

He worried around these questions as he and Hailstorm flew over the snowy landscape, dotted with sheer cliffs and pure blue lakes, and the sky grew darker and darker. A couple of white owls swept past below them, pale flickers, like moths in the moonlight, screeching to each other. A herd of shaggy caribou surrounded one of the lakes, stamping nervously as the dragons passed overhead. Winter thought about grabbing one to eat, but they'd already stopped earlier that day to hunt and now, with home so close, he just wanted to get there and face the queen already.

It was close to midnight when they saw the lights of Queen Glacier's palace ahead of them, shimmering blue-green-silver, like captured starlight. The dark ocean acted as a mirror, sending the same lights dancing in blurred mimicry around the base of the palace. A galaxy of smaller lights spiraled out in five curved arms from the palace, illuminating the dwellings of lower aristocrats, the training schools that were open all night, and the shimmering ice sculpture gardens.

Winter heard Hailstorm catch his breath beside him.

"It's beautiful," he murmured. "I'd forgotten . . ."

"Wait until you see it up close," Winter said, his chest swelling with pride. The Ice Kingdom *was* beautiful, without question.

He wished he could show it to Moon.

But she would never get past the Great Ice Cliff alive — and his parents would send her to the bottom of a frozen lake if she did.

They swooped down to land at the grand entrance of the palace, a set of crystal-studded gates about halfway up the central keep. The gates were carved in the shape of giant dragon wings, matching the small ice sculptures of dragons and wings and talons that topped all the columns and finials.

Although it was possible to fly over the palace walls straight into the interior courtyards, it was considered gauche and therefore career suicide. According to protocol, visitors waited at the gates to be admitted.

Queen Glacier's astonishing palace was also animus-touched — the gift of splendor, designed, built, and enchanted centuries ago by a pair of animus twins, with magic that ensured its walls of ice would never melt, never crack, and never be harmed by outside attack. It soared miles into the air, with towers and balconies and spires that pierced the clouds. There were so many rooms on so many levels that Winter, who had lived there his entire life, had never seen them all.

A low-ranked guard stood outside the gates, wearing the chain of five concentric silver circles that marked him as Fifth Circle in the adult rankings. His posture and form were perfect, although his eyelids were drooping dangerously. He snapped to attention as they landed, stamping his spear twice.

"Nephews of Queen Glacier," Winter announced, although he was sure the guard must recognize them. He hesitated. IceWing etiquette demanded that the higher-ranked dragon should be introduced first — but Hailstorm wasn't even listed in the rankings anymore. His name had been scratched out along with all the other murdered IceWing prisoners.

But surely the correct introduction was still "Hailstorm and Winter," wasn't it?

The guard saved him the trouble. "Hailstorm?" He blinked and rubbed his eyes violently. "Aren't you Hailstorm?"

"I guess," Hailstorm answered, in the least convincing tone of voice possible.

The guard couldn't hide how rattled he was, although he did his best. "My apologies, sir," he said, bowing. "We believed you were dead. It is a wondrous day indeed that you are returned to us."

"We should report straight to the queen," Winter said. "She'll want to be woken for this, if she's not still awake."

Thousands of years ago, IceWings must have been restricted to daylight hours. (Or, as some speculated, perhaps their night vision had once been stronger — but nobody said that too loud, lest it sound like criticism of the animus gifts or the royal family.) But ever since the gift of light, they could stay up all night long if they wanted to, and many of them did, seizing every hour they could for working and training.

"Queen Glacier is on a diplomatic mission," the guard said, flinching in a strange, embarrassed way. "Her brother Narwhal is overseeing palace matters in her absence. Right now he is at work on the rankings in the courtyard."

Our father, Winter thought. Beside him, Hailstorm's wings twitched.

"Thank you," Winter said to the guard with a small nod. The older IceWing looked slightly outraged, but he stepped aside and let them pass without further comment.

It wasn't until they were through the gates that Winter realized he might have handled that interaction entirely wrong. He'd approached it with his last known rank in mind — he'd been in the Second Circle the day he left for Jade Mountain Academy. But perhaps his position had slipped in his time away . . . especially if Queen Glacier knew what had happened with Icicle. If he'd fallen into a circle below that of the guard, Winter should have been much more deferential. But surely it couldn't have dived so low in just a few weeks . . . could it? Into the Sixth Circle? Winter had only ever gone that low after Hailstorm's capture.

Hailstorm was silent as they flew through the vast entrance hall, spiraling down toward the three arched openings that led to the central courtyard. Winter glanced sideways at him, wondering if the familiar surroundings were helping clarify his memories.

All around them, pale blue stars seemed to be drifting slowly through the otherwise bare, translucent walls of the palace. It wasn't until you got close to the walls that you could see the small glass snowflakes encased in the ice, glowing silvery blue as they fell, mimicking the weather outside.

This was the gift of elegance, which Winter appreciated for its beauty but thought was a waste of magic. The phosphorescent snowflakes must have been created in a time when IceWings were comfortable and didn't need anything more urgent — a time when they thought they would always have animus dragons.

Or perhaps it was enchanted by an animus who was artistic but not very practical. IceWing history included a few animus dragons who chose their gifts against the wishes of their queens.

The gift of subsistence was one — a trio of holes in the ice located on the outskirts of the kingdom, where the poorest, weakest IceWings could reach into the dark ocean beneath and always pull out a seal. No ice dragon who cared about the rankings (in other words, no aristocrat) would ever accept food that came so easily to their claws, however. It was a gift that only benefited the lowest of the kingdom, which made it seem narrow-minded and useless to all the IceWings Winter knew.

But perhaps it would seem like a kinder, wiser gift in the eyes of other tribes — RainWings, for instance, who took care of one another so easily and had apparently no hierarchy at all. Winter thought uncomfortably of all the dragons in Possibility, like the wounded MudWing, who could use a source of food like that.

Stop thinking about other tribes. Father will smell doubt on you.

Winter had once dreamed that he was an animus dragon, and in his dream, he gave his tribe the gift of observation: a scavenger den in the Ice Kingdom constructed so the scavengers could survive without freezing. A perfect setup for Winter to study them.

That was probably another example of a gift that a queen wouldn't approve of.

A couple of dragons in the hall did a double take as the brothers flew by, but Hailstorm didn't seem to notice. He swept unerringly through the center archway into the snow-covered courtyard, a vast space dominated by the two most important animus gifts in IceWing history: the gifts of light and order.

As a young dragonet, Winter had loved to climb the tree of light. His small, serrated claws would dig into the ice of the trunk and propel him up into the branches, where he could curl up and pretend he was sitting on one of the moons. Sometimes he would imagine he was the animus who'd created the tree — a dragon named Frostbite, according to his history tutor, who had spent more time and care on her gift than perhaps any other animus the tribe had ever seen.

She hadn't enchanted the ice to sculpt itself, like the designers of the palace or the Great Ice Cliff. She'd spent years painstakingly carving the tree with her own claws, each branch and twig and frost-kissed leaf.

For the first time, Winter wondered if Frostbite had left the Ice Kingdom for a while to study real trees. He'd spent enough time in actual forests now to realize that she had gotten the details exactly right.

The magic came once the tree was finished. The animus touch gave the tree a kind of eternal life and, most important, the moon globes that grew on it all year round.

To Winter's surprise, Hailstorm went to the tree and picked a globe right away, like most dragons did when they first arrived at the palace. Did that mean his instincts were kicking in? The globe floated quietly over his left shoulder, casting pale light that accentuated the shadows between his horns.

Winter followed, choosing a light of his own and releasing it over his own shoulder. A small bud appeared instantly in its place on the branch, where a new moon globe would grow within a day or two.

He turned and realized that everyone in the courtyard was staring at them. He hadn't even noticed the quiet murmur of conversation in the air until it abruptly stopped.

Nine IceWings watched in silence as Hailstorm and Winter walked under the tree and down the long path to the wall of rankings. Standing in front of the rankings, watching them approach with a cold, unreadable expression, was their father, Narwhal.

Winter didn't wait for Hailstorm to bow first; whatever their respective ranking was in whoever's mind, he couldn't face his father's gaze anymore. He dropped into a crouch, spread his wings, and bowed his head. The wet snow crept between his scales, comforting and chilling at the same time.

Beside him, more slowly, Hailstorm did the same.

In the long silence that followed, Winter imagined he could hear glaciers moving, the world spinning, the stars weeping softly.

What is Father thinking? He didn't dare look up. He knew Narwhal's expression wouldn't hold any clues anyway.

"Ssso," Narwhal finally hissed, in a voice that could slice an iceberg in half. "My two sons have returned to me. One I thought could never come back — the other I hoped never would."

Winter lifted his eyes, shocked into meeting Narwhal's gaze. Behind his father, the seven circles of dragonet rankings blazed like comets against a dark sky. This wall was the gift of order, where every dragon in the aristocracy was listed. Their names were all carved into the ice, but enchanted so that the queen and her chosen advisors could slide them around like beads on an abacus. Every dragonet that hatched appeared here as soon as he or she was given a name. Every night the queen considered the current standings and changed them according to the rules and her own judgment.

Winter spotted his name right away.

In dead last, at the bottom of the Seventh Circle, was Icicle's name. And one step above her — second-to-last, lower than all the new-hatched dragonets on the list, lower than any royal had ever been before, was Winter.

⌒ CHAPTER 21 ⌒

A gust of wind swept a cloud across one of the moons, and it began to snow harder. Winter stared down at the tracks of dragon prints that crisscrossed the courtyard. He couldn't think. He could barely breathe.

"We did not think you could possibly be alive, Hailstorm," Narwhal said, inspecting his older son from wings to claws. "Congratulations on your survival. The queen will be pleased to welcome you back to her army."

Hailstorm swept his tail in a slow arc through the snow, his head drooping lower.

"As for you, Winter," Narwhal went on. "We have heard a lot of stories about your behavior. Perhaps you can clarify some of them for us. Attacking your own sister at Jade Mountain Academy. Leaving the school without your queen's permission. Traveling with a *NightWing*. Leading the RainWings straight to Icicle's hiding place so she could be imprisoned. And then abandoning her, unconscious, in the rainforest, where any NightWing might have murdered her. Disappearing into Pyrrhia without consulting your queen.

Consorting with dragons from other tribes. Gone for days with no message sent home and no oversight or explanation for your behavior."

He took a step toward Winter, his talons crunching in the snow. "What were we supposed to think? How were we supposed to account for you in the rankings? What choice did the queen have?" He swept one wing toward the wall.

That's where she's gone, Winter realized. *Queen Glacier is in the rainforest to deal with the Icicle situation.* He wondered if his sister was still asleep, and whether Scarlet had returned to torment her dreams. How would the queens decide to punish his sister for everything she had done? Queen Glory wasn't likely to accept "demotion to the bottom of the Seventh Circle of the rankings" as sufficient justice. No one but an IceWing would understand what that meant.

"Father," Hailstorm said suddenly. "I see I am no longer listed in the rankings, but may I have permission to speak?"

Narwhal inclined his head. "Briefly, if you please."

"My brother acted rashly and without oversight," said Hailstorm. "But he did so to save my life. I would have been executed within hours if he had not saved me in time. He was courageous and honorable in his time away from the Ice Kingdom. I am prepared to attest to that before the queen."

His eyes flickered sideways to Winter, the only betrayal that he was not telling the entire truth. Winter knew he couldn't possibly approve of Winter's friendship with Qibli, Moon, and Kinkajou. But would he hide it to protect Winter?

Was he expecting Winter to hide the truth about Pyrite in exchange?

"Come to my chambers," Narwhal said, shaking snow off his wings. "Tell me the whole story there. Winter, go to your room, and I will summon you shortly."

Hailstorm shot Winter another significant look as he followed their father away. A minute later, the other IceWings in the courtyard had dispersed, leaving Winter alone.

He spent several minutes scanning the rankings, taking note of what had changed in his absence. His cousin Snowfall was the new top of the First Circle on the dragonet side, which was disheartening, as she was already abundantly blessed with mean smugness. Lynx was in second place behind Snowfall, and that was much better news; she was only the daughter of a minor noble, but a hard worker and very smart.

On the adult side, he saw that his parents had fallen several spots, nearly into the Third Circle, which meant they were almost in danger of losing their right to live in the palace. *That's our fault,* he realized. *Having me and Icicle at the bottom of our rankings reflects badly on them. We dragged them down.*

No wonder Father is so angry.

At least, Winter *thought* he was angry. It was hard to tell; Narwhal's outward demeanor was much the same whether he was proud or furious.

That wasn't quite the homecoming I was hoping for, he admitted to himself. But he hadn't exactly expected a parade either. A nod of approval was as much as his imagination had been able to come up with, but apparently that was still hoping for too much.

He dragged himself through the palace to his old room, bowing low to everyone he passed — most of whom were too startled by his appearance to respond. In a way, it did make things simple, being at the very bottom. He didn't have to keep the list memorized when he knew that everyone was above him.

He hoped seeing his old room would cheer him up, but instead it struck him as a bare, joyless box that seemed to have shrunk while he was away. The one window overlooked the courtyard, which he definitely did not want to look at right now. The snowflakes in the walls had become a blizzard, matching the oncoming snowstorm outside. Winter set the moon globe on his desk, turning it one rotation to dim the light to a sleep-appropriate glow.

He dropped onto the shelf of ice that served as a bed, and then after an uncomfortable minute, he got up and pulled the two polar bear rugs up onto the bed with him.

Perhaps sleeping in grass had made him soft, but he was too tired to punish his aching bones any more. He curled into the warm white fur, remembering the bright colors of the rainforest, the busy sounds and smells of Possibility, the voices calling and talons thumping through the halls of the Jade Mountain Academy.

The flash of silver scales against black; dark eyes in the moonlight; the fire that roared forth to protect her friends.

Don't dream about Moon, he told himself with his last waking thought, and then fell asleep knowing perfectly well that he would, and unable to feel anything but relief at the prospect.

He had expected to be prodded into wakefulness with sharp claws by some messenger from his father. So it was unsettling to wake up slowly and realize that morning light was pouring through the window.

It was even *more* unsettling to roll over and find his mother's eyes fixed on him from only a few inches away.

Winter let out a yelp and sat up fast, knocking one of the rugs to the floor. Tundra frowned at it for a moment, looking more puzzled than disapproving, and finally kicked it out of her way with one foot. The SkyWing teeth in her necklace made the jittery, small clattering sound they always made when she moved — a sound that still made Winter want to run and hide in a snowbank.

"The sun has been up for an hour," she said.

Winter took a deep, stabilizing breath and tried to match her flat "here is some information" tone. "I did not stop to sleep after finding Hailstorm," he said. "We flew home as fast as we could." *Apart from one detour to drop an injured*

RainWing in a town of overlapping dragon tribes that you would hate on sight. He wondered how Kinkajou was doing, and whether she'd woken up yet.

Tundra studied him for a moment with her stormy gray eyes. "Good," she said at length. "No apologies. But now it is time to rise. There will be a ceremony in the courtyard in seven minutes that you must attend."

"Yes, Mother," Winter said, stepping off the bed shelf. A ceremony — most likely restoring Hailstorm to the rankings. But where? At the top, where he'd been when he was captured?

Winter hoped he'd get to see Snowfall's face if that happened. That would make the torture of a rankings ceremony worthwhile.

His mother paused in the doorway and gave him another assessing look. Finally she said, "Thank you for bringing Hailstorm home."

What is this feeling? Winter wondered. *Elation? Pride?* He'd never felt anything quite like this swelling in his chest before. He dared to give her the smallest of smiles.

Tundra blinked slowly. "It was the least you could do," she added, and then she turned and left.

Winter could practically hear Qibli's voice in the room beside him: *So THAT didn't last very long.* He startled himself by laughing.

I'd better not do that again, not in front of Mother and

Father. I'm going to have to work harder than ever to climb back up the rankings now.

He scooped some snow off the windowsill and rubbed it all over his scales, polishing them as clean as he could get them in three minutes.

He made it down to the courtyard two minutes before the ceremony. Almost every dragonet in the palace was there, lined up in order, wings folded in attention position. He found his way to the end of the line, in the back corner farthest from the rankings wall. The tiny dragonets back there with him gave him curious looks and whispered to one another in voices that were really not whispers at all.

Adult dragons were gathered around the perimeter of the courtyard — more than were ever usually present for a dragonet-ranking ceremony. The sun glinted off white scales in many of the windows, indicating that even more were watching from overhead.

They want to see how Father will handle this situation, Winter thought. *Can he be impartial with his own son? Will everyone still think his decision is fair?*

Tundra, Narwhal, and Hailstorm swept into the courtyard in a triangle formation with Narwhal at the front. This was something Winter had seen so many times growing up, but had never expected to see again. Their tails swept majestically through the snow, leaving long snaking trails behind them.

Narwhal pivoted to face the gathered dragonets, who all fell instantly silent.

"We have some changes to make to the rankings of which you all should be aware," Winter's father said, his resonant voice echoing around the courtyard. He sounded just like Queen Glacier — straight to business without any meandering preambles.

"Several months ago, a dragonet was removed from the wall due to reports of his death. He has now returned to us, alive after all. This is my son, Queen Glacier's nephew, Hailstorm." Narwhal indicated Winter's brother with a sideways flick of his wing. "Therefore he must be added back to the rankings."

He turned to Tundra, who flexed her claws, ready to write. "At the time of his capture, Hailstorm was in first place."

Winter risked craning his neck to see Snowfall, right at the front of the crowd. Her face was turned away from him, but he could see rigid tension all the way through her spine and wings.

"But he has been without oversight for almost two years, and by his own admission, in that time he has not behaved according to our IceWing standards. We must also factor in the clumsiness of allowing himself to be caught by SkyWings in the first place."

Winter flinched. What a thing for Hailstorm to hear upon his homecoming.

"Therefore, after careful consideration," Narwhal announced, "we are slotting Hailstorm into last place in the Seventh Circle. May he claw his way back up with his own talons."

A collective gasp and a murmur of bewilderment ran through the gathered dragons. Even the most rigorously trained IceWings couldn't suppress their reactions. No one had ever, *ever* expected to see Hailstorm's name at the bottom of the rankings list.

Tundra bent toward the wall, scratching Hailstorm's name below Icicle's.

Wow. Winter felt faintly dizzy. It had to be unprecedented in IceWing history for one set of parents to have all *three* of their nearly grown dragonets in the last three spots. This would be devastating for Tundra's and Narwhal's rankings as well. Would they all have to move out of the palace? Where would they be assigned? What would Mother and Father do if they were no longer advisors to the queen?

At least no one could accuse Narwhal of sentimentality or favoritism.

Hailstorm was watching their mother with a perfectly impassive expression. Did he remember that he'd once been on track to be ranked even higher than his parents? No one had ever been number one in the dragonet rankings for as long as he had been. Expectations had been high for where he might climb once he turned seven and shifted to the adult rankings.

A deep chill suddenly ran through Winter's scales. Turning seven. He'd completely forgotten — he hadn't even thought about how old Hailstorm was. Hailstorm's seventh hatching day was only twelve days away.

And wherever he was in the rankings on that day would determine the course of the rest of his life.

Could even Hailstorm rise back to the top that fast? Would he choose to risk the Trial? Or would he be exiled to an island outpost two weeks from now?

Perhaps Winter had rescued his brother from one terrible fate only to doom him to another.

"One more announcement," Father said brusquely. "Another dragonet was recently shifted to the bottom of the list due to unsupervised, unauthorized activity. However, new light has been shed on his behavior for the last week. According to the newest information, he has conducted himself with courage and intelligence befitting an IceWing. While we cannot approve of any dragonet acting outside approved orders as he has, in this case the final result — returning a missing dragon to the tribe — outweighs our disapproval."

Winter could scarcely believe his father was talking about him. The balance of praise to criticism had never tilted in his direction before. Would this get him back up to the Fourth Circle? Maybe even the Third?

"Therefore, we are obligated to adjust his ranking accordingly. All present advisors have been consulted, and by general agreement, we are slotting my other son, Winter, into first place in the rankings."

Tundra lifted her talons and stabbed Winter's name on the wall. With a crackling sound and a shower of icy sparks, she slid the name sideways and up, flapping her wings to reach the very top of the First Circle.

First place. ME. WHAT.

Hundreds of eyes were staring at Winter now. The crowd reaction was less shocked than the reaction to Hailstorm's placement. Other dragons had performed deeds worthy of jumping to the front of the rankings before — although perhaps there was an undercurrent of surprise that it was Winter, of all dragonets, who'd managed it.

Did I really earn it, though? Winter wondered. *What did Hailstorm tell them?*

Also, although he didn't want to admit this to himself, he couldn't fight off the lurking suspicion that this was truly Narwhal's way of maintaining his own status. A son in first place would counterbalance the weight of one in last, and if the story of his heroic rescue was impressive enough, it might even drag Tundra and Narwhal back up a few numbers.

"Winter," his father said, indicating the front row with his tail. Winter wondered if he was the only one who could hear the tiny note of impatience in Narwhal's voice.

He spread his wings and rose into the air, feeling the wide-eyed gaze of baby dragonets following him. As he flew to the front, he passed Hailstorm in midair, but his brother only nodded on his way by.

The glare Winter got from Snowfall should have melted all the ice in the courtyard. She edged sideways to let him take her spot, fuming.

First place. Number one.

It was really up there, his own name shining at the very top of the rankings.

Maybe I can take a minute to enjoy it, even if I'm not quite sure how I got there.

He gave Snowfall a dazzling smile and she hunched her wings with a scowl. On her other side, Lynx smiled back, mouthing the words, "So *great.*"

Narwhal cleared his throat. "As per the usual protocol, the queen will review the new assignments upon her return, which we anticipate will be tomorrow. Further changes may be in order then." Winter saw his mother glance at Icicle's name, then drop an expressionless mask over her features. "But for now, these are your new rankings. Dragonets dismissed."

The courtyard instantly filled with the murmur of shocked conversations. Winter saw a few older, extremely high-ranked dragons coming toward him. He wished he could cover himself in snow and hide.

"Well," Snowfall said, looking down her nose at a spot just behind his left ear. "That was unexpected."

"Yes," he agreed.

"Congratulations," Lynx said. "You must have had such an adventure." She had an unusual pattern of dark blue scales scattered across her white snout and wings. Winter had always found them pretty, but now they just reminded him of Moon's silver scales. He wished he could tell Moon that he was number one in the rankings . . . although, of course, that wouldn't mean anything to her.

"Indeed," said Snowfall. "I can't *wait* to hear all the details."

On that ominous note, Winter was swept into a whirl-wind of congratulations, questions, bowing, and advice. Every adult dragon in the palace had an opinion on how to maintain your spot, and many of them had suggestions for his future if he could keep first place all the way until his seventh hatching day. Behind them, Snowfall's smirk clearly expressed that she didn't expect it to last even a week.

One week, Qibli's voice echoed in Winter's head.

He still had five days to decide to go back to them. Four, since one would be needed for traveling.

What am I thinking? No one would EVER leave after reaching first place. This is every IceWing dragonet's dream.

Firmly he focused his mind on the nobles around him.

Was it hours later that the courtyard finally cleared? The last noble gave him a respectful nod and flew away. Only a few dragonets remained, including Snowfall and Hailstorm, who were both staring at the rankings as if they could reshape them with the sheer force of their eyeballs.

Winter's stomach ached with hunger, but he needed to talk to Hailstorm before going hunting. Maybe they could even go together — one of the things Winter had missed most while Hailstorm was away.

Was the dragonet in first place allowed to hunt with the dragonet in last? Could he lose his new ranking if he associated with someone in the Seventh Circle? There had never been such a gap between family members before, so he wasn't quite sure what the protocol should be.

But he was going to talk to Hailstorm anyway. The watching dragons could eat the moons if they cared. He needed to reassure his brother that climbing back up the rankings could be done — and remind him that it *had* to be done fast, in case Hailstorm's muddled memory couldn't recall his hatching day.

The snow was packed down by the hundreds of dragon feet that had passed through this morning. Shards of blue sunlight reflected off the tallest towers, illuminating odd splotches of the courtyard.

Snowfall watched the brothers with slitted eyes as Winter slid up to Hailstorm.

"Are you all right?" Winter whispered.

Hailstorm frowned at him. "That's not a very IceWing question," he pointed out. He hesitated, and then bowed deeply to Winter.

"Stop it, stand up," Winter hissed. What a horrible feeling, to have his exceptional older brother bowing to him like that. It made the whole world feel out of order, as if the palace had been flipped upside down. He tried to hide how flustered he was as Hailstorm stood back up. "It seems like a good sign that you remember what is and isn't an IceWing question," he pointed out.

"Of course I do," Hailstorm said in a distant way. "Everything is very clear now that I'm home."

And yet — the way he glanced at the sky . . . Winter wondered if he had really shaken off all those SkyWing memories yet. Perhaps he remembered how to be an IceWing, but he hadn't yet found his way back to being Hailstorm. The brother Winter had missed for so long would have had a laughing comment about Winter's new rank.

"Hailstorm," Winter said hesitantly. "What did you tell Mother and Father?" He wished they'd thought to compare stories before coming home. He needed to know what he should say about Pyrite and where Hailstorm had been for the last two years.

"I told them the truth." Hailstorm drew himself up, looking offended. "What else would I tell them?"

"The truth about . . . everything?" Winter asked. "About . . . about my friends, too?"

Hailstorm's expression now was pure IceWing. "If that's what you want to call them," he spat. "Yes, I told them about your little band of misfits. I hoped they would promote you up the rankings — I owed you that much. But I did not expect them to raise you so high, not with the entire truth in front of them." He fell silent, scowling at the wall again.

"This is *sssssssssssssssssssssoooooooo* interesting, isn't it?" Snowfall strutted toward them, casting arch looks at the circles. "Three moons, Hailstorm, I bet you feel so peculiar right now."

"Leave him alone," Winter growled.

She laughed. "There's not *quite* enough distance between our numbers for you to be giving me orders," she said. Her snout was smiling, but her voice was all murderous stalactites. "Besides," she added, "I'm sure I won't be the only dragon who wants to ask Hailstorm about the Diamond Trial. Are you considering it, Hailstorm dear? With only twelve days until you're seven, I certainly hope so."

Hailstorm didn't answer her. Winter wondered if he remembered what the Trial was. It had never been attempted in Winter's lifetime — he wasn't even sure it had happened in his father's lifetime. It was so rare for a dragonet to still be in the Sixth or Seventh Circle when he reached his seventh hatching day . . . and rarer still for any dragonet that inadequate to risk his life on the mysterious Trial.

But Hailstorm wasn't inadequate; it was pure bad luck that had him so low right now. Whatever the Trial involved, surely he could conquer it easily.

"I mean, if you succeed, you'll move up to first place," Snowfall said archly. "Your life would be right back on track *instantaneously*."

"You're going to do it, aren't you?" Winter asked his brother. He couldn't understand why Hailstorm was staring fixedly down at his talons.

"Oh, how funny, I wouldn't have thought *you'd* want him to," Snowfall went on, her voice sugary-sweet and mocking. "Have you forgotten that the Diamond Trial must also be undertaken by a defending challenger? That's whoever is currently in first place, of course. But only one dragon can survive the Trial. Dear me, that means it'll be brother against brother, won't it? Tsk, tsk. What a conundrum for poor Hailstorm."

Winter felt ice grip his heart and spread down to his talons, rooting him to the snow.

He had forgotten about that part of the Trial rules. Or rather, it had never occurred to him that *he* might be on the other end — the defending first-place dragonet instead of the struggling lower-circle challenger.

But Hailstorm knew exactly how it worked. He knew it would have to be him or Winter; that only one could survive.

And of course, Winter's parents did, too.

This was their plan — to move a dragon into first place who would be no trouble for Hailstorm to defeat. Snowfall was Glacier's daughter and formidable in her own way, only a few months from her hatching day. But Winter . . . Winter was expendable.

Sacrifice one brother to save the other.

They couldn't give both of us high rankings — someone would have called it unfair. This is more dramatic, more like my parents; a higher risk for much higher gain.

They had to do it. Hailstorm's future is too valuable to throw away.

He understood his parents' motivations completely. Whatever happened at the Diamond Trial, they'd end up with a son in first place — and they'd get rid of a disgraceful last-place offender.

But Hailstorm . . .

His brother finally looked up at him, with those blue eyes sharp and alert once again. *This is what you told me to do,* his eyes seemed to say. *You wanted me to be a true IceWing again. Well, here I am.*

And without a word, Hailstorm turned and left the court-yard, leaving Winter behind as a new snow softly began to fall.

CHAPTER 22

The summons arrived later that day.

Hailstorm's messenger found Winter on one of the tallest spires, gloomily picking apart the seal he'd caught. He hadn't been able to find anywhere else to eat in peace; everywhere he went, dragons bowed or hurried over to offer him things or buzzed around with a million questions.

And as the day wore on, he'd heard the whispered phrase more and more.

The Diamond Trial . . . the Diamond Trial . . .

Every dragon over the age of three knew what it was, but no one could give him any details. The Trial was shrouded in mystery, and there was no one left in the palace who'd survived it, since it hadn't been used in so long.

"Prince Winter," said a clipped voice behind him, shaking Winter out of his thoughts. The messenger handed over a small slab of ice marked with precisely carved letters. She stepped back and bowed deeply. "Good luck, sir."

According to the brief, impersonal message, the Trial was scheduled for sunset the next day.

What would happen if I did something terrible between now and then? Winter wondered. *If I snubbed the wrong dragon, or dripped seal blood in the pristine courtyard, or broke one of the queen's ice sculptures? Would I drop down the ranks? Would someone else have to face the Trial with Hailstorm?*

He had a feeling nothing like that would work. The plan was in motion. And Narwhal wouldn't put Snowfall into the Trial, no matter what Winter did. Queen Glacier would be too furious if she came back and found her daughter's life in jeopardy.

And if he fled or tried to refuse the challenge, he'd bring shame upon his whole family, and cost Hailstorm any chance he had at climbing the rankings before his hatching day.

For a moment Winter turned the message slab over in his talons, and then he spread his wings. The only thing he could do was fight. Fight for his new position at the top of the rankings. Fight for his family's melting honor.

Fight for his own life.

It was what Hailstorm and his parents would want him to do, even if they hoped he would lose in the end. He still had to go down like an IceWing warrior.

He spent the rest of the day in the palace library, looking for the Diamond Caves mentioned in the summons. He'd never heard of them, but there they were on an old map. If the Ice Kingdom's peninsula was shaped like a dragon's head, the caves were located where her frostbreath would come out.

Diamond Caves. The most famous Diamond in IceWing history was Queen Diamond, the mother of Prince Arctic, the animus who had been stolen by Foeslayer and the NightWings. As a young dragon, Queen Diamond had given the tribe the gift of healing — five narwhal horns enchanted to cure frostbreath injuries in case any IceWing ever wounded another. But there had been a few other Diamonds over the years as well. He wondered if the caves and the Trial were named after one of the historic Diamonds, and why.

He slept poorly that night, troubled by dreams of Moon and Qibli and Hailstorm all in danger, their scales melting and shifting into other colors as he searched for them in the halls of the ice palace. Every time he woke, he wondered why he hadn't been visited by Scarlet again. He could only imagine her wrath when she discovered that Pyrite/Hailstorm was gone.

The next morning he found Lynx and asked her to train with him. The familiar fighting patterns came naturally, and focusing on her attacks helped drive out all the other worries in his head. They leaped and wrestled in the snow outside the palace until they were exhausted.

Afterward, as they washed each other's dark blue blood off their claws and scales, they heard wingbeats and looked up.

Queen Glacier was back. Behind her flew two generals and Icicle.

Winter watched them soar into the palace. He wondered what the queen would think of Narwhal's scheme. Would she stop it? Would she rearrange the rankings before sunset? Could she do that, even with the summons already issued?

If she could, she didn't. A few hours later, she was among the twelve dragons assembling in the courtyard to fly to the Diamond Caves.

"Prince Winter," she said, and he bowed as deeply as he could. The IceWing queen was huge and majestic, far more beautiful and imposing than any other queen in Pyrrhia. He wondered if he was only imagining that he could see sympathy in her eyes.

"You've served the tribe well, returning Prince Hailstorm to us," she said. "I wish you luck in the Trial."

"Thank you, Your Majesty," he said. There was an uncomfortable prickle at the back of his neck that he suspected meant Hailstorm was nearby, staring at him.

"You will fly alongside me on the way to the caves," she said. "I wish to hear about everything that has happened since you left us for Jade Mountain. I've heard your sister's version of events, but I suspect another perspective would be instructive."

"Yes, Your Majesty," he said. "May I ask what's going to happen to Icicle?"

She looked grave. "It's a good question. Queen Glory is . . . not like other queens. I thought she would demand Icicle's execution, but instead she said she would leave Icicle's punishment entirely to me in exchange for something unusual: a cutting from our moon globe tree."

"What does that mean?" Winter asked.

"I wasn't sure either," said the queen. "Apparently with plants, you can take a piece of it and bury that somewhere else, and then a new plant will grow from that piece. The idea, I think, is that she wants to grow moon globe trees in her rainforest, to bring the gift of light to the RainWings and NightWings."

"Oh," Winter said, startled. He didn't know quite how to wrap his head around this. "Will it work?"

"It might," said Queen Glacier. "The tree is enchanted to behave like a real tree. And I can see how such a thing would benefit her tribes greatly, although, as I said, it's an unusual queen who would choose a path toward peace and cooperation over clear and simple vengeance." She flicked her wings, frowning thoughtfully. "The question is whether her tribes will be satisfied with this solution. I suppose we'll see. It may partly depend on how I ultimately punish Icicle, but I haven't decided that yet."

They lifted off into a cloudy gray sky, flying southwest with Tundra and Narwhal in the lead and Hailstorm trailing at the back, as befitted his last-place ranking. Winter had to struggle to keep up with Queen Glacier's pace, but she didn't seem to notice.

And since he had a feeling he was about to die, he told her almost everything — about Icicle trying to kill Starflight and how Winter stopped her; about the rainforest and the volcano; about going in search of Scarlet, meeting

Pyrite, and encountering the mysterious NightWing in the valley.

He left out a few things, though. Moon's powers and her prophecy. The fact that his friends were waiting for him in Possibility at that very moment. The way he felt about them, especially Moon.

The queen only stopped him once during his story. "Who?" she asked.

He paused, startled. "Your Majesty?"

"You said there was an IceWing with the Talons of Peace." Queen Glacier shot a glance at the hole in the clouds where a piece of sunlight had muscled through. "Who was it?"

"His name was Cirrus," Winter answered. "I didn't know him and he didn't know me. He was . . . confusing."

"We haven't had a Cirrus in many years," the queen mused. "And I don't recall any IceWings leaving us for the Talons of Peace — unless they were from the lower classes, outside the rankings. Perhaps that's why I don't know him. Or perhaps he changed his name."

"He acted like an aristocrat," Winter said. It hadn't even occurred to him that Cirrus might be from the outskirts of the Ice Kingdom. That would explain why he didn't tell Winter his ranking, though. "He implied that he knew my parents, but in a way that seemed like he was lying."

"Hmm," Queen Glacier said. "I'll look into it. Go on."

Most of the clouds had cleared and the sky was shading into a brilliant orange-red when they finally dove out of the sky toward a snow-covered evergreen forest clustered at the base of an enormous white cliff.

Pine needles jabbed Winter's snout as he dropped through the trees to the forest floor. The scent of the pines surrounded them and the snow crunched like crushed paper under their talons. He thought of the Pyrite scroll spell, now carefully tucked away in the skyfire pouch around his ankle.

A cave mouth yawned in the side of the cliff, glittering with stalactites as sharp as teeth. Ice covered the walls, floor, and ceiling all the way into the tunnel, as far as Winter could see before darkness took over. He touched the moon globe over his shoulder, making sure it was there and still working.

"Princes Winter and Hailstorm," the queen said briskly. "Your task is simple. Enter the Diamond Caves and search until you find the frozen dragon by the river chasm. Touch one of these spears to her." She took two gleaming, diamond-tipped spears from one of her guards and handed them to the brothers, one apiece. "Whoever returns shall take first place in the rankings. The other . . . we bid farewell."

Huh. Ominous and unspecific, snarked Qibli's voice in Winter's head.

Narwhal stepped forward and tipped his long snout down to study his sons. "Remember, be strong," he said. "Be vigilant. Strike first."

"Restore our family's rank," added Tundra.

Narwhal's gaze rested on Winter for a moment. "Farewell," he said finally. "Whichever of you does not return, I know you will accept defeat with honor."

Sounds great, Winter thought, feeling light-headed. *Always wanted some defeat with a side of honor.*

He had a feeling he should say something here, but Hailstorm was already pivoting and marching into the cave. Winter glanced around at the assembled IceWings one more time. Was this the last time he would see his parents? His queen and the sky?

When he'd said good-bye to Moon — had it really been forever?

He found he didn't have anything to say to his parents after all.

Winter turned in silence and followed Hailstorm into the icy tunnel.

The Diamond Caves, according to the one map Winter had found, apparently stretched for miles in a kind of underground labyrinth with only one exit. Walls of ice hemmed them in on all sides, glittering blue-white in the light of their moon globes. In places, the ceiling brushed the horns on Winter's head. In others, they had to creep along narrow ledges over dark crevasses, gripping the ice with their claws, because if they tried to fly into that vast dark space they might not find their way back before tiring and falling to their deaths.

Hailstorm glanced back at Winter once or twice with a frown, as if he'd expected Winter to choose a different path. But Winter did not want to wander this labyrinth alone, with no way to know if Hailstorm had completed the task yet or not. Better to stick together and know for sure.

They wandered for hours, perhaps in circles, perhaps in spirals ever downward. Winter was beginning to wonder if the frozen dragon even existed at all when they came out of a narrow tunnel and found the river chasm before them.

This had to be it — a wide slash in the ice ahead of them, with sheer walls that plunged down into a darkness that echoed with the rushing sound of a river.

Winter lifted his moon globe higher, scanning the cave, and felt a terrible chill run through his veins.

The cave was *filled* with frozen dragons. Nearly a hundred of them glittered in the moon globe's light — some on this side of the chasm, but most of them on the other side. The one closest to him looked like an ordinary IceWing with an almost cheerful expression on his face, stepping toward Winter as though he were about to saunter out the door.

But others were frozen in positions of terror, their talons covering their faces or their wings flung out as though they were trying to leap away. And he could see a few that had clearly been fighting when they were frozen, wearing expressions of fury.

There were no other ways in or out, apart from the chasm and the tunnel behind him. Eerie blue bubbles morphed and twisted within the shining ice walls, moving as though the cave itself was breathing.

Which statue was *the* frozen dragon? Which one were they supposed to touch with the spear?

Hailstorm was staring around at the ice sculptures as though he were one of them. Winter took a step into the cave and noticed a sparkling pile of crushed ice near the entrance. He nudged his moon globe toward it, wondering why the pile was so big — and then he saw a dragon's talon buried in the ice with a few of its claws snapped off.

Maybe this one had been midflight when he was frozen, and he smashed to pieces when he fell to the ground. Or maybe whoever froze him decided to finish the job by bashing his frozen corpse to smithereens.

Winter shuddered, his tail spikes rattling along the floor.

Suddenly Hailstorm leaped forward. Winter whirled and saw him racing toward a dragon on the far side of the chasm — a dragon larger than any of the others with her claws outstretched and her wings flared.

Hailstorm sailed across the gap, landed, pivoted, and struck the statue with his spear. It all happened in a moment, like a burst of lightning. By the time Winter landed beside him, Hailstorm was in battle position, brandishing the spear against whatever happened next.

A crackling sound came from the dragon.

And then, slowly, bits of ice began to break off, splintering into falling shards and shattering against the floor.

The frozen dragon comes to life, Winter realized. It made sense. *Then we fight her, and she kills one of us, and the other wins.* He looked around at the frozen statues and winced. *Or she freezes one of us. These must be all the dragons who've lost the Trial.*

And I could be one of them soon.

He looked back at the large frozen dragon and realized that she was not actually *made* of ice. She was encased *inside* the ice, and as her prison came apart, he saw her scales, and they were dark as a moonless night.

This was a NightWing.

She pulled in her wings and then flung out her claws, shaking the last of the ice off. Only two spots still glittered against her scales — a pair of shackles around her back ankles, although they didn't seem to be connected to anything.

With a hiss, she turned in a circle, then whipped around to drop the full force of her glare on the princes.

"Oh, good," she rasped in a hoarse voice. "More IceWing dragonets with spears."

"I'm here to kill you," Hailstorm announced, without a tremor of insecurity in his voice.

"Aren't you all," she said drily. "Shall we introduce ourselves first?"

Hailstorm and Winter exchanged glances. Was that normal? Conversation with a creatively imprisoned NightWing?

"I'm Prince Winter," said Winter after an awkward pause. "And this is my brother, Hailstorm."

"Brothers, oh my, how devastating," said the NightWing. "Welcome to my prison. I am Foeslayer."

Winter started back, his head reeling.

Foeslayer?

The same Foeslayer who stole the IceWing animus prince, Arctic?

The mother of Darkstalker?

CHAPTER 23

"You've heard of me," she observed with a hint of amusement.

"That's — you're — you don't mean —" Winter couldn't seem to put words together.

"Yes," the NightWing said. "Your ancient and terrible enemy. Everyone is always surprised. I want to know what the point is of abducting and freezing your archnemesis and then never telling anyone about it? Don't you want to shout it from the clouds? So everyone will know how dangerous and powerful you are?"

"You can't be alive after all this time, though," Winter finally managed to get out.

She folded in her wings. A curl of smoke rose from her snout. After a moment she said, "No, don't tell me. I don't want to know how long it's been. I'll never see them again anyway." Her tail flicked toward the icy cave walls. "It's part of your queen's gift, IceWing. I have been frozen in time, so I only age in the moments when I'm unfrozen like this. The plan, evidently, is to keep me here a very, very long time."

Thousands of years, Winter thought, aghast. *She's been down here for two thousand years already.*

"The gift of vengeance," he said. But Queen Diamond had already given the tribe her gift, long before her son was stolen. Which meant she must have used her animus magic again to create this prison. Had it driven her mad? He couldn't remember anything in the history books about what happened to her after Prince Arctic was gone.

"Indeed," said Foeslayer. "You could say my mother-in-law and I have a . . . complicated relationship."

He heard the scratch of claws on ice behind him, and then suddenly there was a blur of blue-white motion. Hailstorm launched himself at Foeslayer, swinging the spear around to stab her through the heart.

The NightWing dodged aside and seized the spear, jerking it out of his talons. Hailstorm caught his balance, whirled, and attacked again. His claws slashed at her throat and she slammed the blunt end of the spear against his side, knocking him into the wall.

With a roar he was up again, this time seizing her tail and clambering up it onto her back. He sank his fierce claws into the flesh between her shoulder blades and heaved up as though he was trying to yank out her spine.

Foeslayer shrieked and threw herself into a roll, tucking her wings and landing heavily on Hailstorm. He lost his grip on her amid an explosion of sharp cracks, which sounded to Winter like bones snapping.

The NightWing leaped free again and came straight at Hailstorm while his underbelly was exposed. Her back talons pinned down his tail, and she raised the spear to impale him through the heart.

Winter threw himself at her without a second thought, tackling her to the ground. They rolled and twisted and slid across the icy floor, kicking at each other with their claws.

"You idiot!" she yelled at him. His head bashed into the cave wall and tears of pain sprang into his eyes. "Do IceWings get dumber every year? Don't you want to win?"

He flung her off so hard she spun across the ice and nearly slid over the edge into the chasm.

"That's not what I want!" Winter shouted. "I don't want to win if it means Hailstorm has to die!" He whirled to face his brother, who was on his feet and panting, his sides splattered with red and blue blood. "What are we fighting for? A number on a wall? Your life is more important to me than the rankings, Hailstorm."

Hailstorm growled. "I would have said the same thing, brother," he said. "But I sacrificed myself for you once already, and it was the worst thing that ever happened to me. You can't imagine how it feels to know what I've done — to have these memories in my head." He clawed at his temples. "I want my life back. I want my *self* back. And I won't get it if I reach my hatching day in last place. I have to be first again."

The old, familiar guilt was surging back through Winter. *My fault, my fault, my fault.*

"I didn't think it would be you I'd have to destroy in order to get back to first," Hailstorm admitted. "But it had to be someone. I won't be a traitor to my tribe anymore. When I'm number one, I can prove it."

Winter looked back at Foeslayer, who had slowly risen to her feet and was listening with a curious expression.

"Is there any other way?" he asked her. "A way we can both live?"

"I'm not the right dragon to ask," she said. "Frankly I'd rather see you all dead."

"I'll take last place," Winter said to Hailstorm. "What if we told the queen that? Would she let us switch?"

Hailstorm snorted. "Where's the honor in that for me?" he asked. "No, they won't agree to it. If we both come out of the caves, they'll just kill one of us — and probably leave the other in last place." He picked up the spear Foeslayer had dropped and twisted it between his talons.

The NightWing breathed a jet of flame that melted the wings of the statue closest to her. "This is very moving, but would one of you please kill me already?" She paced toward them, her dark eyes reflecting the light of their moon globes. "I'm tired, I haven't eaten in hundreds of years, and these days it's more painful to be awake than to go through the process of dying again."

"Dying?" Winter asked.

"Yes," she said, stopping in front of them and spreading her wings. "You stab me, I die painfully, and then I go back to being frozen until someone wakes me up again. It's a cunning enchantment. The first forty times, Queen Diamond killed me herself." Foeslayer let out a bitter chuckle. "I suspect the original point of the spell was that she wasn't satisfied with killing me just once. But then the forty-first time, there were two dragonets here . . . so she must have decided I could be used for this other purpose, whatever you two are here for."

"So you just get murdered over and over again?" Winter asked.

"That's my punishment." Foeslayer shrugged eloquently. "Here's some advice for you — never make an animus angry."

Winter turned to Hailstorm, puzzled. "Then how did all these other dragons get frozen? Maybe that's part of the spell, too. One kills Foeslayer, and then the other one freezes?" It seemed more complicated than the usual animus spell.

Hailstorm's eyes were fixed on the spear. "You do it," he said gruffly. "You kill her."

"No," Winter said. "Hailstorm, you're right. You've already sacrificed yourself for me. I've been waiting for two years to make it up to you."

"Winter —" Hailstorm said.

"I'm not going to be responsible for your death a second time," Winter insisted. "It's my turn. And let's face it, this is what Mother and Father would want."

Hailstorm winced, but didn't argue.

"Just be a great IceWing," Winter said. "Help keep the tribes at peace. That's what *I* would want."

"This is peculiar," Foeslayer spoke up. "But not as peculiar as you might think. I've seen a surprising amount of this 'I'll die for you!' 'No, *I'll* die for *you!*' 'No, let *me* be the brave sacrifice!' nonsense from IceWings over the years."

"Do it," Winter said to Hailstorm. "I'm ready."

"Me too," said Foeslayer. "As fast and clean as you can, please."

Hailstorm took the spear, leveled it at Foeslayer's heart, and drove it swiftly through her chest. She gritted her teeth, her face twisted in pain — and then the ice came crawling up from the shackles on her ankles, freezing her from her tail forward to her wings, neck, and head. Hailstorm pulled the spear free before the ice got there, and Winter saw the wound heal over just before Foeslayer was completely frozen.

He closed his eyes, expecting the world to go dark.

But it didn't.

Nothing happened at all.

After a moment, he opened his eyes again and saw Hailstorm standing by the edge of the chasm.

"Why didn't it work?" Winter asked. "I'm not frozen." He looked around at the other statues. Something whispered in his mind — an explanation, although it still didn't quite fit together.

"Right," Hailstorm said. He turned to look at his brother. "That's because it's not part of the original enchantment. The spell on the NightWing isn't what froze these dragons." He lifted the spear. "That's what these do. That's what . . . that's what I'm supposed to do to you."

Winter was silent. Everything was starting to make a kind of awful sense.

"Mother and Father told me earlier today." Hailstorm's wings drooped to the floor. "They told me that no matter who killed Foeslayer, I was the one chosen to win. That I was to take this spear and stab you the same way I stabbed her, freezing you like all these other dragons. Then I was guaranteed first place."

Do they do this every time? Winter wondered. *Choose one dragonet to win? Tell only that dragonet the secret of the spears and how to freeze the other?*

He shouldn't have felt surprised, or betrayed. Of course his parents would choose Hailstorm. This was really quite normal, given the patterns of their lives so far.

But it still . . . it still *hurt*, deep inside him where he'd thought his family couldn't hurt him anymore.

Moon, Qibli, and Kinkajou wouldn't do something like this to me, he thought.

"All right," he said out loud. "Then I guess that's what you have to do." He set down his own spear and braced himself.

"You know I can't," Hailstorm snapped. "You're the one who rescued me. You're my *brother*. I'm not going to murder you now, so you're just going to have to do it to me." He tossed his spear to Winter, who jumped aside and let it clatter to the ground.

They stared at each other for a long moment as the rush of the river below filled the cavern. All the frozen dragons seemed to be waiting, like a captive audience enjoying the suspense.

"If we can't kill each other," Winter said, "maybe we leave it like this. You go out and claim victory, and I wait to sneak out later. We both live."

Hailstorm shook his head. "As soon as you got home, they'd throw me back into last place, and probably you as well."

"I won't go home," Winter said. He felt a lump forming in his throat, like frostbreath icing over his windpipe. "I'll stay away from the Ice Kingdom."

It didn't sound possible. His whole life was about being an IceWing, being Queen Glacier's nephew, proving something to Tundra and Narwhal. He believed in the perfection and superiority of the Ice Kingdom. How could he ever be happy anywhere else?

But now he'd been to so many other places — he'd seen the world beyond the Ice Kingdom, and it wasn't so terrible really.

Because happiness is not where I am . . . it's who I'm with.

And he knew exactly who he wanted to be with.

Hailstorm's claws curled in and out as he thought. He reached out and picked up one of the diamond-tipped spears, and Winter felt a quick bolt of fear that his brother had decided to kill him anyway.

But Hailstorm just bowed and took a step backward.

"Thank you, brother," he said. "I hope — I hope one day I'll see you again."

Winter nodded, not trusting himself to speak.

Hailstorm turned and flew across the chasm. In the entrance to the tunnel he paused, glancing back at Winter . . . and then he fled, his footsteps echoing behind him.

A long time passed. Winter tried to keep track of the hours in his head, calculating when it would be dawn.

Finally he stood up, stretched, and picked up the other diamond-tipped spear.

Taking a deep breath, he reached out and tapped Foeslayer with it.

~ CHAPTER 24 ~

The ice around the NightWing cracked and splintered just as it had before, and Foeslayer slowly opened her eyes. Surprise flashed across her face when she saw Winter there.

"This is a first," she said. "I've never been brought back by the same dragonets before. Did you want a chance to kill me, too? Seems a little over the top, if you don't mind my saying so."

"Listen," Winter said, "I don't know if you even realize how much you stole from us when you took away our animus magic."

The gifts of light . . . of order . . . and, running like a hidden current through every dragonet's understanding of himself, the gift of faith in their tribe that came from the indisputable wisdom of how IceWings handled their magic.

"Imagine what our kingdom would be like if we still had animus dragons," Winter went on. "What else would we have invented?"

"I suspect you wouldn't have stayed in your little kingdom

much longer," Foeslayer answered him. "Have you considered that your perfect tribe might have used the magic for evil as well as good?"

Was that true? *Would we have done something terrible with it? What kind of gift might Queen Glacier have asked for during the War of SandWing Succession?*

He shook out his wings. "When you stole Prince Arctic, you stole all our future gifts, everything that we might have become, and I can see why some dragons would think that's unforgivable." His scales felt heavier and heavier as he went on. "But . . . this. This imprisonment, for centuries, keeping you alive only to die over and over again. I feel like . . . I feel like perhaps you've been punished enough."

Foeslayer turned away from him and rested her talons on one of the frozen dragonets, hiding her face. After a moment she said, in a muffled, fractured voice, "I didn't steal him."

"Prince Arctic?" Winter said.

"I didn't steal him." Foeslayer lifted one wing so she could meet Winter's eyes. "I fell in love with him."

An entire history of a tribe, the story of a war, the foundation of an ancient hatred — it all shivered in Winter's mind like stepping onto the thinnest layer of ice.

"And he loved me, too," Foeslayer said. "That's the truth, although no IceWing has ever listened long enough to hear it before."

Everything was splintering apart.

"We didn't mean to ruin everything," she said. "Or start a terrible war, or make two tribes hate each other for all eternity. We just wanted to be together."

He believed her. He wouldn't have a month ago, but now he believed her because he knew exactly how that felt. Because he could imagine throwing everything away, too, for the chance to be with Moon.

If they dared to start something . . . could he and Moon end as badly as Foeslayer and Arctic?

Would he risk it, even after seeing where it might lead?

It's different, he told himself. *Queen Diamond cared very much what happened to Prince Arctic. No one cares at all what happens to me.*

"So now you know," Foeslayer said, rolling the spear over to him. "Ready to kill me?"

He shook his head. "I'm getting you out of here."

The NightWing's eyes gleamed, dark and glittering in the light from his moon globe. "That's impossible, I'm afraid," she said. "Every time I've tried to cross the chasm, some kind of invisible wall drives me back. I assume the enchantment was crafted to keep me here forever."

"Maybe," Winter said. "But IceWings are careful planners, especially when it comes to animus gifts. I'm sure Diamond left a way to free you, in case they needed you to negotiate with the NightWings." He stepped back, studying her from wings to tail. "It must be your shackles — that's what's been animus-touched, right?"

She lifted one back foot and then the other. "Well, they're impervious to fire," she said. "And nothing happens when I smash them against the walls, except it makes my ankles really hurt. So I'm guessing they're enchanted, yes."

"Whatever will break them," Winter said, "I bet can only be done by a member of the royal family. If I know IceWings anyway. But you're in luck, because that's what I am." He tried not to think about his name on the rankings wall — his name glittering at the top, and then Tundra's claws scratching through it, marking him as dead.

He picked up one of the spears and pointed it at the shackles. "Hold still."

"Oh dear," Foeslayer said, closing her eyes.

With a swift jabbing motion, Winter struck the closest shackle with the tip of the spear.

It bounced off, reverberating in his claws. The shackle looked untouched.

Winter set the spear down again and crouched to examine the shackles. There was a small diamond shape indented on the side of each one. Carefully he poked the diamond with one claw, but that didn't do anything either.

One more possibility. Something only an IceWing could do, which made it safe because no IceWing would ever, ever free a NightWing.

He reached inside him for the lurking snowstorm and then breathed out, covering the diamond with frostbreath.

The shackle sprang apart, clattered to the floor, and shattered into tiny pieces.

Foeslayer sat up, staring at the other shackle with hope and disbelief warring in her eyes.

"Wait," Winter said. He touched the other shackle. "I should — I have to make sure of one thing. If I free you, you have to promise you won't go hurt any IceWings. I don't want a whole new cycle of vengeance and war to start. Do you understand? It ends here."

"I never want to see an IceWing ever again in my whole life," Foeslayer said fervently. "Set me free, and I'll go straight home to the Night Kingdom, and you'll never see me again."

The Night Kingdom.

The lost city of night — Foeslayer knew exactly where it was. She could help them stop the prophecy.

"Actually," Winter said, "I want to come with you."

This was his future now. Not prince among IceWings, not Queen Glacier's nephew, not a warrior struggling his way up the rankings under the disapproving gaze of his parents.

He was a dragon who had friends from other tribes. And he was going to save Jade Mountain with them.

He leaned forward to breathe frostbreath on the last shackle.

Moon, Qibli, Kinkajou . . . I'm coming. Wait for me. I'll be there soon.

EPILOGUE

Alone and buried in rock, Darkstalker waited, and listened.

Twenty-six dragonets remained of the thirty-five who had started at Jade Mountain Academy. And their minds were full of secrets.

In the art cave, a NightWing wondered where Moonwatcher and the rest of the Jade Winglet had gone. He dipped his brush in paint and worried about the secret letter he had just received from old friends. *Is it true? Have they escaped Thorn's prison? Are they really coming back soon with an army?*

And, *does Mother know?*

And, *will she join them? Which side of the coup would she be on?*

And *would I want her to . . . or are things maybe better the way they are, even with a RainWing for our queen?*

He didn't know. He'd have to make a choice, probably sooner than he wanted to, and he had no idea what the right decision would be.

Darkstalker knew. He knew which option would lead this dragonet to a long, safe life, and which would end in death within the year. He also knew which choice would be better for his own plans. But which path the dragonet would take . . . that was still uncertain.

Outside, on the sandy bank of a mountain stream, the mind-shrouded SandWing took off her necklace, hid it carefully under a rock, and waded into the frigid water. Darkstalker narrowed in on her, knowing this was a rare few minutes of exposure.

Cold, cold, cold, she was cursing as she splashed. *Stupid, stupid, stupid three MOONS why is it so cold I've got to get back to the desert —*

Abruptly, out loud, she said, "Are you listening? You'd better be."

For a moment, Darkstalker was startled into thinking she meant him, but then she went on.

"This plan is inane. I haven't learned anything new here and I can barely get near the daughter, especially after all the aggravation with caves exploding and other inconvenient nuisances. I thought I had an idea, but then he up and vanished from the school. You have no idea how frustrating it is. It's like four hundred other stories are going on around me and nobody has noticed that *I'm* the one who's going to shape the future of Pyrrhia."

She brooded for a moment, thinking jumbled thoughts about castles and crowns and power. Finally she said, "There's one more possible option if I stay a bit longer. A dragonet, as loyal to that Thorn character as anyone, and I think she's connected to one of Thorn's generals. She might be my in. I'll give it a try, but if it gets too annoying, I'm coming back to the Scorpion Den."

Onyx climbed out of the stream and shook her wings furiously. "Send me a message the usual way," she snapped.

I will be queen within the month, whether that old dragon helps me or whether I have to kill him and do it myself.

She dropped the necklace over her head, and all Darkstalker could hear was fuzz.

Interesting.

Who was she talking to, and how?

He wished he could tell Moonwatcher. He wished he could tell *anyone*, but with her gone, he had no one left who could hear him.

Come back soon, little Moonwatcher. Bring me my talisman, and come back soon.

Deep in the underground lake, another dragonet was swimming, although the temperature of the water didn't bother her.

Fathom's great-great-great-great-great-great-great-great-great-great-granddaughter dove to the bottom and then shot up out of the lake, soaring to the ceiling and spiraling back down with a splash.

"Very impressive, Princess!" called the SeaWing named Pike, paddling in a small circle nearby. "Such speed! And grace!"

The SeaWing with the skyfire bracelet snorted from the top of a rock. "Anybody can do that," he said.

"Not when you're tied to your mother," his sister said, squirting water at him with her talons. *I've never flown as fast as I wanted or soared as high as I could go. Now I can do anything,* anything I want. "Stop being such a mope, Turtle. So what if your entire winglet is gone? You've still got us." She thwacked her tail into the water, sending a wave over the other three SeaWings in the lake with her.

Unless Mother comes and tries to take me home. But I won't let her. I won't. I might be the most powerful dragon in the world, and if she didn't learn that from what I did to Whirlpool, I can teach her some other way.

The spell on Auklet's harness should keep her away from me, though.

If it doesn't, I'll come up with something stronger.

"Tag! You're it!" Barracuda called, tapping Anemone's tail and racing away.

The rest of the SeaWing princess's thoughts scattered into laughter and the game.

Darkstalker studied her possible futures thoughtfully, then tucked them away and moved on.

There. Now this was the most interesting mind in the school.

This poor dragon, pacing in an empty cave, afraid of her own scales.

Her mind was a blazing mess of flames, hot and fierce and self-destructive. Her dreams were haunted by a hissing queen with a melted face. Her heart was given, entirely and forever, to the only dragon she couldn't hurt.

Was she "the talons of power and fire"?

Darkstalker wasn't sure. The paths ahead of her were all confusion, like trying to follow a map into a forest fire. But on the other side, something flickered through the smoke. Something like hope.

Something shaped like a scroll.

He didn't have to see exactly what would happen. He was already sure of one thing.

This dragon could change everything.

WINGS OF FIRE

will continue . . .

TUI T. SUTHERLAND

THE NEW YORK TIMES BESTSELLING SERIES

WINGS OF FIRE

ESCAPING PERIL

There! Talons thumping on stone! The rough slither of a tail! Was it him?

Peril nearly leaped into the corridor — and came within a wing flicker of colliding with a dragon who definitely wasn't Clay.

The dark green SeaWing dragonet didn't scream or faint or stagger back in terror. He simply froze, slamming his eyes closed as though danger would obligingly disappear the moment he couldn't see it anymore.

"What are you doing?" Peril yelped, jumping away from him.

"Um," he said in a low, rumbly voice. "Walking? In the halls? Back to my cave?" He risked opening one eye to peer at her.

"Well, that was VERY STUPID of you!" she snapped.

He thought about that for a moment, then opened both eyes and regarded her peaceably. "Oh," he said. "Sorry."

What a peculiar dragon. He seemed to have no fire about him at all. That wasn't a SeaWing thing; Tsunami was a fireball that blazed up and down and sideways at everything that made her mad (which was most things). And her sister, the little SeaWing princess, at least from a distance seemed to be a shower of bright orange sparks on the inside.

This SeaWing, on the other talon, was a puddle. A fireless

puddle, blobbing quietly into the rocks in front of her, not even trying to get away.

"You're Peril, aren't you?" he said. "Queen Scarlet's . . ." He trailed off, perhaps realizing there was no good way to end that sentence. *Champion? Weapon? Notorious death monster?*

"Yes," she hissed. "I'm Queen Scarlet's notorious death monster."

He made an odd hiccupping noise and ducked his head. "Ah, OK. I'll just . . . go, then."

What would Clay want her to do in this situation? *Maybe you'll make some friends here,* he'd said, in that oblivious magical way he had of thinking that any other dragons in the world might have open hearts like his.

"Who are you?" she asked. *Hmmm. That came out more menacing than it sounded in my head.* "I mean, who *are* you?" she tried, adding a Sunnyish cheerful lilt to her voice. *Now I sound manic.* "I'm not being creepy," she added hastily. "I'm not, like, putting you on a murder list or anything. I don't have a murder list! Not a to-be-murdered list, I mean. Wait, no — to be clear, I have no kind of murder list at all. Definitely out of the murdering business, me. Maybe I should stop saying the word murder."

"That would be great," the SeaWing said. "If you wouldn't mind."